WHO
IS MARY?

AN AMISH ROMANCE

STEPPING STONES
BOOK ONE

LINDA BYLER

New York, New York

WHO IS MARY?

All rights reserved. No part of this book may be reproduced in any manner without the express written consent of the publisher, except in the case of brief excerpts in critical reviews or articles. All inquiries should be addressed to Good Books, 307 West 36th Street, 11th Floor, New York, NY 10018.

Good Books books may be purchased in bulk at special discounts for sales promotion, corporate gifts, fund-raising, or educational purposes. Special editions can also be created to specifications. For details, contact the Special Sales Department, Good Books, 307 West 36th Street, 11th Floor, New York, NY 10018 or info@skyhorsepublishing.com.

Good Books is an imprint of Skyhorse Publishing, Inc.®, a Delaware corporation.

Visit our website at www.goodbooks.com.

10 9 8 7 6 5 4 3 2 1

Library of Congress Cataloging-in-Publication Data is available on file.

Print ISBN: 978-1-68099-916-7
eBook ISBN: 978-1-68099-929-7

Cover by Godfredson Design

Printed in the United States of America

CHAPTER 1

SHE WAS BORN AND RAISED IN UPSTATE NEW YORK, THE YOUNGEST child in a family of eleven, living all her life on a hardscrabble farm devoid of loamy soil or any amount of good management or profit. She had always been reasonably happy as a child, the knowledge of her lower status on the food chain undetected, struggling along in school until she acquired the wisdom of her place in the order of things, which was being one of Amos Glick's girls. Amos was one of five brothers and five sisters who dotted the community of Amish inhabiting the Pinedale Valley, all of them married and raising families of their own.

Amos and Barbara were honest, God-fearing members of the Amish who held strictly to the traditions and *ordnung* (rules) of the church. They farmed the stony soil with rusted machinery and tired mules well past their prime, milked a small herd of cows, and grew tobacco for a cash crop. Amos wore a serious expression, if a bit bewildered at times, was soft spoken and sincere, and his wife Barbara was submissive in all her ways. She made her own butter in a glass churn, and yogurt and sourdough bread were a staple, made with her own hands that were misshapen by hard work and arthritis. Her back was bent, her shoulders rounded, her dress front straining at the straight pins that kept it together across her ample chest.

Where she was of rotund build, her husband was thin as a rail. His large, ill-fitting trousers held up the worn suspenders across his shoulders and his Redwing work shoes were perpetually coated with the manure residue he could never quite avoid. Barbara never raised her voice in disapproval. She merely grunted a bit as she bent over her rounded stomach to wipe up mud and gravel, manure or wet grass, her face darkened with exertion.

All the children, from Ezra to Lydia, were mild mannered and obedient to the counsel of their softspoken parents, never questioning the stringent requirements of their upbringing. They had a deep respect for their father and took the voice of the minister as a direct gateway to a home in Heaven and ruled their existence accordingly.

That Mary was born five years after the youngest, Abner, came as a bit of a surprise, with Barbara at the ripe old age of forty-five. Amos chuckled softly when his wife imparted the news, held her hand in his, and pronounced it good.

Mary was born with a round face and an unruly thatch of hair the color of an old penny, a cry erupting from her open mouth with the startling clarity of a crow's raucous clamor. Never satisfied, she yelled with a bellyache after being fed, yelled with boredom in her little swing, yelled with indignation when she was put on her back, and became redfaced and unable to breathe on her stomach.

Even the calm Barbara was pushed to her limits, weary of the grating cry, so she put Mary in her crib, shut the door, and let her cry herself to sleep.

In school, Mary was brilliant. By the time she was in second grade, she was reading anything she could find, even encyclopedias and history books, and could recite all the states and capitals and the names of all the books of the Old and New Testament.

She surpassed all the older children in German, seated in the small dark living room on Sunday forenoon, reading from the German Scripture. Amos heard her recite the twenty-third Psalm in German to the barn cats who rubbed their arched backs across her stockings and purred appreciatively. She sang hymns as she washed the milkers, and Amos told Barbara he believed she was born to be a minister's wife, creating a quick rush of emotion in them both.

Yes, Amos was a blessed man, his children around his table, his quiver full of good, strong arrows, raised to be upright citizens, obedient in all their ways. His heart was full.

No matter if his farm never appeared as successful as his neighbors'. He knew a man's worth was not measured by dollar bills, but by the content of his character. His good wife Barbara never questioned the struggle to make ends meet, always breathing a sigh of relief after the monthly mortgage payment had been met.

It simply never occurred to her that she could make extra bread or yogurt or grow tomatoes and green beans to sell at a roadside stand. Instead, she focused on being a good helpmeet to Amos and being frugal in all her ways.

So Mary was sent to school with hand-me-downs, every stitch of her clothing having been worn by Lydia or Rachel or Becky. Her lunch box was a scratched and dented red Rubbermaid, stained by years of use, containing a sandwich, two cookies, and a jar of peaches or pears.

For a time, Mary rested in the childish security of caring parents and loving siblings. But by the time she entered fifth grade, she had begun to notice her classmates' way of dress, the beautiful hues of a rainbow, the long skirts and new sneakers with various colors and stripes. She began to keep her own feet tucked under her seat, the frayed edges of her inexpensive black sneakers suddenly repulsive. She started to wonder why she and her siblings couldn't have nice things like the other kids. Weren't her parents hard workers? Was there something wrong with them?

She didn't know her girth was widening, expanding with the calories of many slices of sourdough bread and "smear cheese," the shoofly pie she soaked in milk, or the homemade sweet bologna she rolled around a dill pickle spear. Her kind, soft-spoken mother would never hurt her feelings nor mention the fact she was becoming quite chubby.

When Katie Ann, who was a seventh grader and the captain of everything, including ball games, told her she could run faster if she wasn't so fat, Mary's face became even redder and she blinked back scalding tears of shame. This was new and uncomfortable. She'd had no idea someone could make her feel so shameful and worthless.

She tried harder, gritted her teeth and swung mightily, sent the ball over the schoolyard fence and made a homerun, her round form nearly level with the ground as she raced across the bases.

She looked around expectantly for cheers and flowery praise, but found none, the cruelty of the pecking order in a schoolyard fully visible for the first time. Katie Ann didn't like her, so no one else was allowed to either.

Her remaining years of school were spent in a haze of bewildered shame, hurt pride, and an ever increasing sense that she was simply not worthy. She always stayed on top of her class, receiving searing looks of jealousy when her one hundred percents were called out. She went home and did her best to forget about school the minute her feet crossed the threshold.

She never mentioned any of this to her mother. Feelings and emotions were not something you discussed, and especially negativity. It was all right. Swallow it. Stay quiet.

And she did.

By the time she was in vocational class, however, she was tired of stumbling along with her hand-me-down clothes, her too big yellowed covering and torn black sneakers. She took a good look in the mirror and decided she wasn't that bad, really. With some decent clothes, she'd look just fine. She gathered her courage and asked her mother for a new covering that would fit her like the other girls', and if she could have a new dress that was longer and made to fit her better.

Barbara was taken aback, to say the least. Why, after raising ten children who never questioned her decisions, would this one require anything she perceived to be out of the *ordnung* (Amish rules)? Surely it was prideful for her daughter to be discontent with what she had, and vain to long for fashionable outfits to draw attention to herself. She raised the subject with Amos and was comforted with the soft, understanding voice packed full of wisdom.

It was a passing phase. She'd come around.

Yes, yes, Barbara reasoned to herself. She would. But this was unthinkable, one of her girls being concerned with something as worldly as fashionable clothes. What would people say?

Needless to say, Mary's requests were met with a resounding no. She would have to be content with the clothes she had. Fancy clothes were not something any obedient young woman should be longing for.

Mary felt the now familiar weight of shame settle over her. She hadn't meant to be vain or ungrateful, but clearly she had let pride get the best of her.

When she turned sixteen, she was allowed to join the *rumspringa*, a group of young men and women who gathered for games of volleyball and hymn singings. The popular girls would start dating almost right away, while the less attractive or social girls might attend the gatherings for years, some eventually becoming "leftover blessings," single women who never had spouses or families of their own. Dressed in her humble attire, she wet her copper-red hair so she could roll it into submission in the modest style her community required. She joined the others and tried to feel like she belonged.

She soon discovered a deep sense of boredom, coupled with an overriding anxiety about the possibility of finding a suitable mate. Every last one of the young men were childish, immature, as simple as a barn cat. They didn't seem to think much of her, either.

At eighteen, she'd had enough. She most certainly was never getting married, so she might as well give that thought up. On her day off from work, she began driving the family horse to the library, where she spent hours escaping the ties that bound.

Her remaining time was spent helping her adult sisters or brothers, depending on who had a new baby, was behind with her house cleaning, or was hosting church services at her house. She was a maid to her family, working hard for twenty-five dollars a day. Twenty of that went to her father. She sweat profusely in summer, froze her fingers hanging load after load of laundry on freezing lines in winter, learned to cook and clean and perform every household duty expertly and efficiently.

Her sisters sang her praises and her brothers smiled at their wives' descriptions of Mary's capability.

"I don't know where she gets it," Lydia said to her new husband as she rocked her firstborn. "She simply accomplishes so much, with such a small amount of effort."

Her confidence increased a bit as the years went by. She gleaned knowledge from her books, looked at the world with wisdom, and realized she lived on a dreary farm close to an even drearier town. There were Amish bulk food and dry goods stores, a dusty hardware store, and in her twentieth year, a yellow Dollar General appeared along Route 276.

She was one of the first customers, curious, eager, the store containing several aisles of colorful and enticing products—sandals, pink T-shirts, lipstick, and makeup to hide blemishes. She guiltily pushed her stockinged feet into a pair of white sandals and took a few steps before putting the sandals back.

But she smiled to herself.

That day, she purchased hairspray, new shampoo, and body wash that smelled amazing. She went home and practiced doing her hair only a wee bit differently, not enough that her mother would notice. She felt attractive, had a spring in her step.

Her mother noticed and took the hairspray from her with a sharp reprimand. Her father's sad eyes followed her.

They lived on the hope that a young man would ask for her hand. She needed to settle down, start a family, become securely entrenched in her role as a wife and mother. This acting up was not something they had bargained for, and an unsettling emotion ensued.

After turning twenty-one, she was allowed to keep the entire twenty-five dollars she earned for a day's work. Four days of work meant a hundred dollars. Her father opened a bank account for her, with his name on it, so he could check her input, keep track of her deposits, and question her withdrawals.

She stopped working for her siblings, laying out in careful detail her valid reason. She was twenty-one, her own adult now, and there were jobs that paid three or four times what they paid.

She faced disapproval, tight-lipped rebukes, her mother's tears, but would not be deterred. Her father said it was the book reading. Her mother said she had not received enough discipline as a child.

She began having stomach issues and terrible heartburn, so her mother gave her comfrey tea and homemade yogurt. Her headaches turned into a roaring in her ears, her sinuses dripped and burned. Natural remedies helped for a while, but mostly she suffered discomfort after eating, which was quite frequent, food being her only source of comfort after the hawkish attacks from her disapproving family members.

"Why can't you be like the rest of the family?" her mother pleaded.

Her father rebuked her, saying no child of his would go out in the world to find a job.

"No one will hire you," he finished.

For a while, she stayed on the farm, nursing her heartburn and sinuses.

She felt a vague sense of unease, a chafing of restrictions. For a summer, she helped her father till the stony soil, watched the clouds of dust waft across the rolling hills, listened to the songs of migratory birds, and soaked up the sunshine. She did love nature in all its forms, the budding trees, the shy squirrels and wheeling birds. She could name every wildflower, every weed and herb growing along fencerows.

She still loved to get lost in books, and she relished the adventures of heroines who traveled to far-off places around the globe.

Torn between her vivid imagination that was fueled by the steady influx of borrowed library books and her stringent upbringing and guilt because of her inward disobedience, she finally came to the conclusion she needed to get away from Pinedale Valley.

But how?

She prayed. She sought after God's leading, finally bringing up the subject to her mother, who was ironing in the kitchen.

"Mam."

"Hmm?"

"What would you say if I asked to move to Lancaster?"

Without skipping a beat, she said, "No."

"But I want to, Mam. I need to get away. I'm getting old and have no idea what to do with my life here."

"What is that supposed to mean? You'll find a husband eventually."

Mary hesitated before blurting out, "What if I don't want to get married?"

Mam gave her a sharp look. "You have to. Being single is no way to live. Marriage is every young lady's dream."

"Not mine."

"Why not?"

"I don't know why not."

"Oh Mary." Mam's voice softened into a sort of pleading. "You'll break our hearts. Lancaster is no place for you. You need to stay here, where we are more secluded from the world. Where our *ordnung* is kept."

"I don't want to disobey, but I feel as if I can't breathe." She desperately hoped her mother might understand. "I feel as if these mountains are crushing my spirit."

"Where do you get thoughts like that? From the devil, that's where." Her mother's lips formed a thin line, her eyes pools of rebuke.

"Go talk to your brother Abner. He is very level-headed. He'll show you what it means to be *gehorsam* [obedient]. If you can't give in to man, how can you give in to God?"

Mary shook her head in confusion.

"I don't know, Mam. I truly don't."

"Well, then, straighten yourself out."

SHE DID AS her mother asked, driving the horse and carriage to her brother Abner's welding shop. She stood in the doorway, silently watching him pound out a piece of steel. The shop was small, dark, and filthy.

Mud-splattered children shrieked and played in the driveway, hopping puddles.

He looked up and laid down his hammer, a grin spreading his face. "Imagine this," he said.

She smiled. "Yes, imagine. I came to see you."

"Great. Glad to see you."

"The children are really getting muddy."

"I see that."

He went to the door, called, "*Kinna!*"

They obeyed immediately, stepping away from the mud puddles.

She said ruefully. "I wish I was their age."

"Oh, come on, Mary. Time goes on. What gives?"

"I want to move to Lancaster."

He drew himself up to his full height, put out both hands.

"Whoa."

"I know. I know. It simply isn't done."

"Well, it is, but not in our family. Lancaster is a big city, Mary. I'm afraid you'll be misled."

"How could I be? I'm smart."

"Yes. That's true. But a humble spirit and true obedience is better than all the wisdom in the world."

Mary stared at the floor, her heart racing. Another headache was coming on. She felt like if she heard the word "obedience" one more time, she might explode.

"The *ordnung.* Honor thy father and mother. Going against their wishes will bring a curse."

Mary sighed. "How do you know that?"

"It's all over the pages of the Bible. The children of Israel repeatedly disobeyed and were conquered by the enemy. Same thing today. If you don't obey, God will discipline you. Out of love, of course."

Mary heard his voice, but her thoughts churned on in so many other directions.

"Abner, stop. Why do I feel so restless? Perhaps God has something for me in Lancaster. I'm an adult now. If God is calling me to Lancaster, wouldn't it be disobeying Him *not* to go?"

"There are only two ways. One is right and one is wrong. God will never direct you to go against what the Bible says, and it says to honor your father and mother."

Mary sighed, then said she was going to the house to visit with Arie.

She found her sister-in-law amid a clutter of half folded laundry, unwashed dishes, clean clothes hanging from makeshift lines in the corner of the kitchen, her distended abdomen speaking of another impending birth. She lifted tired eyes to Mary, waved a hand as she apologized for the disarray.

One-year-old Annie howled from her playpen in the corner. Mary went to her, caught the scent of a soiled diaper.

"Do you have clean diapers?"

"Here's one."

She reached for one from the mound of graying cloth diapers.

"Why don't you use disposables?"

"Oh goodness, Mary. Abner would never allow it."

Mary watched her rub a palm across her stomach. Obedient to parents, then the church, now her husband. Did God expect this of every woman in the Amish church? She remembered Arie as a younger woman, energy sparkling from her large brown eyes, and here she was, seven or eight years later, hardly recognizable. She was worn down with constant childbearing, a workload that Mary knew was monumental to some wives, the daily grind almost more than they could tolerate.

"You're going to have three babies in diapers. Sammy isn't trained yet, is he?"

"No. Potty training is too much to even think about right now."

"*Ach, my,* Arie."

Arie looked away, blinked. "Don't pity me. It's the way of women."

And Mary wanted to yell, to wave her arms and shriek of the unfairness of her husband's expectation. She thought of the words she'd so often heard: "Women shall be saved through childbearing, submit to

their husbands, and live a life of servantly duty to them, calling them
'Lord.'"

Did it have to be this way?

Yes. It did if you chose to walk this path, but no one would ever
persuade her life had to be quite this difficult.

"Arie."

"Yes?"

"Are you happy this way? Are you content with your lot in life?"

"Mary, what kind of question is that? Of course I'm happy.
Contentment is great gain."

But when she met Mary's gaze, her eyes slid away, as if to conceal
the truth.

Mary left that day with the ever-growing conviction that there had
to be something better in life. She was not cut out for the mind numbing drudgery she had experienced too many times as a maid in her
siblings' homes.

She attended the Sunday evening hymn singing, cast discreet
glances along the row of single men opposite her, and wondered. Every
one promised the life of her sister-in-law, every one would require the
companionship of a dutiful wife, also known as a willing slave. The
conviction bloomed in her chest, took her breath away.

This was not who she was or wanted to be. God had given her brains,
a mind to analyze and comprehend things perhaps others didn't. She
would wait and see what God had in store for her.

Was that so wrong?

Her father cornered her in the milkhouse, his aging straw hat torn
at the brim, stained with sweat and dust, his eyes sparking disapproval.

"I talked to Mam."

"Yes?"

Mary didn't look up, but kept washing milkers. The tank purred as
the agitator spun, stirring and cooling the fresh milk.

Outside, rain dripped steadily from the eaves. A sparrow twittered.

"I hope you know you are forbidden to go."

She didn't answer.

She gasped as her forearm was caught in a vice-like grip. Drawing back, she lifted bewildered eyes, her mouth going dry.

"None of my children has ever gone against my wishes, so I can only warn you not to disobey."

She stared at him, a little in shock. He seemed to realize he'd gone too far and dropped her arm, took a step back. She gathered her thoughts, speaking in what she hoped was a respectful tone. "Dat, I won't leave the Amish. I just want to broaden my horizons. I want to experience new things."

He lowered his face. "If you leave, you will be shunned."

Now her heart lurched again, pushing blood up to her temples. "You can't, Dat! I won't be banned from the church for going to Lancaster. Our relatives live there."

"You heard what I just said."

With that, he was gone, his thin, stooped back rounding the corner. Her heart ached for him, and for herself. She went back to her milker washing, more confused than ever. *God, help me to know what to do*, she prayed silently, a sob stuck in her throat. *If I'm supposed to stay here, help me to be content. If I'm supposed to leave, please make a way.*

WHEN ARIE GAVE birth to Moses, Mary was there, bathing the infant, dressing and swaddling him in cheap flannel blankets, washing sheets and towels, cleaning the house, and trying to keep the four siblings in line. Five children, all preschoolers, cloth diapers, and no money for groceries after the midwife was paid.

She cooked oatmeal and fried eggs for breakfast and tried to maintain a cheerful attitude, at least until she discovered Abner was pouting and wouldn't speak to her. *Well, fine*, she thought. *Absolutely great. You have met your match, brother.*

And she gave him an icy stare and a cold shoulder.

As the days passed, her resolve to leave the area became steadily stronger.

Arie cried with baby blues, and Abner stayed out of her way until she "got over it." When he was finally speaking to Mary again, he told her that Arie always got this way, that it was all in her head and she'd be fine. Women were just weak.

Mary tried to keep the hot rebellion inside but stood up so fast she bumped the couch and knocked over little Annie, who howled indignantly. Mary reached for her, soothed her, and wrinkled her nose. Another mess.

She felt suffocated by diapers, unable to breathe as they piled around her. Arie shuffled around the house, unpinning or pinning her dress front as she changed nursing pads. The baby cried lustily.

Mary made hamburger gravy and opened a jar of green beans. The potatoes boiled over. She plopped a bowl of applesauce on the soiled tablecloth.

At dinner, Johnny was smacked for spilling his water. He opened his mouth and bellowed out his pain and frustration, mashed potatoes spilling out like vomit. Mary grabbed the dishcloth, listened to Abner telling Arie she needed to be more of a disciplinarian with Johnny, and thought, *No, no, no. Never.*

CHAPTER 2

Her Aunt Lizzie came for a visit, an unexpected one, catching them all unaware. She came stalking up the porch steps of Mary's parents' house, opened the door, and called out, "Anybody home?"

Mary was scrubbing the bathtub with Comet. She got up from her knees to see who was at the door, delighted to see Lizzie, her father's sister.

They greeted each other warmly, and Lizzie came straight to the point, after inquiring about the whereabouts of her brother and his wife.

"Oh, an auction. No wonder he doesn't have any money. An auction in the middle of the week."

Mary looked at her.

"Okay, here's what I want. Leroy has to have back surgery, and I have a business to run. I can't leave him without a caregiver, so if I would have you to help me, we'd be in good shape."

"What kind of business?" Mary asked.

"You know. I own a bakery."

"I didn't know."

"Well, I do. I'd train you up for a few weeks, before he goes in for surgery. Do you bake?"

Mary nodded, gesturing at her own ample figure. "Do I look like I bake?"

Lizzie laughed, a sound like pebbles rolling down a hill.

"Oh, you look nice. You just have a few curves, the way a woman is supposed to look."

Mary felt a deep blush. No one spoke so boldly around here.

"Don't you have coffee?" she asked.

Mary blushed even deeper, ashamed of her inhospitable ways. Ashamed of the unpainted barn and thin mules with their ribs like bad slats, the paint peeling from porch posts, the patched trousers on the line, hanging sodden and still. She noticed the couch cover, dark green polyester with a lighter green pleated ruffle around the bottom, homemade many years ago. Cracked linoleum. A vinyl tablecloth in dark blue, faded green blinds with Folgers coffee jars lined on the windowsills and holding tepid pink geraniums ready to be planted in flower beds.

Mary put on the kettle.

"Is that all you have? Instant?" she inquired.

"Sorry."

"Guess it will have to do. Once you have a coffee maker, it's just so much better than instant. But it seems as if this part of New York never changes much, does it?"

"No, I guess we don't."

She almost apologized again, then knew it would be ridiculous. She felt a need to protect her home community for unexplained reasons—perhaps it was only instinct, but it was there nonetheless.

"I'm staying until I can talk to your parents, but then I have to get going. I came up here with a load of Henry Beiler's sisters and they're heading back tonight. I hope you'll come with me."

Mary's head spun. This was her answer to prayer. God had made a way, and much sooner than she'd even imagined! She could be on her way to Lancaster that very night.

WHEN MARY'S PARENTS arrived, Lizzie eyed her mother's shawl and bonnet, sniffed, and adjusted her nice new sweater before shaking hands. Mary sensed her father's disapproval, saw his eyes travel over Lizzie's fashionable white covering, the lack of a *halsduch*, the cable knit sweater, down to the Skechers on her feet. She knew his thoughts were telling him, here was a prime example of why he did not want Mary to go to Lancaster.

Lizzie told them why she'd come.

Amos remained quiet while she spoke, then asked in a tight voice why she couldn't find someone in Lancaster, where she came from.

"Mary needs to get away. She would make an excellent supervisor in my opinion."

"How do you even know? You've hardly spent any time with her," her father growled. Then suddenly he turned to Mary, his voice accusing. "Did you write and ask her for this?"

Lizzie jumped in before Mary could even answer.

"No, of course she did not. I just know that she's getting . . . older," she cast a careful look at Mary, not wanting to hurt her feelings. "And I read the *Botschaft*, you know, and I noticed that she's always someone's *maud*. Probably for forty dollars a day or something ridiculous."

"Twenty-five."

"What?!" shouted Lizzie "That's practically robbery."

Mary's mother almost smiled, but caught it quickly.

"If she goes with me, she'll be making fifteen, twenty dollars an hour. An hour," she repeated triumphantly.

"Money is the root of all evil," Amos quoted dryly.

"You're wrong. The love of money is the root of all evil. Not the money itself. It's the love of it that's wrong."

He gave her a level stare.

"Anyway," she continued, unperturbed, "there are plenty of girls I could hire in Lancaster, and I do have a few working for me now. But I need someone who can hit the ground running and I just get the feeling Mary is that kind of girl. I know I can trust her. You've raised her well." She looked at Amos, hoping the compliment would soften the stern look on his face. It did not.

"Come on, Amos. Lighten up. Mary is of age. She's twenty-one. Let her go see some of the world before she gets married and is stuck in these forlorn hills."

Mary watched her father control his anger.

"They are not forlorn if God is with us, as I believe He is."

"Course He is. But He's in Lancaster as well."

"We hope so. Well, Lizzie, I forbid her to go. It's no place for a daughter of mine."

"Oh, come on, Amos. At least until Leroy heals up. I came all the way out here so I could ask face-to-face. I knew you'd have concerns, but let's be reasonable and talk them through. What exactly are you worried about?"

"It was foolish to come without writing or calling first. You wasted your time."

"I knew that would just give you more time to fret about it. Lancaster is not such a bad place, you know. You grew up there, after all. And I'll keep her so busy there won't be time to get into trouble."

"She's not going."

"Yes, Dat. I am." Mary spoke with a confidence she didn't know she possessed. "I'm twenty-one and quite capable of making my own decisions."

Lizzie's face lit up. "See? She wants to go."

"She won't have my blessing."

"You're just the same as you always were. Determined old stick-in-the-mud is what you are. Crabby as all get out."

It was all Mary could do to keep from laughing out loud. She'd never heard someone stand up to her father like that and suddenly the whole thing seemed comical. She could feel the jiggling inside her stomach. Her mouth twitched.

She looked at her mother, who brought her eyebrows down in stern warning.

MARY PACKED QUICKLY and left with Lizzie that evening, her insides a maelstrom of doubts and fears. The knowledge of her disobedience weighed heavily on her, and she felt cursed by the stern Old Testament God of Abraham. She thought of how she'd left her parents on the porch, bogged down in failure, their eyes swimming with tears.

What had she done?

Her stomach rumbled. She thought she might retch. Her temples pounded.

As the adrenaline from the afternoon wore off, she began to feel frightened. Was she cursed now? Would God punish her for going against her parents' wishes? She endured alarming turmoil in her soul, absolutely certain she was doomed.

Almost, she called out to the driver, "Turn around, take me back so I can experience the blessing of my father. Take me back to marry some man and raise eleven children, suffocating my own will under his rule and a mountain of soiled diapers. If that's what's necessary to obtain the real blessing from God, I'll do it."

When the van pulled into a Sheetz parking lot, everyone clambered out noisily, went into the brightly lit store, and returned with foil-wrapped sandwiches, paper cups of French fries, and bottles of soda.

When Lizzie returned, she sang out, "Don't you want anything?"

"No."

"Sure you do."

With that, Lizzie backed out of the van into the store and returned with a brown paper bag, which she handed back to Mary, saying there were napkins and ketchup. Mary had never tasted soda from a bottle. Immediately her eyes watered and her nose burned horribly when she swallowed.

Her cheeseburger was delightful, the French fries a dream. She wondered how often Lancaster people went to Sheetz. Would it be wasteful to go every few months?

She didn't know how to open the packets of ketchup, so she rolled them in leftover napkins and stuffed them in the bottom of the bag. As the warm food settled in her stomach, her mood lifted.

She was still frightened by her own bold move, still hated the thought of her parents suffering in any way because of her, but it was done now.

It was the middle of the night when they arrived at Lizzie's house after a bewildering number of roads, lights, moving traffic, and buildings crosshatching the dark night. Everything was so alive, pulsing and thumping, cars stopping and starting, trucks shifting gears, and through it all an occasional horse and buggy running alongside.

Country mouse, that was her.

But Lizzie's house was warm and inviting, her husband Leroy getting up from the couch, gasping in pain, but welcoming. Lights were snapped on, and Mary thought there was electricity, but Lizzie said they were rechargeable battery lamps. The house was so fancy.

Mary looked around, her eyes wide, wondering how much she still had to learn. She was shown to her bedroom upstairs in the small Cape Cod, the windows built into dormers, traffic humming below. She had her own bathroom with a shower, a bed that was solid and soft at the same time, a quilt so cozy it seemed like a cloud covering her.

She snuggled in and was immediately attacked by fear of her disobedience. Her mouth went dry. Her stomach heaved. She began to pray, but the ceiling kept her prayers from going beyond.

What have I done? she thought wildly.

Mam. Dat. I'm so sorry. Forgive me. I don't know if it's worth it, this crazy adventure, but I want more from life than what you have to offer. Is that a sin? What is sin? Is everything wrong? Sometimes it feels like it.

She wept a bit that first night. She hated herself a bit, too. Why had she done this? Now it seemed as if Lizzie's invitation had not been an answer to prayer but rather the devil tempting her into sin.

She fell asleep from sheer exhaustion, confused to find herself in strange surroundings when she woke. Guilt stabbed her conscience immediately, the thought of her parent's grief like a knife in her side.

She'd go back today. She'd hire a driver and go back. Fall back into the old routine. Be blessed.

But Leroy and Lizzie were friendly, inviting her to the table for a mug of steaming coffee. Lizzie produced a tall, odd-shaped container that said "Starbucks" on it, opened the spout, and poured a steady stream of thick, creamy liquid into her own mug. She handed the bottle to Mary, her eyebrows raised.

"Is this cream?"

"Better. Caramel macchiato creamer."

Mary looked at her aunt, bewildered.

"Try it."

So she did, and she was pleasantly surprised.

Aunt Lizzie's kitchen was bright and clear, with oak cupboards that seemed to gleam in the sunshine that filtered through the windows. There was a large propane refrigerator and stove and houseplants and ceramic knickknacks everywhere. Artificial flowers in brilliant colors nodded from vases and there were small signs with Bible verses or wise sayings all over the walls. A clock on the wall had a long list of sayings. When music began to sound across the kitchen, she was so taken aback, she set her coffee down and looked for the source.

"Isn't it pretty? That's Amos Raber's songs. He's an accomplished guitar player. Also does the harmonica so well. I just love my clock. The girls went together and bought it for me for Mother's Day."

"Oh."

It was all she could think to say. She thought of her father immediately. He disapproved of musical instruments.

"There's a chip inside. A tiny little thing. You can purchase dozens of different ones. Leroy likes this one best. That song was, 'Daddy's Hands.'"

She hummed a few bars, her fingertips tapping the tabletop.

"Music is good for the soul, Mary. I know some say it's forbidden, but these clocks inject a bit of sunshine in my day. *Gel*, Leroy."

He nodded, said he could certainly use it these days, enduring all this pain from his lower back. Lizzie reached over and patted his hand.

"Poor dear. You have been so patient."

The look they exchanged was one Mary had never seen between her parents. She knew they loved each other, but they would never display affection in the presence of others.

Lizzie made omelets and bacon for breakfast. Conversation flowed freely, Lizzie being extremely talkative, saying she was "worked up" having a new person in the house.

"Yes, Mary, it's a shame, the way my brothers and sisters are scattered. Such an extreme difference in all of us, living in faraway states, some of them choosing other churches. Ben's family has *gonz English* [gone 'English,' left the Amish] now, living in Nevada or Arizona, some crazy place like that. I haven't seen Ben for years. It's a shame. And then there's your father, so strict, looking down on the rest of us."

She shook her head.

Was he strict? Did her father look down on his siblings? He never spoke of anyone, so who knew? A part of her sided with him. He was so sincere in his convictions, his way of life above rebuke. He was her father, and now, hundreds of miles away, she sided with him, in a way at least.

She opened her mouth, closed it again. Perhaps Lizzie would take offense if she sided with her family, and she certainly did not want to start off on the wrong foot, this being her first morning.

"The way that place looks, it's not even *chide* [proper]. You'd think he could at least spread some paint on that barn. I don't know where he gets it, that pitiful attempt at farming up there. You'd think he would have known the area was poor when he bought it."

"The price of the farm was very reasonable."

"But to what end? Everybody is poor up there."

Lizzie hung up her dishcloth, and Mary said nothing. She felt torn between loyalty to her parents and wanting to see the world through Lizzie's eyes.

THE ROOM ATTACHED to the house was like a three-car garage, with windows allowing the sun to cast plenty of light, the interior appearing immense. There were tabletops of gleaming stainless steel, a huge mixer, refrigerator, and what she guessed were ovens at eye level. Mary saw racks with aluminum trays, countless pans and cookie sheets, spoons and supplies, flour and sugar in fifty-pound bags. That was familiar, the way her mother had always done her buying for the household in bulk.

There was a smell of burnt sugar and yeast, coupled with the scent of pine cleaner someone had used on the floor, probably.

"What do you think?"

Lizzie turned, expectantly.

"Oh, it's nice. Very nice. I've never seen anything like it. How many workers did you say you have?"

"Four."

"Including me?"

"No, without you. We make many different things. But I think I'll start you off doing bread and rolls. It's an easy job. Then later you can learn pies, and whoopie pies."

Mary nodded, but said nothing. She'd made pies, bread, cakes, all of that ever since she could remember, but did not want to appear as if she knew more than her aunt. But she thought of flaky pie crust, sweet fillings spilling from between them, loaves of bread risen high and light, whoopie pies like a photograph in a cookbook.

Yes. This was her domain. Adrenaline coursed through her veins. She smiled, ran a palm across a tabletop, felt the gleaming smoothness.

Professional. This was a real commercial bakery, a job paying her real wages.

Her aunt prattled on, a constant stream of instruction and how-tos. She talked about how much they produced, the high prices they could charge, the cost of Leroy's surgery, all the while wiping the sink with squirts of Dawn dish soap, muttering about Ruthann's poor clean up.

Who was Ruthann? Mary wondered. She dreaded meeting these girls, felt her resolve crumble at the thought, painfully aware of her dreadful hair, the large old covering so terribly out of style.

Nothing she could do to change that now.

The bakery was open on Thursday, Friday, and Saturday. All the baking was done on those days, as well as Wednesday. Supplies and inventory were done on Monday, which left Tuesday to run around, go shopping, clean, and do laundry or yard work.

Lizzie didn't have much of a garden, she said. No time. And besides, she didn't need bushes of tomatoes and beans the way she did when the children were home. A bit of canning and freezing was all that was necessary. Her work was cut out for her in the bakery.

MARY LEARNED FAST. Lizzie soon put her in charge of the others, but this did not sit well with the girls who had been there longer, especially the older girl named Rebecca, or Beck, as she was called. Ruthann and Susan, or Suze, accepted Mary, but rolled their eyes behind her back, thought her awfully outdated and backwoodsy. Aunt Lizzie noticed the tension between the girls, but once Leroy's operation was over, she had to focus on caring for him, and she felt she could trust Mary completely.

Mary was a wonder. The most efficient work engine she'd ever seen. She plowed through tubs of dough, even tweaked the recipes here and there until the dinner rolls, sandwich rolls, and loaves of bread were golden perfection. Lizzie sang her praises.

Beck was first, whispering behind a raised palm to Ruthann. Who did Mary think she was, coming from the pitiful Pinedale Valley, dressed like a minister's wife, fat with that awful red hair? Greasy, too. Didn't she use shampoo?

Suze joined in then, and the bakery became a sort of war zone, filled with catty remarks that sent Mary into a reclusive shell of hurt feelings.

She worked even harder, staving off the homesickness and the impending knowledge that she was an outcast.

Her first time at church, she stood on the outskirts of a group of girls that looked like an entirely different species than the girls at home. These were real Lancaster girls with long dresses and tight sleeves, hair arranged fashionably with a much smaller heart-shaped covering setting off tanned good looks. White capes and aprons fit the girls perfectly, and there were shoes with heels, and even slip-ons, the epitome of being fancy.

Mary leaned against a wall, crossed her arms, and put a hand to her chin, wishing she could disintegrate, *poof,* into a pile of ashes and be swept into a dustpan and dumped in the trash.

No one spoke to her. No one looked at her, except for a few sideways glances. But the church service was conducted exactly the same as her home services, the singing from the thick black *Ausbund* hymnal, the minister's voice rising and falling in the common mixture of high German and Pennsylvania Dutch, the prayers on bended knees.

She lifted shy glances as the young men filed in, appalled to find a dozen or more with "English" haircuts, yet dressed in the black trousers and *mutza* (suits) of the Amish *ordnung*. Some of them were breathtakingly handsome, which only made her feel worse about herself.

She tried to concentrate on the sermon, but her mind tumbled off repeatedly, imagining trying to carve out a life for herself in Lancaster County, far away from the restrictions of her iron-fisted father with his rules of discipline, his soft voice and contentment.

Who would keep her from changing her dress?

She was still Amish, still a member of the Old Order, still believed in the articles of faith, in *ordnung* and obedience. But did one have to submit to the point where you have nothing at all, no will or spirit to exercise over your life? Did all women have to be turned into childbearing, diaper-changing zombies? "Zombie" was a word she'd come across in a novel and then looked up in the dictionary at the library. "A human without will or speech, resembling the so-called 'walking dead.'" Sounded an awful lot like her sister-in-law.

She'd tried to explain to her closest friend, Barbie, who simply could not grasp what she was saying.

"But Mary," she insisted. "Marrying and having children is a high calling from God. Our obedience to His will brings us peace and contentment. What is better than the peace of our Father in our hearts?"

"But what about us? What about our own dreams, our own lives?"

Perplexed, Barbie lifted eyes that were blank as clean paper.

"That is our life," she answered.

"What if you don't want a husband and children? Is that so wrong?"

"Why no, of course not. The Bible says it's better to stay single."

"Well then, what's the big deal?"

Barbie shook her head, and for a long time after, her best friend's disapproval haunted her.

Now here she was, loving her job but finding herself on the outside, a guinea fowl with a peculiar way of dressing and strange way of speaking. She doubted herself, doubted God, felt cast away from the blessing of obedience.

Her stomach rumbled and roared, produced debilitating gas and bloating. Her sinuses ached, her nose ran continuously, followed by searing headaches. She discovered Extra Strength Tylenol, and was relieved of all her symptoms, for a while. Her mood lifted after taking three, then four.

And she gained some confidence at the bakery. She told Ruthann a better way of rolling the dough for cinnamon rolls, helped Suze wet her hands to shape monster cookies. She told Aunt Lizzie her pie fillings needed more sugar, a touch of butter, and lemon juice.

Sales increased.

She developed a way of marketing whoopie pies, stacking them upright in plastic containers, checking to make sure the filling was evenly distributed. She added red velvet whoopie pies, and banana nut.

When business picked up so much they were struggling to keep up, another girl was hired, Dan King's Linda.

Over the course of the summer, Mary learned to wash her hair more than once a week, found the heavy red tresses to be softer and more manageable. She used hairspray, learned to comb them into neat, heavy rolls. Aunt Lizzie helped her buy a new covering, stiff and unusual, feeling as if it would fall off her head. Her ears felt positively naked.

She learned to sew her own dresses and wore bib aprons, something that had always been strictly forbidden. She wore the colors of the rainbow, even lavender, pink, and yellow. The girls at the bakery watched the transformation, turned their backs, and sniffed.

Some hillbilly wannabe.

Mary became restless when she wasn't working. She wanted something to do on weekends, but had no way of knowing how to insert herself into the crowds of young people.

Aunt Lizzie hoped the bakery girls would warm up to her, but not one of them welcomed her or made any attempt at inviting her to the gathering they attended. She was heavier than them, she had flaming red hair, and no clue how to dress. She came from upstate New York, for pity's sake. And they turned up their noses.

So Mary spent her weekends playing chess with Uncle Leroy or Scrabble with Aunt Lizzie, or reading magazines and books from the library in Intercourse.

She continued to gain confidence at the bakery as Aunt Lizzie's praises grew. She was told repeatedly she was the best thing that ever happened to her. Lizzie took her to a fancy restaurant, where they ordered salad and steak and shrimp, Aunt Lizzie teaching her how to cut the steak and peel the shrimp. She ate a slice of cake unlike anything she'd ever tasted before, developed her own version in the bakery, and it sold out the first day.

She considered going home for a visit, but could hardly face the thought of meeting her parents dressed in these well-fitting, high-styled dresses and shoes. She wrote them a letter, writing of her beloved job, her love for Lizzie and Leroy, and that she missed all of them very much.

When a letter came back a week later, tears rose to the surface as she read the news of home in her mother's neat, cursive hand.

"Greetings of love *im Namen Yesu* [in the name of Jesus]."

So old-fashioned, so dear, so real. Homesickness threatened to choke her.

CHAPTER 3

Eventually, she decided she'd been lonely long enough and it was time to take matters into her own hands. The bakery girls were never going to be her friends, so she'd have to find some somewhere else. She dressed in an avocado hue, took a long time with her hair and covering, and told Aunt Lizzie she was walking to the supper at a neighboring farm.

Lizzie gasped. "You can't do that, Mary."

"Why not? I have to start making friends somehow. These girls at the bakery won't accept me. Jealousy is a terrible thing."

Hmm, Lizzie thought. *Smart.*

"I'll walk, see what happens."

"*Ach,* Mary. Do you want Leroy and me to go with you?"

"You don't have to."

Lizzie eyed her hair, her cape and apron. Yes, Mary was learning, but she was not as neat as she should be. One side of her cape was crooked, the pin offset.

"Here, let me help you with your shoulder here."

Mary thanked her, looked in the mirror one last time, faced the glow of the late summer sun as it headed toward evening, and walked along the busy highway, her head held high.

Leroy and Lizzie sat on the back porch with glasses of meadow tea and thanked their lucky stars for Mary. They chuckled at her absolute confidence, the way she'd "made herself out," in Dutch words, turning into a young woman that was no longer a shrinking violet.

The fabrics she picked out at the dry goods store!

Oh my, Lizzie laughed. And Leroy's eyes twinkled, knowing exactly what she meant. Brilliant rose, electric blue, dusty orange, and fiery red. Mary's parents would be shocked. Lizzie felt almost guilty, but what really was the harm in a brighter wardrobe?

Mary walked up the drive of a perfect farm setting, gray farmhouse, white dairy barn, clean white outbuildings with a manicured lawn and garden, gleaming carriages parked in neat rows, people milling about as the women set the table buffet style on folding tables in the side yard.

A volleyball game was going on behind the back barn. She entered through an open gate in the white fence.

She said hello to a few of the women, then walked on, looking around and seeing a group of girls sitting on the ground watching the game. She walked slowly now, but smiled when a few of them looked up. There was surprise, almost alarm, a wariness on most faces.

"Hi. I'm Mary Glick. Mind if I join you?"

A silence stretched as taut as an elongated rubber band. Just when Mary thought this might be the worst mistake of her life, a small blond girl with a severe case of acne on both cheeks rose to her feet, extended a hand, and said in a deep, gravelly voice, "Hi. I'm Linda."

They made eye contact, and a friendship was born.

Linda Lantz was the oldest in a family of seven, it turned out. She was only a year younger, had never had a date, or been asked out on a Saturday night, and didn't let it bother her. She lived close to Leola, which wasn't that far away, and she only went to suppers and singings because she had to. Her parents were adamant about attending these functions, saying it was a time-honored tradition, and one they hoped would always be part of their children's lives.

Linda introduced her to Sara Ann, Liz, and Karen, who gave her a friendly smile before turning their attention back to the game.

Just then someone said it was time for dinner and the volleyball game came to a halt. The young men and women all lined up with divided Styrofoam plates and plastic utensils and loaded their plates from the deep aluminum pans of lasagna and scalloped potatoes and took salad from a cavernous bowl.

She was being scrutinized by the group of parents clustered beneath the maple trees. She took a deep breath, exhaled, held her head high. She was stopped by an older gentleman, his beard snow white around a tanned, wrinkled face.

"I don't believe I know who you are," he said, squinting at her with curious blue eyes.

She told him. He calculated shrewdly.

"You say Lizzie's niece? I see. Your dad is her brother? Pinedale? Heard of it, never been there. Who is your father, you say?"

And so forth, other men leaning in to listen.

Linda complained about her lasagna being cold and said it was stupid the way everyone had to know who everyone else was, taking forever to figure out whose cousin was related to whose brother's aunt's grandmother.

"You should have told him you're Sam's, Check's, Amosa, Dannie's Mary. Let him figure that one out."

Surprised, Mary cast her a look, then laughed out loud.

"Well, I wasn't able to think that fast, so I told him the truth."

"Probably the best. I get sick of everyone being so nosy, trying to figure out how everyone fits together like we're a gigantic jigsaw puzzle. It's annoying."

Her rough voice was tinged with irritation. Mary watched her reach up to apply a fingernail to her skin, scratch a protruding pimple. A dot of blood appeared, was scraped away.

"Do you have a Kleenex?" she asked.

"No. Sorry."

"I hate my skin."

Mary searched for something to say. "It's . . ."

"It's horrible. So bad. No boy will ever look at me with this skin."

"Does it matter?"

"What?"

"That no one looks at you."

"Well, yeah. Of course."

Mary took a bite of lasagna, chewed, swallowed, then looked over at her.

"Having a boyfriend isn't everything."

Linda raised her eyebrows. "Boy, you're different."

She dabbed at the bleeding pimple with the inside corner of her black apron, lifted it to the light, then turned her face to Mary.

"Is it still bleeding?"

"No. You know, though, the worst thing you can do is pick at your face, don't you?"

"I know. But I'm always afraid there's a yellow tip. It's so gross."

"Well, it's okay. I'm fat and have red hair, and there's not much I can do about either one. You can go to a dermatologist."

"Whatever that is," Linda said dryly.

When Mary explained, Linda shrugged, said her mother was one hundred and twenty percent natural and didn't believe in antibiotics. She'd tried every remedy available, including organic vinegar and detoxing, clay, homemade soap, and all kinds of crappy lotions. She didn't eat sugar or white flour, ate kale and cabbage and all kinds of high vitamin foods, and her skin still looked like the surface of the moon.

Mary felt the familiar jiggle of laughter in the pit of her stomach. Her eyes crinkled and she tried keeping a straight face, but she had to laugh out loud at Linda's expression. She leaned over and touched shoulders.

"I have a distinct feeling I have a true friend," she said.

Linda looked at her. "You do. You definitely do. I should warn you though that it's not just the bad skin. I also have a nasty attitude. Sometimes I can't stand anyone, and am guilty of letting people know."

"I think you're pretty, Linda. I also think you're refreshingly honest, a quality I find so rare in young women like us."

Their conversation was halted by two young men who flopped down on the grass beside them, their faces gleaming with perspiration.

"Hey, Sis," the smaller blond one said. "You going to eat the rest of that lasagna?"

He reached over like he was going to take her fork. She slapped his hand.

"Get your own."

"Who's your friend?"

"Mary Glick. From New York. Pinedale Valley."

"Where the Harry is that?"

"Halfway to the North Pole," Mary offered.

He laughed. His friend joined in.

"Mary, this is my brother Jimmy. The other guy is Jimmy's sidekick, Davey King's Marcus."

"Hello, Marcus. Nice to meet you."

"Hi, Mary."

"So, Mary," Jimmy asked. "You joining the Diamonds?"

Mary looked puzzled, shook her head.

Linda came to her rescue. "That's our group. The Diamonds. There are so many young people in Lancaster County, we're divided into groups. Every group has a different name, different levels of, oh, how would you word it? Morals? *Chide*ness? Wild or tame? Decent or not? I don't know. You just pick and choose who you want to be, I guess."

Mary had gathered as much from the girls' talk at the bakery, but found this description honest and helpful. Marcus, his brown eyes small and too close to his protruding nose, was intelligent and full of laughter. He filled her in on the wide range of differences, from driving vehicles to still using the old-fashioned courting buggies with no top, only a big black umbrella hoisted in case of rain or snow. The Diamonds were somewhere in the middle.

Mary was unsure of her own honesty. Should she tell these new friends about five years of running around in an old-fashioned courting buggy, the heavy black umbrella an accustomed way of life? Would they poke fun at her if she did? She decided to let it go, for now, afraid of a culture divide scaring them away. Guilt crashed around her, obscuring her view. She was not where her parents thought she should be.

In September, she took the Greyhound bus to Albany, then switched to an incoming bus going all the way north almost to her hometown in Pinedale Valley. She wore her plainest dress, a somber navy blue, an apron pinned around her waist, black shoes and heavy black stockings. She knew her hair and new covering would not be well received, but she couldn't bring herself to go back to the old stained and threadbare one she'd worn before going to Lancaster.

So much rested on her outward appearance.

She tried setting her face to a pious expression, but was rigid with fear of her father's words, spoken softly, but steely with menace, and her mother's weeping, and all her sibling's disapproving looks. She missed them all and knew this visit was a necessity, one she had looked forward to for a month, despite the tension she knew would meet her. When she stepped off the bus, she breathed in the scent of pure mountain air, of tumbling water and whispering firs, sun-warmed rocks and cool pockets of air beneath them. Almost, a lump formed in her throat, knowing how much she had missed about her home in New York.

She'd missed the clean, cold air as she hung out laundry, trimming wick on kerosene lamps, washing the glass chimneys until they sparkled, new calves and squealing litters of piglets, bare feet squishing in the mud. The scent of boiling apple butter beneath the glory of an orange sugar maple in the fall.

She was brimming with nostalgia when she got out of the car, paid Ernest Decker his ten dollars for picking her up from the bus station, and made her way to the porch. Her heart pounded as she opened the screen door and her mother hurried across the living room floor.

Her expression turned from one of joy to consternation as she said, "Mary."

"Hello, Mam."

"My, it's good to see you."

Mary watched the display of changing emotions on her mother's face.

Gladness, then a reaction to her hair and covering, her eyes raking in the *hochmut* (pride) of her dress, an all-consuming sadness mixed with real fear. But wasn't there a hint of appreciation at her youngest daughter's blossoming?

"*Ach*, Mary. It spites me."

Mary looked away, unable to face the raw disappointment in her mother's eyes.

"What will Dat say?"

Mary swallowed, cleared her throat.

"Mam, does it matter what he says? I am an adult. I make my own choices. I am still Amish. Why must it be this way?"

"Honor thy father and mother," was her stiff reply.

They tried a united conversation, but both knew her *ungehorsam* (not proper, disobedient) appearance had efficiently severed the close ties of familiarity.

Mam abhorred style of any kind, had never imagined any of her children dressing in this manner. She dreaded her husband's arrival, which was every bit as hard as she had feared, the way tears swam in his tired eyes and he sat down heavily, his thick gnarled hands clutching each other on the tabletop, as if for support.

"Mary, is this really what you want?"

"Dat, I am still the same Mary. I just live and work among people who dress a bit differently than here in Pinedale Valley."

"The devil is cunning, devising ways to devour the soul. *Hochmut* was taken out of Heaven and will never enter back in. You are already misled, traveling on the broad path of destruction, and if you don't change your ways and come to repentance, you will burn in eternity."

"Dat."

Her cry for mercy came from the heart, a plea to be understood.

"What if *hochmut* is pride at the heart and not of the outward appearance? Perhaps some of the plainest among us is guilty of having the spirit of the Scribes and Pharisees?"

"Mary."

The word fell heavily, a gavel of doom. She knew she was being taken as a true heretic, fallen away, when in truth, she didn't feel any different inside, only experiencing life more fully, taking in color and light and a release of choking restraint. She knew her father was firmly soaked, marinated in his version of right or wrong, his version of who would enter into Heaven and who would burn in hell. There was only the black and white, the *ordnung* kept or the *ordnung* ignored. Heaven or hell.

"Please come home now, and follow God's will," he said brokenly.

Who could resist the pleading voice of a father? Mary was dizzy with fear of disobeying, torn by her devotion to Aunt Lizzie.

"But, I don't want to. I may be guilty of appearing different, but still feel God's will in Lancaster."

"I don't believe that," her father growled.

Round and round they went as the golden light of a New York September evening turned into a pink and gray twilight. Chores were done, and Mary took her old place washing milkers in the double stainless steel sink, humming in tune to the soft whir of the agitator in the bulk tank. She smelled wet concrete, fresh creamy milk, the yellow soap and the underlying scent of lime and cow manure. She hadn't known she missed the milking so much.

Her parents fell into a saddened acceptance of their errant daughter, listened as she told them news of seldom visited relatives, the unbelievable land prices, the hundreds of thriving businesses and frenetic work pace.

"Prosperity will be the downfall of the Amish," her father predicted, his face sagging with disapproval, his mouth pinched with the uncharitable attitude he hosted.

Mary said nothing but thought of him dragging his rusty farm equipment through thin, stony soil, the skinny, lop-eared mules plodding on, his mind occupied with a thin, stingy God eager to mete punishment on anyone and everyone who stepped out of line. And his line was thin, exacting, leaving no room for any slip-ups. She felt the hum of rebellion, a jagged cut of lightning that sizzled between them.

She spoke out.

"Dat, don't you believe in the blood of Jesus Christ being the only way?"

For a long, cold moment there was only silence, then a "yes, but obedience must follow faith, and there are many sins that will take away grace. Grace is a vapor. We need to strive after it at all times."

Before she left, her mother assured her of her father's love for her, reminding her that he was a steadfast man in all his ways, and would remain attached to his stringent rules. She confessed that she was often of a different mind, but chose to give herself up to her husband's tutelage. Her eyes wandered out across the yard, to the screen door as she spoke, finally giving a small laugh.

"I guess your ways come from me, Mary. My heart often rejoices in the truth of God's grace, but perhaps it's my obedience that brings me to that. I don't know. I don't have to know."

"So, you think I'm alright, Mam?"

She sighed, then reached over for an uncharacteristic pat on the shoulder.

"Just keep love in your heart and obey the rules where you are, Mary. And don't do anything I wouldn't do."

Mary was so shocked her eyes opened wide, and her mother gave her a broad wink, before a smile spread across her face.

"I am always side by side with your father, you know that. But I also have a mind of my own, tucked away safely."

"Mam, I had no idea."

"Well, you do now. I know, with a mother's intuition, that you won't be back, that your home is in Lancaster now, and we need to accept that, which in time, we will. Your way of dress is a culture shock to us, but you're old enough to make your own decisions now."

"But, Mam. I don't want to hurt you. I just feel like I'm not cut out for life here."

Wisely, her mother nodded. "I know."

She traveled south that day, heartened by her mother's words, but a bit mystified at the thought that she wasn't quite on the same level as her father. She had always appeared to be in perfect unison, but really she'd been concealing her own, different thoughts and beliefs the whole time?

Mary's heart was glad to return to Leroy and Lizzie. She'd grown fond even of their married children who dropped in unannounced, a genuine love between them. Leroy was now back to work at the welding shop where he obtained a job in the office.

Sales increased at the bakery until Lizzie threw her hands in the air and said this was it, she was no longer knocking herself out, she had had enough. If they ran out of an item on Friday evening, well then, they were out. Customers could come back the following week.

They added another worker, a sullen fifteen-year-old neighbor boy who sneaked cigarettes behind the barn and stepped on the cat's tail on purpose, laughing when the cat yowled and jumped. But he hoisted fifty-pound bags of flour with ease, emptied garbage cans, and peeled neck pumpkins with more accuracy and speed than any of the girls could.

Then came Thanksgiving, with dozens of pumpkin, mincemeat, sour cherry, and lemon sponge pie orders. They rose at three in the morning, set the bread and dinner rolls to rise, and mixed pie crust.

Mary still loved her job at the bakery and was getting along better with the girls now that she looked like everyone else and had learned the modern slang. Jealousy had been gradually replaced with respect as she took on the bulk of the work and never complained that the others were less skilled and efficient. She gave them gentle suggestions for improving, but never made them feel badly.

Her weekends were now entertaining, Linda an unexpected source of unending amusement, her brother Jimmy their willing driver, often with Marcus in tow. They went bowling, played miniature golf, went to concerts and Saturday night "picture shows," as they called movies to set their guilty consciences free. They played volleyball at Saturday night gatherings and came home in the wee hours of Sunday morning, dressing for church bleary-eyed but happy.

No one had curfews. Parents knew their teenagers were at the home of other Amish parents, so they didn't worry about their safety.

Mary discovered a new sense of humor, delighted in the laughter coming free and easy. She learned how to order in restaurants, how to lay a cloth napkin across her lap, how to cut a steak and to eat mousse with a spoon. Her world was a clean palette, and she held the brushes in her hand, choosing the colors and creating the life she wanted.

Only on occasion, the sad eyes of her father came to haunt her, bringing a sort of vague pity. Sometimes her siblings, Lydia or Abner or Rachel, wrote her a letter containing verses from the Bible, meant to keep her in line, which mostly served to irritate her.

Caught up in the dashing life of a young woman in the humming community, she was happier than she'd ever been.

She had a substantial nest egg, a new set of bedroom furniture, her upstairs bathroom done in the latest style, a closet filled to overflowing with brilliant colors, sweaters and jackets and shoes. Not a day went by without a full appreciation of all she had acquired.

She went to the local clinic for an evaluation of her sinus headaches and the rumbling in her intestines. Sent for an ultrasound, she was humiliated beyond words, and when the results came back, with all signs clear, she told Linda it was ridiculous, spending three hundred dollars for a test that showed absolutely nothing.

Linda's mother, Mima Stoltzfus, told her to try organic vinegar, and she told her she'd already done that. Enzymes? Done that, too.

Linda asked if she'd ever heard of a disease of the mind called being a hypochondriac, and Mary thought that was rude and hurtful.

Of course, she wasn't one. Her stomach hurt, her sinuses raged, and that was a fact of life. Linda said she might be infested with parasites and could take Ivermectin, the way a lot of folks did when they contracted COVID-19.

Mary told her she was not a horse or a cow and she was not taking medicine meant for one, and Linda laughed till she cried.

Oh, they had so much fun, joking and laughing, having deep, serious talks about their futures, and if and when they would ever be asked to be someone's girlfriend. Mary wrinkled her nose, but Linda lived for that moment, naming five or six different young men she would definitely accept, then ran her fingers down her pockmarked face and despaired, saying who would even want to touch this mess? "I look like I have leprosy," she lamented.

They tried not to laugh, since leprosy wasn't funny, but they couldn't help it if they did laugh, then. Linda was just naturally funny, without trying, and Mary told her she had the gift of humor.

Linda said there was no such thing, women were supposed to be sober, keepers at home, loving their husbands and all that good stuff, and they nodded their heads in silent agreement before laughing again.

CHAPTER 4

She went home for Christmas, the last fifty miles spent bracing her feet against the seat in front of her, the huge Greyhound wallowing through a New York snow storm as it sped down the interstate. She had never been so glad to arrive safely at her parents' house, to be held by the warmth of four walls and a good wood stove in the kitchen.

She dressed in dark colors and a black belt apron, but endured the quiet stares of disapproval again, her father's thin frame folded into a rocking chair drawn up to the woodstove, her mother nervously chattering as she cut up celery for the *roascht*.

Mary loved a white Christmas, loved the whirling quiet of a snow storm, the falling flakes creating a soft swish around her as she went for an evening walk. White pine trees and snowy owls, twittering titmice and nuthatches at the feeder, the flash of a male cardinal followed by his humble brown mate—she soaked up all of it. She would always love the snow, the cold wind that blew in from the north, the pristine drifts crafted in layers by the force of it.

Her siblings arrived in bobsleds or carriages drawn by spent horses, traveling in half plowed, drifted country roads. The house overflowed with children, toddlers, and crying babies, but the double doors were taken out, creating a large open space for tables and a seating area for the men.

Greetings were stiff. Mary was examined through the microscope lens of centuries' old tradition, her gaze held steady, a small smile of welcome on her lips. She was a disappointment to them all, she knew, but she held her own, talking and laughing as if nothing was amiss.

Abner and Lydia cornered her after dinner, firing questions like missiles. She shrank back, her pupils dilated with fear of judgment.

Abner loomed above her, his dark beard wagging, and warned her of being a poor example for the grandchildren with her modern dress. Her sinuses dripped, her stomach popped and growled.

Lydia told her to hang on to the old ways, to come back home where temptations were few. She said Dat had grown old since she had decided to take her own way.

But most of them were warm toward her, thankful she was still in the fold. She had been to council meeting *uns' nachtmal* (communion) and therefore was still a part of them, in the spiritual sense. Mary held new babies, praised the two-year-old's growth, and handed out a large swirled lollipop to all the little ones as a Christmas gift.

She sat on the old couch covered in dark green polyester with a lighter green ruffle and knew this was her true family, with ties so strong there was nothing else in all the world to compare.

When her sister Annie asked when she was going to get a "chappy," she had almost forgotten the old-fashioned term for boyfriend.

Chappy. Oh my.

"No one has asked me," she answered. "And I might not accept if one did."

"But you want a husband and children, Mary."

It was said in a clucking tone that set her teeth on edge, the condescension thick enough to cut with a knife.

Between clenched jaws, she managed a stifled, "Yes."

Ill at ease now, she slid away to find her mother and helped cut Rice Krispie treats and the puffed rice candy she always made. There were chocolate-covered peanut butter crackers, hard candies in a pretty glass bowl, party mix, and caramel popcorn balls.

Her mother told her in hushed tones about the quilt she'd sold at the summer school sale and how she'd saved the six hundred twenty-five dollars for Christmas money.

"Thank you for the head scarf, Mam. It will always mean a lot to me, the way you have to quilt for money."

There was a quiet moment of warmth between them as they worked together in the kitchen, refilling trays of treats and wiping crumbs from the old counters.

"Mary," her mother said quietly. "I'm glad you are happy in Lancaster. And I appreciate what you do to keep respect toward Dat. I know you dress plainer when you come home."

Mary pretended to be shocked. "Why would you think that?"

"Oh, Mothers know things."

"Well," Mary admitted, smiling, "maybe a little plainer." The two of them laughed, feeling close in a way they never had before.

MARY WENT AWAY with a renewed sense of belonging to her family while at the same time knowing she would never return to their way of life. It was strange to belong to two places, but she no longer felt the intense guilt of leaving her parents. Her father and siblings might never understand her, but maybe she didn't need them to. It was a blessing to know that her mother, at least, was glad for her.

JANUARY WAS A slower month at the bakery, so they took a few days off and went to Leroy's brother Henry's cabin in the mountains of Bedford County. There was no snow, so the trip was uneventful, going west on the Pennsylvania Turnpike. They passed through three long tunnels that fascinated and frightened her. She tried to imagine how men could build a tunnel through a mountain without modern equipment. Once at the cabin, she talked about it with Leroy, who seemed to have a better grasp on the dynamics of tunnel building, but it was mostly a mystery.

"*Ach* Mary, let it go," Aunt Lizzie said. "You think too much about things that don't concern you at all."

The cabin was more like a lodge, a huge log structure with eight bedrooms, a kitchen with a built-in grill, and a commercial refrigerator. Amish didn't have electricity, so why was this cabin fully wired, Mary wondered?

"Oh, it's an Airbnb," Leroy said. "It's a business, so electricity is allowed." He proceeded to answer her questions about what exactly an Airbnb was.

"So, anyone can come in here and spend a week or two?" Mary asked, incredulous.

"Sure. But it's not cheap."

"Like a few hundred dollars?"

"Try a few thousand."

Mary was speechless. So much of the world was a mystery to her. How could anyone make enough money to own something like this in addition to the home they lived in?

That was her next question.

"*Ach*, Mary," her aunt said again. She was beginning to worry about Mary just a little. With such a bright mind and ambition stirring in her heart, it would be hard for her to settle down and be content as a submissive wife and devoted mother. She thought about how Mary charged ahead at the bakery, quickly taking over by devising new and better ways, unafraid to express her opinion.

While Leroy and Lizzie found relaxation and renewal in the vacation, Mary found the idle hours annoying, her mind crowded with questions no one could answer. She went for a long hike on a secluded trail, her energy taken up in hard physical exertion as she climbed the mountain to a rocky overlook, taking in the barren view of leafless trees. She saw deer and soaring eagles and examined the ice along creek beds, wondering what happened to fish, turtles, and frogs in the winter. She'd have to look that up.

She learned to make mountain pies in the fireplace, ate French toast with Nutella between slices of buttery bread, and kept up a lively conversation about everything that popped into her mind. Without the duties of the bakery and the entertainment of friends taking up her time, she had a renewed sense that there was so much to learn, so much to experience, and she had no intention of missing out on anything.

On the return trip, she noticed missing tiles on the sides of the tunnels, lights needing repair, and had to know who took care of these things. The driver kept her informed, telling her about the hired employees whose work involved maintenance of the interior.

Then why was it in disrepair? She wanted to know.

THE YOUTH SUPPERS and singings became boring to Mary in the winter. Uninterested in the young men who came and went, tired of Marcus and Jimmy's lame jokes, and sick of eating casseroles and salads that always tasted the same, she told Linda she was going to stay home Sunday night. It was cold. She was tired. There was nothing to do at the supper. Why not stay home and catch up on sleep?

Linda was incredulous. Of course they couldn't do that. Going to the supper and singing was a vital part of the Amish community, like going to church. It was where most young people met and started dating.

Mary sat on her bed and applied a coat of clear nail polish, her face sullen.

She held up one hand, turned her nails to the light, and blew on them before emitting a long sigh, setting the bottle on the nightstand, and blowing again.

"It's just not fun anymore, Linda."

"I don't know what to tell you. My parents will never put up with me not going. It's a rule at our house."

"Leroy and Lizzie don't care."

"I bet they do."

"Maybe, but they'd never make me go."

Linda snorted her disapproval. "I never met anyone like you."

"Good for you."

"Hurry up, Mary. Get dressed. Marcus is coming in an hour."

"I don't feel like going."

"Come on. Get over yourself."

She went, but she didn't make much effort getting ready. Her colorful dresses no longer seemed exciting and she really didn't care what anyone thought of how she rolled her hair or which shoes she chose to wear. The clear nail polish was mostly to help keep her dry nails from breaking, not to impress anyone, though she did enjoy glancing down and seeing a bit of shine.

On the way to the supper, she took in the cold, lowering sky, the sullen sun hiding behind swollen, gray clouds above dull brown fields of dormant hay and broken corn stalks. Horses drew carriages with windows closed, lap robes drawn over the occupant's knees.

The weather was depressing.

Mary glared straight through the front window, grunting answers, half-heartedly smiling at offhand remarks, and wondered if this was what the rest of her life would be. Work, go to church, go to social functions whether your heart was in it or not.

The supper was a good distance away, over on the west side of New Holland. Impatient drivers honked horns at red lights and Marcus made unkind remarks that Mary thought were self-centered and rude. Horses and buggies were a hassle to the general public, slowing them down when the roads were too narrow to pass, sometimes forcing cars to cross over into the oncoming lane to get around them. The least buggy drivers could do was show a bit of courtesy.

She told Marcus outright.

He didn't bother answering, but he thought there was a reason this girl was going on twenty-two years old and was still single.

Once at the gathering, Mary played cards, filled her plate from another chicken casserole, and hoped the time would pass quickly.

She was on her way up the basement stairs when she tripped on the top step, caught herself with one hand, and righted herself immediately. Embarrassed, she looked up to find a large young man looking down at her, his eyes squinting with laughter.

"You okay?"

"Does it look like I'm okay?"

She pushed past, her face flaming.

He turned to his companion, shrugged his shoulders, and let himself down the basement steps.

Later, she found him at the singing table. Someone new.

He was wide, with full arms, heavy shoulders. He weighed over two hundred pounds, she guessed. He wore dark-rimmed eyeglasses that did nothing to improve his looks.

But she kept looking toward him, although she told herself it wasn't the same as looking at him, or for him, as in searching for him. She only glanced in the general vicinity of where he may be. Or might have been. Or, he might glance in her direction, which wouldn't matter at all, because she wouldn't be looking back at him anyway. And if he did look at her, that made no difference at all.

She sang the German hymns but had absolutely no idea what she was singing, her mind fully occupied by the big guy in glasses.

Her chest felt as if there was a brick on it. Her stomach rumbled and churned. The two boys opposite her got to their feet, leaving the space unoccupied, which put another brick on her chest. What if he slid into the empty space?

And then he did.

He sat directly opposite her. He looked straight into her alarmed eyes, his own squinting with laughter, and said quietly, "Hi."

She thought she might have a full-blown seizure. She gasped, swallowed, looked away, looked back again, and said, "Hey," in a very tiny way.

"Are you new here?"

"Kind of."

Someone picked another song, and the only thing to do was join in. So she sang, switching to tenor halfway through and nodding at Linda, the cue for her to join in. Their voices blended in perfect harmony, rising above the bass and soprano. He looked at her, but she pretended not to notice.

After the singing was over and chocolate chip cookies, cheese, and pretzels were passed, he asked what her name was.

"Mary."

"Mary what?"

"Mary Glick."

"You're from around here?"

She shook her head, reluctant now. Linda chimed in, telling him where she was from, where she was staying, and why. He nodded, his eyes never leaving Mary's face.

"I'm Ben. Ben Stoltzfus. I know there are hundreds of Ben Stoltzfuses, but there's only one of me."

He grinned easily. She couldn't bring herself to meet those squinty eyes. The glasses were just horrendous.

"So, besides working at your aunt's bakery, what else do you do?" he asked.

"Weekends are boring in winter," she answered. "Suppers. Singings. Hang out on Saturday night."

"Hang out with who?" he asked.

"Linda and her brother Jimmy. Marcus."

"Marcus?"

Mary shrugged.

"She's not dating him," Linda said, shoving Mary a bit with her shoulder. And she found herself fiercely happy that Linda provided that important bit of information.

Up went his eyebrows. His glasses slid down his nose a bit. He pushed them up with a forefinger.

"So is Pinedale Valley close to the Canadian border? Ever been to Niagara Falls?"

"Fairly close. No, never been there. My parents are poor. We couldn't afford going anywhere like that. My family is . . . well, different. I mean, they're very plain, with extremely conservative ideals. I don't fit in very well. Anymore."

She thought, *Take it or leave it, Ben Stoltzfus. I am who I am. No more and no less.*

He wrapped a pretzel in a slab of cheese. She was sure she could sense his disappointment.

So be it.

"So, you're saying you left and made a big change? You're basically *opp ganga*."

To have left the way of the Old Order. *Opp ganga*. The words struck fear in the hearts of parents everywhere, the ultimate blow. When a son or daughter decided to leave behind the "outdated" traditions of their Amish culture and turn to the ways of the world, there was nothing to do but let them go, let them be excommunicated and accept the resulting expectations of shunning.

Mary spoke quickly then to set the record straight. "No, I'm still Old Order. The order just isn't quite as old as Pinedale's."

She only stated a truth, knowing full well the diversity among the plain people, not having meant for it to be humorous.

He shook all over, laughing.

"You nailed it with that statement, Mary."

She blushed. Linda looked from one to the other, delight written all over her features. *Aha*, she thought.

MARY WAS FROZEN, even her bones like icicles. The dry, hard wind had no mercy as they huddled in the machine shed waiting on Marcus, who obviously wasn't concerned with their welfare at all. Linda's teeth chattered as she poked her hands into her coat pockets and whirled around in a sort of dance to stay warm.

"See, Mary, he doesn't like me at all. If he did, he'd be worried about leaving me here in the cold. And Jimmy's just a loser."

"He's your brother, for pity's sake."

"Stop saying that. It doesn't make a bit of sense. What kind of sake does pity have? It's stupid. My feet are so cold I could whack my toes with a sledge and they'd never feel it. I hate running around in winter. You want to know something else? If Marcus cared for me at all, he'd be here."

"You already said that."

"Well, he obviously doesn't. Probably if I had good skin, he would ask me for a real date."

"Stop. We've gone through this before."

The wind picked up. They stepped back even farther. The scent of diesel fuel, cast iron, and rotting hay was overwhelming. A cat streaked past in the dark. Linda shrieked.

"Let's go sit in Marcus's buggy," Mary suggested.

"Good idea. I don't like cats. I also don't like running around in winter."

Mary chose not to remind Linda that she'd been the one who convinced Mary to come.

They made their way to the thin line of buggies, many of the young folks in the process of hitching eager horses to cold shafts.

Friends called out to one another as they dashed between parked buggies, headlights slicing through the cold, dark night. Red and yellow lights blinked from the backs of carriages being drawn swiftly away, the horses cold and hard to manage. Linda opened a few doors, switched on interior lights, discovering the wrong color of upholstery, the wrong dashboard, before locating the right one.

Gratefully, they sat on the front seat and drew the laprobe over their legs, which didn't seem to make much of a difference. They huddled together. Linda reached into the glove compartment and extracted a pack of Wrigley's spearmint gum, silently offering one to Mary. They laughed when the frozen stick of chewing gum snapped in two.

Finally, the sound of voices, the hoofbeats on the frozen ground. The door was opened, and Jimmy yelped.

"Scared me. Why are you out here in the cold?"

"Where else would we be, Mr. Night Owl? Seriously, you've been gone for, like, an hour," Linda yelled.

"Wasn't my fault. Marcus was talking to Kate and Liz."

Linda elbowed Mary's side.

"See? I told you," she hissed.

Marcus unhooked the bridle from the headlamp, struggled to adjust it to the reluctant horse's mouth, before slipping it up over his ears, fastening the chin strap. Jimmy lifted the shafts and Marcus backed the shivering horse between them.

"Sorry," Marcus murmured. "We got held up."

There was no sound from the back seat, Mary and Linda in misery with painfully cold feet, nursing grudges toward the unsuspecting young men.

"We were waiting for a long time," Linda said sharply.

"Well, I did apologize, Linda. Kate can get pretty talkative."

"My feet are blocks of ice," Linda complained.

Mary knew her lament was deeper than the cold and discomfort. She had admitted her deepest secret, the hope she had for Marcus, and this created a bond even stronger as the weeks went by. Girls needed a friend to confide in, a platform of assurance, someone to support and encourage them to navigate the bewildering labyrinth of *rumschpringa*, the once in a lifetime opportunity to decide with whom you would spend your future, or if you would spend it with anyone at all. If you were liberal, ran with the wild crowd, unsupervised, or if you chose to respect your parents' line of boundaries.

But the important part, whether anyone admitted to it, was finding someone who would be your companion till death parted you. There would be no divorce, no putting aside of sacred vows, except in extreme cases of mental illness, occasional adultery, or alcoholism.

Did anyone take dating and marriage seriously enough? Mary felt a deep empathy for Linda, knowing the weight of her insecurities about her skin. It wasn't supposed to be this way, and no doubt, in a perfect world, it wouldn't be, but life wasn't always fair. Everyone wanted the pretty girls, the slim, popular ones with good skin, and she knew this to be a cold, hard truth. No matter how well this fact was hidden behind pious fronts, it was there.

She sniffed, leaned over, and touched Linda's small, thin shoulder with her own, a wave of love and loyalty warming her through and through. Linda pushed back on Mary's shoulder, the silent signal receiving the encouragement.

It will be okay.

CHAPTER 5

MARY WAS STARTING TO FEEL DISCONTENT WITH HER JOB AT AUNT Lizzie's bakery. She found herself daydreaming of owning her own establishment, adding coffee, a few tables and chairs. She would decorate it herself, use cloth napkins and neat cups and small plates.

All of this swam in her head as she punched down bread dough, rolled it out with a rolling pin, then spread softened butter and scattered brown sugar, cinnamon, and nuts over the top, her movement swifter than the eye could follow. She'd wanted to try raspberry filling with cream cheese frosting but Lizzie said no, absolutely not. They had enough.

Leroy's back improved. He was back to work full time and could lift whatever he wanted. Mary had no obligation to continue at their bakery at this point. She kept an eye out for a space to rent, without telling a single soul. Not even Linda. She felt a sense of guilt, knowing how kind Leroy and Lizzie had always been. They'd become dependent on her. What would they do when she left? Was it wrong to take what she'd learned from their bakery and apply it to her own business? She wasn't sure, but she decided it didn't hurt to daydream . . . and maybe start taking a few steps toward owning her own bakery. If she actually found a place to rent that she could afford, then she could think about the right way to discuss it with Leroy and Lizzie. Until then, there was no sense getting anyone upset.

BEN STOLTZFUS BECAME a regular at the Diamond group, sometimes alone and sometimes with a friend. When the weather turned a bit warmer in early March, Mary felt a sense of renewed interest in being with the youth, without admitting Ben's presence had anything to do with it. Her mind was often full of work at the bakery and how to start her own business, wavering between guilt and excitement.

She went on a diet, eating nothing containing carbs, which made working at a bakery tough. Was life even worth living if you could only eat vegetables and fruit, grilled chicken breast, and cold lunch meat?

She lost five pounds and gave it up. She felt slimmed down, attractive, really. But what was wrong with eating bread? It was the staff of life. "Give us this day our daily bread," she reasoned. The Bible said so, and she planned on perfect obedience.

The days turned into soft, velvety sunshine and sun-dappled spots as buds broke into leaves as delicate as new lace. Birds traced acrobatic flight in their frenzy to find a mate and build a nest to raise a brood of young fledglings, their full-throated songs rising above the dull, monotonous roil of traffic. It never failed to surprise her, the amount of birds and small creatures coexisting with the steady hum of commerce.

It was an ordinary Sunday with an ordinary church service, going to the supper with a clueless Marcus and the lovelorn Linda, Jimmy in tow, cracking jokes and admiring himself in the mirror. Mary was glad to be among close friends, grateful for her life here in Lancaster County.

Volleyball games were in full swing. She was soon in the middle of the action, surprised to find Ben step in beside her. He was looking good in a light blue shirt, his height and width formidable, as usual. She glanced at him, then glanced away as quickly.

He said hello, and she answered, stepping away a few feet.

Standing beside someone to play volleyball was a thing, a sort of honor, especially if you liked someone but weren't sure what to do about it. So she smiled to herself, tried to make a few impressive moves, and was rewarded by his nearness, his quick smile of approval. She thought she might lift off and sail away, like an untethered hot air balloon.

WELL, SHE THOUGHT that following week. *Well.*

He was seriously attractive, even with those awful glasses. In the sun, his hair shone black, his eyes were brown and crinkly, his smile as quick and glowing as the waters on a rippling stream.

But he wouldn't ask her, she reasoned, keeping her feet firmly on level ground.

The letter arrived in Thursday's mail. It was an old-fashioned letter that arrived in the mailbox, delivered by the putting little mail car.

Leroy brought it into the bakery, waved it for everyone to see. Mary was instantly alert. She grabbed it, successfully hid the beating of her heart, and said mildly, "from my brother."

"Don't believe it," Leroy chortled. "Don't believe it for a minute."

Lizzie gave him a blistering look, but the girls smiled, raised their eyebrows. The letter crackled in her dress pocket the remainder of the day, but she showed no sign of agitation, until everyone reasoned among themselves, saying it might be true, what she said.

Very clever, she knew. She was an actor and a good one. She smirked her way through the remainder of the day, acting out her boredom, saying her brother had a case of shingles.

Which he did. Her mother had written last week.

"Was that letter from your brother, then?" Leroy asked later.

"Sure."

She hoped God would forgive her. This Ben could be classified as a brother, a brother in the church. She wasn't lying outright, just muddling the facts a bit. Leroy was too noisy anyway.

She didn't go to her room at all, in spite of desperately wanting to open the letter, but helped Lizzie mulch the roses and asparagus, then read the rest of her book before yawning and saying goodnight.

Leroy looked at Lizzie and she looked at him, and she said he'd jumped to conclusions. Mary honestly was telling the truth.

"I am still not sure. I could almost guarantee I saw that Harrisburg seal. Maybe not."

"No, she would have showed a bit more excitement, Leroy. Besides, who would ask her?"

"She's not that bad."

"I didn't mean it that way," she said, a bit muffed over the whole thing.

Upstairs in her room, she shut the door firmly, sat on the small sofa, and slowly opened the plain white envelope.

Her eyes went up to the signature, her heart racing.

Marcus? Oh, please. Not Marcus.

She threw the letter down as hard as she could, but it only floated to her feet and lay there, mocking her in its simplicity. A betrayal.

She had no feelings for Marcus. None. Poor Linda. Her first unannounced visitor was guilt, her constant bedfellow. She'd talked too freely, too friendly, too inviting. Flirt. She was a despicable flirt. Ashamed of herself, she put her face in her hands and wept.

Her father always predicted a bitter harvest for the sowing she had done. Was doing. She gazed at the opposite wall, seeing nothing.

Well, here it was, then. Marcus had written a letter, asked her for a date on Saturday night. It would be like dating her brother. Absolutely not.

She sat up, wiped her eyes, went to her dresser drawer and got out her tablet, bit her lip, and penned a polite refusal, apologizing if she had led him on, then crumpled the whole thing and started over.

She addressed the envelope, put a stamp on it, and vowed Linda would never know.

HER ACTING SKILLS came into full play after that fateful letter. Neither Jimmy nor Linda suspected anything, or if they did, no one said a word. Mary hid her attraction to Ben, never showing her happiness if she saw him, always cool and fairly distant.

As the weather warmed, she turned twenty-two years old and had a birthday party with Leroy and Lizzie's family. She felt very much like an old has been, been there, and done that. It was now time for something new, but she was not quite sure how to proceed.

She missed her mother, but could not bring herself to pay another visit to Pinedale. The letter still reminded her of her father's words.

Then, she was standing alone in the warmth of an early summer evening, before the singing was about to begin, wearing the deep teal dress she loved, feeling at peace as she listened to the trill of a Baltimore oriole, the sound like water splashing over rock. She had no expectations, no deep regrets of her past as she stood by the gate to the garden as she watched for the familiar flight pattern of the brilliant bird.

"You waiting for someone?"

She turned around. Ben was there, the sunset behind him. She couldn't read his expression, could only see his silhouette.

"No. Listening to an oriole."

He held very still. The sound rose, clear and precise.

"Hear it?"

He nodded, but he was looking at her.

She smiled. "Beautiful, isn't it?"

"It is."

Then, "Mary, I got your address from Linda, but I saw you here and decided I'd just ask you. I want to know how you feel about me."

Her eyes opened wide, "You? I mean . . . as in?"

"Just how you see me, or if you ever think about me."

"Well, you're a friend," she said carefully.

"But what if I wanted to be more than a friend?"

She could not meet his eyes, so she pushed at a broken twig with the toe of her shoe.

Dozens of answers flashed through her mind, but they were all the wrong one, so she kept pushing at the twig.

"That poor twig," he observed.

She raised her eyes to his, courage flooding her view.

"I would say yes. Yes, Ben. I would welcome being more than what we have been."

He drew in a deep breath, his eyes never leaving hers.

"You're being honest?" he breathed.

"I am. But, are you sure? I'm not much, and you surely cannot know where I come from."

"None of that is significant. I think you are an attractive young woman, and I would be more than happy if you'd agree to begin a relationship."

That took her breath away. Finally, she said softly, "Okay."

"Wow."

And he laughed, a soft laugh filled with happiness. He stepped closer.

"I'll pick you up on Saturday afternoon and we'll attend a campout with my family."

Quickly, without thinking, she blurted out, "No. No. We will not do that."

He laughed, looked around at the stream of young people headed to the shop to start the hymn singing.

"Just kidding. It's meant as a joke."

"No. It just terrified me. Save the jokes until I know you better."

"Do you look forward to that?"

And she knew by that very small jingle of happiness starting in her heart, creating an unexpected panorama of unnamed emotion that yes, she was looking forward to it very much. In fact, she had never imagined this kind of joy, this wild elation mushrooming in her heart, taking her breath.

"Getting to know you? Yes. I am very happy."

"I love your straightforward answers."

They stood in the waning twilight, their eyes reflecting their new-found treasure, the future before them infused with possibility. It was this possibility, this aura of hope in one another, knowing one was the recipient of true interest in the other, bringing a shared sense of awe.

He would pick her up at seven, and the rest was a surprise.

SHE TOLD LIZZIE first, who promptly got down the new fisher book, traced down his father and mother's name, where he lived and how old he was, how many siblings he had, and how many were married.

She knew some of his family, she said. Oh, she had to let the girls know.

And she ran off to use the telephone in Leroy's office.

She wrote the news to her parents, told the bakery girls, basked in the congratulations. The bread rose light and fluffy, the rolls were perfect.

She hummed as she worked, skipped, and whirled.

But she could not bring herself to tell Linda. It was just too cruel.

She sewed a new dress, a soft shade of green to match her eyes. She gave up carbs again, at least for two days until Leroy came home with pizza and cheesesteak subs from Brother's.

From the first bite, she'd fallen in love with "bought" pizza, and could never refuse it, or a sub in any form.

"You're not fat," Lizzie kept saying. "Now just look. Here this Ben asked you, and he would not have done that if he found you unattractive."

"But Lizzie. It gives me the shivers. What if he tries to put his arm around me or something?"

And Lizzie laughed, saying he probably wouldn't. These days, the classy, Christian thing to do was to have a distant courtship, and he might be one of those. She couldn't imagine getting married like that, but to each his own. She and Leroy hadn't been that good.

And she laughed again.

Guilt creeped up again as she thought of her own parents' very conservative rules about dating. Absolutely rigid. No romance, no touching, the devil's wiles completely unpredictable. Her mother's words had been like brimstone shooting from dark clouds of foreboding.

Prayer and the feeling of God's will were the two most important things in the start of a pure courtship. To dress modestly, to revere one another in all respects were next in importance.

Well, she'd certainly be off to a good start. She could easily summon the reverence part. She was amazed that he found her attractive.

Maybe he didn't. Maybe he wanted her to be a helpmeet, a wife to him and mother to his children, a good, strong, solid girl who could undertake the crushing weight of a dozen children and help make ends meet on the farm.

Was one man so different from another?

She asked dozens of questions, sending Lizzie into a tailspin, raising her hands, and rolling her eyes in exasperation.

"I don't know the answer to all of that, Mary. I don't know. Marriage is not one size fits all. It's different for everyone. You didn't even have your first date, your best friend doesn't even know, and you're worried about farming? Ask him about eleven children. Tell him you don't want eleven children. Why in the world are you stuck on the number eleven?"

"I don't want to be a poor farmer's wife with a pile of kids."

"Tell him, not me. You're driving me slightly crazy here."

"But how do I know he won't be sweet and loving and sincere, and the minute we turn our backs to the preacher he'll be a real jerk?"

"Oh my word, Mary."

"I mean it. I don't want the kind of life my mother has. Had. I guess she doesn't anymore, since the children are grown. Do you think she knew what she was getting into the day she put her hand in his long, skinny one and said, 'Ya?'"

"I doubt if she did. Does anyone? If they knew what they were getting themselves into, probably not. But, there are many blessings along the way, Mary. Times are hard sometimes, of course they are, but for most of us it's well worth it."

"Should I wear sneakers or Sunday shoes?"

Lizzie eyed her with concern. "I'm not sure you're quite right in the head, Mary."

"I'm not. I can tell you honestly. I'm going straight off the rail."

"Well, you better get back on because Saturday night is coming."

SHE WAS ACTUALLY a glowing picture of happiness when it was time for Ben to arrive. She wore her new dress and shoes suitable for almost any occasion, a brand new covering, and her hair was rolled to perfection.

She chewed Wrigley's spearmint gum as if her life depended on it, snapped a ponytail holder on and off her wrist, and asked Lizzie what to do in case he took her to a restaurant too fancy for her.

She worried about getting into the buggy gracefully, and what if her weight tilted it too far to the left, and he knew right then and there he would always be stuck with a hefty wife.

"What about my sinuses? You know how my nose runs when I eat hot food. It's not acceptable to blow your nose in public at all?"

"Well, not blow, as in honking, but you could wipe discreetly."

Mary groaned. "I don't want to go. I'll just do something dumb."

"Here he comes, so you better make up your mind."

Mary shrieked, raced to the mirror, looked imploringly at her aunt.

"You look beautiful. Now go."

Her voice was thick with emotion, realizing she loved Mary like her own.

He was out of the buggy, tying the horse.

"Hi, Mary. You look great."

His smile of appreciation put all her doubts away. She asked him to come in.

"I would like you to meet Leroy and Lizzie, if that's alright with you."

"Um, yes. Of course."

This was strange. No one ever did this in New York. To be dating someone was a time of secrecy, of being ashamed to be seen together.

Again, she wondered what her father would say, how her mother would surely disapprove. Their teaching was Rebecca and Isaac, the humble shame she felt at his appearance, so strong she covered her face with a cloth.

It was the pinnacle of Christian courtship.

He shook hands, introduced himself, and said he was glad to meet them.

Leroy, eager to please, pressed his hand warmly between both of his. Lizzie beamed like a lighthouse, and Mary felt a rush of love for them both.

They spoke politely of the weather, the new building going up between Leola and New Holland, how glad they were winter was finally over. Then Ben thanked Leroy and Lizzie for giving Mary a home in Lancaster. If they hadn't done that, he would never have had this opportunity.

Mary watched him as he spoke, reassuring herself.

He spoke without shame or self-consciousness, merely stood tall and wide, relaxed, and said what was on his mind, leaving Leroy and Lizzie quite impressed.

When he was finished saying what he needed to say, he turned to Mary and asked if she was ready.

She was, so they wished her aunt and uncle a goodnight, and left.

His horse and carriage was spotless, but nothing too fancy, the buggy having seen quite a few years on the road, the horse a nondescript brown Standardbred. Sitting beside him on the gray upholstered seat, she realized with a sense of despair, they were sitting very close. It was her, being so wide. Mortified, she shifted her weight against the side of the buggy, imagining a prominent bulge from behind.

"Well, Mary, we fill up the buggy pretty good, I'd say."

He laughed comfortably, as if he was proud of that fact.

"It's me," she said, in too small a voice.

"What? It's not you. I was over two hundred pounds last time I checked."

He chuckled.

Mary smiled. She shifted her weight back again, rubbed shoulders comfortably, looked down at her lap, glanced at his knees, and felt small in comparison. She took a deep breath.

"Where are we going?"

"I told you, to meet my family. Camping."

She jostled his shoulder, and he looked down at her, a twinkling, squinty-eyed look of good humor.

"You'll see."

They arrived at a farm, an ordinary white farmhouse, white barn, one of dozens scattered over the area. Mary had passed the place before but had no idea who lived here. She said nothing as he drove through, straight between the house and barn, past a corn crib and a machine shed, down a rutted field lane to a small copse of trees around a stone fire pit. A graying wooden picnic table lay on its side.

"Um, this is nice," she managed.

"I think so. A quiet place to spend the evening together."

He stopped his horse, climbed out, and swung the reins out the window.

She wasn't sure how to proceed, but knew that every young woman should always help unhitch, so she did that. She watched as he tied his horse to a tree and returned to the buggy for a can of spray, making his horse comfortably free of flies.

She stood watching, her hands at her side. She had never felt quite as awkward. Her mind reeled. She had to know what was going on. She was never good with surprises. Had he planned a cookout for the two of them? Where was the campfire? Did he bring food? Were they expected to sit around these black ashes with remnants of burnt wood and pieces of baler twine with nothing to eat or drink? Could she trust him? What if he was mentally ill and was thinking of something awful? A stab of fear left her mouth dry, her heart racing.

He came back, dusted off a chair for her and one for him, then proceeded to fold his bulk comfortably into one of them, saying nothing.

Since there was nothing else to do, she sat on the edge of the other chair, folded her hands in her lap, and stared into the black ashes.

"So, Mary, here we are, on our first date. What do you think?"

"It's . . . it's very peaceful."

He merely smiled, looking off into the distance.

The silence stretched on, until she thought she might not survive this strange scenario. What was he thinking? Why didn't he explain?

When she thought she might have to get up and start walking home, she heard the muted sound of hoofbeats accompanied by the rattle of a buggy.

A brown springwagon drawn by a small Haflinger pony came around the bend in the field lane, with two people seated side by side.

She leaped to her feet, recognizing her friend Linda, with none other than Marcus King driving.

"Seriously," was the only thing she could utter.

CHAPTER 6

THE HAFLINGER STOOD STILL, BUT HIS EARS FLICKED FORWARD, then back, hearing the girlish shrieking coupled with the deep laughs of the young men.

He swished his thick tail to rid himself of a few flies before tugging on the bit, impatient to either have his bridle removed or to be able to move along.

Linda sprung off the small springwagon, bounced around like an overeager puppy, hugged Mary, and said, yes, she had a real date with Marcus. The happiness in her eyes was like the sparkle of noon sunshine on water, her laugh frequent and infectious.

More chairs, food, firewood. A coffeepot. Marcus had thought of everything. As the fire crackled to life, the girls righted the weather-beaten picnic table and spread a cloth, unwrapping a package of paper plates. There was potato salad, fresh spring onions and radishes packed in ice cold water, the best hot dogs and potato rolls.

It was a blissful evening. Mary felt wanted for herself, not just for her ability to accomplish work. She couldn't remember the last time she'd felt that way. Ben's approval shone from his eyes, his smiles accenting every word she said. They talked, laughed, and ate until the stars began to appear. And even then they lingered, none of them anxious for the evening to end.

After that evening, they spent as much time together as they could, taking long drives in the buggy, having picnics in sunny parks, enjoying deep conversations punctuated with laughter. He was intelligent, funny, kind. Mary felt accepted, cared for, in a way that was new and intoxicating.

THE MESSAGE ON Leroy's voicemail snapped her back to reality. She gasped and then sank to the floor, the news so cruel it took her breath away. Her brother Urie's two-year-old daughter had been run over by the massive steel wheels of an old Massey-Ferguson tractor and killed instantly.

Riding back to Pinedale Valley, the bus swaying along the northern route to New York, she could not stop the tears. Her sweet niece, so innocent, gone in an instant. Mary had been on cloud nine ever since that first evening with Ben and their friends. How could she have been so full of life and joy and excitement at the moment when her niece had died? Of course Mary couldn't have known until she received the voicemail, and yet she felt guilty for her own happiness. Happiness shouldn't exist in a world where a child could be crushed to death.

When she arrived home, exhausted physically and emotionally, her parents were stoic, faces unmoving, their eyes taking in every detail of her dress from the top of her head to the shoes on her feet. In her haste to get home, she hadn't bothered to dig her old dresses out of the back of her closet.

Finally, her father's lips parted, and in a brittle, raspy voice, he intoned judgment.

"You come to us dressed like a Philistine. An abomination. God has sent a curse on the family, as there is an idol among us. You must repent of your ways and come back to the fold, embrace the old ways and make a fresh start. God has not spared little Barbara, but used her to open your eyes."

For a long moment, Mary sat, her hands folded in her lap, her head bowed as the words rained like hot embers, painfully burning their way through her shock and into her battered conscience. Her parents, aging, sorrowful, believing she caused the pain was like a spike through her heart.

"Dat," she said finally.

He slowly shook his head and said he did not consider her his daughter, not with the rampant *hochmut* adorning her body. Her mother kept her eyes on her lap as she listened to the words of her husband.

"We adhere to the *ordnung* to remain separate from the world. The world is filled with the lust of the eyes, the lust of the flesh. The dress you wear shows your form, thereby inciting lust in young men. You must understand the ruination of your soul."

"Dat."

He held up a hand to stop her.

"The farther you stray, the farther your children will stray. The heartache you force on us will be forced on you by your *ungehorsam* children. The sins of the fathers rest on into the second and third generation."

She didn't try to speak again. He had his own meaning of life branded deeply into his existence, and no one would change him.

As he quoted Scripture, dire warning rained down until she felt soaked, marinated in the dangers of falling away from strict principles, a narrow path of perfect obedience requiring the spiritual blindness he wore.

His measure of her left no room to spare, no mercy, and no understanding.

To greet her siblings was a bitter, difficult task, a sea of them clad in black, sorrowful faces, all long vertical lines of grieving.

A few discreet tears escaped, but it was the will of God and they must give themselves up to this. Sisters clasped her hand even as she was measured, judged, evaluated, and written up as *ungehorsam*. A heretic, deserting the fold of righteousness. She sat with the family at the funeral and greeted well-wishers, former friends.

The small, angelic body was returned from the funeral home, dressed in a plain white muslin dress with a white organdy apron, the simple white headcovering, bruises hidden as best they could.

The viewing and funeral were endured beneath the harsh gaze of her family, the warnings as frequent as the breaths they breathed.

Her sister Annie pulled her aside to cast her judgment in hushed tones, provoking Mary to tears.

"Annie, you simply don't get it."

Annie's eyes narrowed. "You are the one who doesn't get it."

"Look, I haven't left the Old Order Amish. Why do you all feel as if I'm already lost? Why? I am helping to build the church, upholding the promise I made on bended knee, living for Christ."

"With those clothes on? No, Mary. You are not."

"It's not all about my clothes. I fit in perfectly in Lancaster."

"Your *hochmut* portrays your heart. You must come back, Mary, before it's too late."

Mary shook her head, back and forth, over and over.

"It isn't true. I don't feel that way."

"That's because you have been lulled to sleep by the devil's wiles."

Annie explained Christ expected perfect obedience, that to take up the cross and follow Him meant denying self, and that included all forms of pride, which came out in the way one wore clothes. Only those who kept the *ordnung* to the letter would be saved.

Mary was incredulous. Here they were mourning the tragic loss of their niece, and all her family seemed to care about were Mary's clothes.

As she watched the small casket being lowered, many opposing thoughts chased around her head. The sky overhead was a brilliant sun-washed blue, the white clouds like clumps of quilt batting thrown randomly across it, the white fence lined with gray carriages and mostly brown horses, the mark of the Amish community. And she a part of it.

The way of the Amish was beloved to her, the order in which funerals and weddings were conducted, the order of having services in the homes. And how much, really, did all of it have to do with anything?

She told no one about Ben. She would wait until they became used to the idea of her staying in Lancaster. She rode the bus home in a cloud of confusion and sadness, fear like stray lightning. What if her family was right and she had to return and dress in those very plain clothes in order to get to heaven?

There she was, her small heart-shaped covering tucked behind her ears, glossy red hair in thick rolls sprayed into shape by a bottle of Pantene hairspray. Her dress was made in the latest style, with the tight short sleeves, the skirt dusting her heels.

She told herself over and over she was still Amish, still helping to build the church, still following the way of the cross. But her confidence was crumbling. She felt nausea returning as the guilt weighed down her soul.

Like acid, the grating lamentations of her sour siblings wore away at the fresh light that had entered her life after being with Leroy and Lizzie.

HER NEXT WEEKEND with Ben was a dizzying blur of troubled thoughts, until finally, after the singing, they sat together with cups of coffee and fresh shoofly whoopie pies with molasses icing, and he asked her outright what was troubling her.

She was ashamed to tell him, but he coaxed it out of her, gently. After she told him of her time in New York, he gave a low whistle.

"So, it's like you're *opp ganga* [left the church]."

"I guess."

"Pretty harsh, huh?"

She looked into his kind eyes and felt a swift rush of emotion.

"The thing that intrigues me about the Amish is exactly this situation. There is, and always will be, a wide margin of conscience. No one is exactly the same. But we try to accept each other as best we can, and we're taught to encourage one another along the way, bowing to the other in love. Right?"

"I'm not sure I understand."

He changed the subject, telling her he was sorry about her little niece. They talked for a while about the funeral and what life was like in rural New York, and then he asked what she would enjoy doing next weekend. Would she like to be with Linda and Marcus again?

She thought not. She wasn't in the mood for Linda's giggles.

"I think it's time you met my only sister," he said. "She's married and lives over past New Holland. She wants us to come for a Saturday night as soon as you'll agree."

Mary's eyes narrowed. "I don't know. Is she nice?"

"Of course. She's my sister."

Mary smiled, then nodded, said okay.

"You need to read this book I got at Gordonville Bookstore," he said.

She bit her lower lip.

"I was never allowed to read any books pertaining to spirituality. My father says they're misleading. That's why so many leave the Old Order."

Ben was clearly taken aback, but tried not to show it.

"Oh, well then, I don't want to do anything your family will disapprove of."

He looked at the clock.

"Thank you."

He hesitated.

"Does going home always do this to you?"

"What do you mean by that?"

"It's almost as if you have an aura of fear, as if you were actually physically afraid of something."

Her breathing became labored, her eyes opened wide.

"What if I am?"

"Mary, what are you afraid of?"

"Nothing. Don't worry about it. You wouldn't understand. How could you? You weren't raised the way I was."

"Can you explain?"

"No."

He looked at the clock, emptied his coffee cup, then got to his feet. He came around the table. She caught the scent of his cologne, noticed the neat crease in his trousers, the fit of his vest and cream-colored shirt. He reached for her hand. She jerked it away.

"Don't. Don't touch me. Among all the other sins heaped on my head, I won't be guilty of touching a man."

"Mary!" alarm edged his voice.

"Ben. I feel unclean. I feel condemned, unworthy. I think maybe we had better just forget about dating for a while."

"Because of your family? Maybe if they meet me, they'd feel differently. Can you take me to see them?"

"Never."

He stood close to her, his hands at his sides, feeling helpless.

"But . . ."

"Just go."

"Can I see you next weekend?"

"May I have two weeks to think things through? I'm sorry, it's just . . . this week was a lot, and I don't know what to think or feel right now."

She was a pitiful sight, to Ben. He wanted to comfort her, to tell her there was no need to be scared, but how could he?

"Here's my telephone number. Call me if you want to talk."

He closed the door softly behind him, hitched up by himself, and drove away, his hopes and dreams dashed to the ground.

SHE WORKED HARD for three days straight. She unsnarled the tangle of her thoughts by cultivating, edging, mulching, planting, and trimming the small garden she'd started.

She cleaned her bedroom, stood back, and surveyed the room with satisfaction, then ran down the stairs to retrieve the bedding and curtains off the line. When everything was completed, she realized how much she loved her room. The quiet, the calm beauty of muted colors, the one place she could truly be herself.

Was it lust of the eyes?

She had never known of beautiful bedroom furniture, or fashionable decor, had never seen anything like it until a few years ago. It was now an accepted source of comfort, a pleasure to be surrounded by things she loved. There, that picture of her and Linda in the white frame. That was not allowed. What had she been thinking, exalting herself like that? Pictures. Photographs were idolatry. She was bowing down to an idol. Quickly, she grabbed the offensive item and stuck it in the bottom drawer of her nightstand, face down.

Cleansed.

She was clean. She drew a deep breath of satisfaction. Yes, she was able to get back on the straight and narrow way now. And she felt much lighter.

But wait.

The greenery was artificial. Was it a sin to have a mockery of God's creation? They never had anything like it at home. She put it in the drawer with the photograph and placed a plain wooden box in the empty spot.

Better. That was perfect. Relieved to find a measure of peace, she gathered her cleaning supplies and headed downstairs.

She found Lizzie slaving over her bookwork, the least favorite of all her bakery duties. Mary knew to stay out of her way, so exited the house quietly and sat in the shade of the back porch. She felt as if her feet were on level ground again, but she could not risk a conversation about inward struggles with anyone just yet.

She could handle this by herself.

Lizzie looked up when she re-entered the kitchen.

"What's up, Mary?" She leaned back in her office chair, kicked off her Skechers, and stretched, her face elongated into a massive yawn.

"I'm done with my room."

"You have been working hard these past couple of days, and you have no idea how much I appreciate it. How did I ever manage without you? You're such a blessing."

Lizzie watched Mary's expression, fully aware of skewed emotion, some missing cog in the wheel of harmony.

Instead of answering, she simply got to her feet and went to the living room, where she stood with her hands clenched, staring out the window, watching the stream of vehicles, an occasional horse and buggy.

She might be a blessing to Lizzie, but she was a curse in New York. Could a person be both, or did the curse overpower the blessing?

She turned around, faced her aunt with haunted eyes.

"I'm not a blessing."

"How can you say that, Mary?"

"I was at home. Remember?"

She told Lizzie about her father, about Annie, her voice shaking with the inner turmoil, the roiling of accusations devised against herself, finishing with the dreaded question.

Did God use the life of a child to bring a disobedient person to her knees? Should she go back home and submit to the way of life her parents required of her, when every fiber of her being rejected it?

"Mary," Lizzie breathed softly. "My goodness, Mary."

For a long moment, Lizzie simply didn't know how to answer. She knew her brother well, knew he had always had a keen conscience about every single thing, but this? This was unfair.

"Mary, who knows why God allows awful things to happen to innocent children? But you didn't have anything to do with it."

"But you can't be sure," Mary said quickly.

"No, we are never sure of much of anything. But this is . . . Seriously, I don't think it's worth a discussion. If you feel you should go back home, be obedient to your parents, I certainly do not want to stand in your way. Each and every one of us must do what they feel is right."

"What if little Barbara died so I can see the path of destruction?"

"Mary, Jesus died for you."

"But not really. I mean, yes, He did, but I have to do my part or I'll be lost."

Lizzie quickly grasped the delicate tightrope they were on, and knew well the unwavering line of discipline in which Mary had been raised.

To offer false comfort would only double the unsettling thoughts, and she knew well the ways of an unstable heart. She had been unstable herself.

How she longed to hold Mary, to give her an immeasurable amount of grace and peace, but she knew only God could do that. Only the power of the Holy Spirit.

"I think you're doing a great job of that," she said.

"You do?"

"Yes. I do."

"They'll never accept Ben."

Lizzie knew Mary was right about that. Ben would not be accepted by Mary's parents unless he decided to turn to their strict lifestyle, move to New York, and convince Mary to do the same. The futility infuriated her, but she fought it back.

"Mary, if it's God's will, He has a way of working things out."

But Mary didn't look convinced.

THE BAKERY HUMMED with life. Mixers whirred, girls chattered, the door opened and closed, the bell above it tinkled. The cash register clanged, voices rose and fell, laughter rang out.

Mary's hands flew, the rolling pin spun across the sweet yeast dough, elongating it into strips. Butter, brown sugar, cinnamon, and walnuts.

Starting at one end, she began to roll the dough, creating a perfect pinwheel, before taking up the serrated knife and cutting two-inch pieces, filling pans, and popping them into the proofer.

"What are you and Ben doing this weekend?" Ruthann called.

"We're having an off weekend."

"Already?"

Mary nodded, her eyes averted.

"You're not breaking up, are you?"

"No."

A bright smile, a flash of eyes, and Ruthann's curiosity was satisfied. The minute her back was turned, Mary's eyes filled with quick tears. The time to break up wasn't yet, but she could see the white flag of surrender in the distance. Even Lizzie, who had been her staunchest supporter, had told her she must do what she felt was right.

How could one make the right decision every time? Was every choice life altering, or could you skip happily through life not worrying quite so much?

A sense of failure dogged her footsteps, the whole foundation of her being tilted on an unsafe angle. Over and over, the image of little Barbara in her coffin flashed before her, the sound of clods of earth hitting the wooden coffin, young men pushing back their thin hats to mop brows beaded with sweat in the bright spring sunshine. The funeral procession, dark and solemn, crows cawing their portent overhead.

She shivered, looked over her shoulder. Her breathing became rapid, shallow. The bakery spun.

It was only by sheer force of will that she slowed her breathing, acquired a sense of normalcy. She resumed her duties, but her face remained pale, perspiration beading her upper lip. She threw herself into the hardest tasks, lifted fifty-pound bags of sugar, but remained quiet and withdrawn, colliding repeatedly with the hurdles she had set against herself. Nothing made sense if everything was wrong. She, herself, was wrong, was on the wrong track. She had lost her way. The way back was through perfect obedience to her father. Her father and mother were the way to peace. They would provide the comfort and rest she earnestly needed.

But there was Ben. And Lizzie and Leroy. There were Marcus and Linda. Everyone had been so kind, and supported her when she needed it most. None of them, though, had been aware they were helping her on the road to perdition, ambling along in her fancy clothes, acquiring a boyfriend who would never be accepted by her family.

The next week she sat in her room, a palm on each side of her head, her eyes squeezed shut with the effort to control her pounding thoughts. She needed to talk to Ben one more time, then she would confront all her demons and return to the place of her birth to be a blessing to her family. She would help her father on the farm, be a maid to her siblings, and this would bring peace of mind.

She talked to Ben on the phone, agreed to a Saturday night with Marcus and Linda, wore a dark blue dress that accentuated the pale blue circles under her eyes, and sat with her hands clasped in her lap to quell the shaking.

As they drove through traffic, Mary gasped repeatedly, the oncoming cars a collision waiting to happen. Ben laughed at first, but slanted her a look of concern later. When she asked to be taken home on a more rural route, he didn't laugh at all, or smile, knowing something far more serious than approaching traffic was going on.

CHAPTER 7

THE EVENING WAS DISASTROUS. MARY WAS PALE AND TENSE, scratching at her forearms, wiping imaginary spots on the table, biting her lower lip as she repeatedly peered through the slatted blinds. The server at their table had to rewrite her order four times, until Linda waved her away and told her to bring whatever she wanted. They all laughed except Mary, who bit down on her lip so hard she tasted blood.

She knocked over a tall glass of Coke, then panicked and rushed to the restroom where Linda found her in a stall, her face pressed into her hands as she fought for control of her anxiety.

"Mary, seriously, what in the world? Are you alright?"

Her head bobbed up and down.

"No, you're not. What is up?"

When Mary let her hands drop, Linda recoiled at the black depths of her eyes, her face ashen, her breathing in short, hard puffs.

"Mary."

"Get out. Get away from me," Mary hissed.

Linda backed away, frightened. She stumbled back to the table, and with wide eyes proceeded to tell them of Mary's condition, finishing with, "She's not okay, guys."

"It's since her niece died," Ben said softly.

"Well, that is tough," Marcus said kindly. Linda softly slid her hand in his, nodded solemnly.

When Mary returned, her hands were still twitching, her eyelids fluttering as if they had a mind of their own, her lips pressed together in the effort to calm herself down.

"Sorry about the Coke," she grated.

"It's no big deal," Ben said.

The food came, but no one had much of an appetite. Mary pretended to eat, but actually speared her fish, then let it lay on her plate, picked at her salad, looked as if she might throw up.

Everyone was relieved to exit the restaurant, but Ben felt the responsibility after Marcus and Linda left.

"It's a lovely evening, Mary. You want to go to the park?"

"We . . . we can."

The sun was getting low in the sky as he tied his horse at the rail, then turned to look at her, before saying, "This way."

A path through the woods led them to a field of mown grass, a clear, rippling creek. A pair of mallard ducks lifted off, their short wings flailing in the air. Robins chirped repeatedly, calling to each other before ending their day, roosting in branches surrounded by thick leaves.

Mary noticed the pink reflection on the water, but everything blurred, sky melding with trees, trees liquified and floating in dark grass.

A sense of unreality pressed heavily.

Ben spread the lap robe on the grass. He sat cross-legged, his elbows resting on his knees, a blade of grass worried between his fingers.

Hesitantly, she sat beside him. They said nothing as vehicle doors slammed, engines started, children called out. Dogs barked.

"Mary, can we talk about this?"

"What?"

"How you're doing. Something is obviously very wrong."

"I'm okay."

"No, Mary. You're not okay."

She swallowed, rubbed at the sole of her shoe, watching intently as her fingers moved back and forth.

"Mary."

"Stop it, Ben."

"I'm not going to. If you don't talk about what's troubling you, I'm making an appointment for you."

She stared at him, open mouthed. "Why?"

"I'm worried about you. Tell me."

She sighed. "I was at home."

"Yes. Go on."

She stared at her hands for a while and then fell apart. The guttural sobs from her throat were dry, hard animal sounds, telling of a despondency so deep and so raw he wasn't sure how to respond. He reached over to touch her shoulder to let her know he was there for her, and she did not push him away. He allowed her to have this moment to come in touch with her true self, and he waited till she was ready to talk.

When the words poured from her mouth, he was angry, then hurt, then angry again. As the words kept coming, he knew without a doubt that he had to let her go. Still, he felt a conflict in his chest that took his breath away—the desire to keep her with him so strong it was like a war between his own will and God's will.

At long last, she quieted. He handed her his clean, white Sunday handkerchief, and she took it, pressing it to her nose and mouth. Her red rimmed eyes were closed, tears still quivered on downcast lashes.

"I have to go back," she whispered.

He gazed deeply into her sad, swollen eyes. He lifted his hand, and with one finger, he brushed away the last, glistening tear. Her skin felt velvety, the freckles visible beneath his hand. He looked at her trembling mouth, before lowering his mouth to touch hers, very lightly, then even closer.

She gasped, drew back, her eyes wide with guilt and fear.

"Mary, I love you. I have never been more serious a day in my life. I know you have to go back, to find who you truly are, and I'm willing to let you go. Not that it's easy, believe me."

"But you have made it so easy for me. Even as we sit here, I know I have to go. And I can feel my craziness, that black fear, leaving." She opened her eyes wide. "Suddenly, I'm free."

"I have set you free, Mary."

"Yes. Thank you. I feel as if the rest is easy. I can tell Lizzie with assurance. I need to go home. I just need to work out the knots in the rope of my life."

"Mary, I hope at some point it will include me. I know that's selfish, but is there still a possibility?"

She opened her mouth to say something, then closed it again, before searching his gaze.

"I have a feeling I'll have a hard time forgetting your face. And . . ." she waved a hand weakly. "The . . . the other."

"Say it," he said softly.

"I can't. It's *verboten* [forbidden]."

He smiled. "I almost lost my glasses."

"Probably a good thing you didn't."

What was this? A circling, a steady drawing together, creating an invisible bond not soon forgotten. She had never felt more comfortable in a man's presence.

The anxiety eased as darkness fell. They talked at length about many subjects, mostly about her return. She felt going back would enable her to sort out her own sense of identity, of incorporating the ultra-strict heritage with the will of God for her life.

He told her he was willing to wait, willing to go the extra mile, but would she please hurry up? She plucked at his sleeve, gave it a small tug, which she had not meant to do, but did, and he leaned into her, an arm around her shoulders.

This was their last night together. They saw falling stars, found the pattern of familiar ones, created wishes, and kept them secret. Crickets chirped, and katydids chimed in, a high, trilling tenor to their soprano. Bullfrogs along the creek's edge created a deep bass.

The night contained a bit of magic, a dusting of melancholy, the air heavy with the sadness of parting.

He began to hum the traditional goodbye song, and she joined in lightly.

"Goodbye, goodbye. Goodbye, dear friend,

If on earth we meet no more."

She cried softly, blew her nose and laughed. He wiped his tears in the dark night and wondered if he'd be able to do this.

As passersby watched the ordinary horse drawing the nondescript buggy through the night, none of them could guess at the modern day version of an old-fashioned tragic love story within.

At the door, he kissed her one last time, so tender, so gentle, and whispered his love. She could not say it, could not bring herself to say the words, had never spoken them to anyone in her life.

"You don't love me?" he asked.

And she told him she thought maybe she did. He went away happy, although unsure of all his tomorrows.

LEROY AND LIZZIE were not surprised, and told her they understood her need to go back home. Linda was aghast, rearing back in her dramatic way, and asked if she was actually going to wear that thin, sloppy old covering and those awful dresses. They clung to each other, saddened at this departure, but knowing it was a part of life.

In her beloved upstairs bedroom, packing a suitcase with the few clothes and belongings she could take, she felt the scrim of fog, the black questions forming, desperately wanting to stay.

She couldn't take her furniture, but Lizzie told her if she ever married, they would always send it. Her good spirits and encouraging words boosted her own courage, and she was reasonably happy as she boarded the thrumming bus in the city of Lancaster.

She watched out the window as the city was left behind and only rolling farmland prevailed. Verdant hayfields outlined by swatches of forest, a few crooked fencerows and curving roads.

She tried not to think of her parents' poor farm, the screech of rusting disc blades on rock, the tired plodding of skinny mules.

HER SISTERS WELCOMED her warmly, relieved that their stern warnings had finally brought Mary home. Her father's lengthy speech left her cold and rebellious, but her mother's words softened. Mary swallowed angry retorts and set to work digging borders, dividing hosta and perennials, trimming shrubs and overgrown lilacs.

She showed them how to create compost, how to mulch the garden with old, rained-on hay.

Every night she went to the dull, nameless bedroom with the old iron bedstead, waterfall dresser, and rough, green, plaster walls, swallowing the longing for the things of beauty she enjoyed so much. She cried, missing Ben. Almost, she went to the phone booth to call him, but she knew she could not.

Definitely, this was the epitome of denying self.

Onward, Christian soldiers, she told herself, when she missed him too much or felt starved for any kind of beauty. A newly painted barn. A bright battery lantern. The tufted pillows she'd left behind. But there were June roses, the peach-colored ones climbing the rotting old trellis, the scent thick and heady, alive with honeybees drunk on nectar. The sight of a newborn calf on deep green pasture, a galloping horse flying across a mowed field.

Her mother seemed to reverse in age. She smiled more often. One day she stopped Mary and said she looked so nice in her new covering, which was made in the conservative style but out of new fabric that was bright white and didn't need regular ironing. And did she have any idea how happy she had made them? *Anvot tzu gebet.* Answer to prayer.

Mary waited for fulfillment. Like an empty vessel completed in faith, she waited every morning for the sense of peace and joy that would rain down on her from the heavens, an inward fulfillment and peace brought on by obedience. The guilt and fear were gone, that was certain, but she still went about her days with a sense of emptiness, although she reasoned it could be the lack of pleasure, the stark blue walls of the house, the dog-eared feed store calendars on either side of the homely old clock on the shelf.

She had a satisfying reward in the quiet, shining welcome of the women in church, the shy, happy smiles of her friends. Two of them were married now, one with a round-faced squalling little boy with a thatch of blond hair and an endless appetite. Mary tried to stop the edge of her sharp observation, but it came anyway. In ten years Fannie would be worn out, nursing little ones and caring for them on an unbelievably tight budget.

She told her mother, whose mouth twitched a bit, but was drawn into firm control.

"Mary, the Bible says women are saved through the pain of childbirth."

Mary nodded, thinking Jesus hadn't died only for men, but whatever. Oh, she was steeped in modernism. She had to stop.

Over time, her father's face become young with smiles, too. He commented on her nice covering, how the belt apron pinned with safety pins made her thin. And she thought, *Yes, Dat. I know. Straight down the narrow path I go.* It had a rhythm to it, that thought. But she did experience a certain sense of belonging, a feeling of having done something right.

They picked string beans in stoney soil, wrestling a tin bucketful from skinny bushes. Her mother commented on the good crop, which Mary deemed pathetic, but she couldn't say it. They sat together in the shade of the maple tree, clipped the ends, broke them in half and stuffed them into jars with water and salt. The old granite canner boiled on top of the stove for three hours, filling the house with a familiar sound.

And she thought of Ben, when she was alone, and she felt the blush spread across her face. There was not one person there who would ever know about him.

She was asked to teach school but shook her head no. There was another sacrifice, one she shouldn't think about. The school board was desperate. The men pleaded.

In the end, she weighed the hard work on the farm and being a *maud* when babies arrived against the teacher position and decided to take the job. But she required a new coat of paint in the classroom and a fresh coat of polyurethane varnish on the wooden floor. The grass cut and the fence repaired. A proper backstop.

Her parents smiled, hiding pride in their daughter. Her stomach churned, produced volumes of gas. She swallowed a tablespoon of organic vinegar in a glass of warm water every morning, rifted and burped, hated the taste. Her sinuses ran. Allergies swarmed like honeybees.

The community showed up by the springwagon to perform the required work on the school. The women washed windows and polished desks, applied paint and varnish. A few of the women eyed her covering and put a hand to their own. Didn't have to iron it? How could that be? Well, she was definitely starting something new, which would not be a good example to the upper grade girls.

Tongues wagged and Hannah Beiler approached Mary, saying she was only doing this out of the goodness of her heart, and because she loved her in Christian love, then proceeded to ban the covering on her head.

Mary's eyes snapped, and she said her father had no problem with it, so she shouldn't either. Hannah marched off with set shoulders and a shower of dandruff from her greasy scalp and never looked back.

Her mother fussed and hovered as she sewed school dresses. "No, no Mary, not that way. You must remember you are in New York."

"No, no, Mary, longer sleeves than that. You can roll them up. Winter will be here soon."

The day before school opened there was a letter, a plain white envelope with no return address. Her father raised his eyebrows, his eyes concerned. Her mother was bursting at the seams, curiosity filling her like helium gas. "A friend," Mary informed them airily.

A friend, indeed.

She devoured the words, the way a starving animal wolfed food. He missed her, he loved her, and he was struggling to make sense of this parting of ways. They were both Amish, both dedicated members of the Old Order, how was he expected to plan on a future together?

His handwriting was good, his words spelled correctly, and there at the bottom, a phone number. His new cell phone. To stay in touch. Her heart raced.

She walked to the neighborhood phone, a telephone house in a crude, but weathertight shed, posterboard on the wall with a list of drivers for hire, places of business, dentists, doctors. A mishmash of crumpled papers, pens, bits of baling twine, mud gravel, a stained seat on the barstool, more clumps of mud on the runs. She sighed, thought of tobacco-stained teeth, gnarly hands with fingers stained from hard work, and took the corner of her apron and wiped the receiver.

She looked at the phone number, steadied herself, and dialed. Her hands shook in spite of her best efforts.

"Hello?"

"This, this is Mary."

"Oh, Mary. How are you?"

"Good. I'm doing well."

She told him about cleaning up around the home place, the offer of teaching school, her acceptance. He congratulated her. She thanked him. An awkward silence ensued.

Then, "Mary, may I come see you?"

Quickly, she weighed the risk. Ben, short hair, polo shirts, sneakers, well-fitting trousers. Her father would not be happy. And she could not expect Ben to understand. He was not under the same harsh scrutiny, could not be expected to comply to her father's eagle eye.

"Just once. Let me try to win their approval, Mary."

She knew it was highly unlikely, knew the risk, but her heart fluttered in anticipation, yearned toward him. She said ok.

WHEN SHE TOLD her parents, the vertical lines surrounding their mouths deepened. Eyebrows lowered, lips pursed.

"Who is this chap?" her father grated.

Mary winced at the word chap.

"Ben Stoltzfus. A friend from the group I belonged to."

"Mary, you know it won't work. He is probably *behofft* with *hochmut*."

Her mother's head wagged like a pendulum.

A shot of anger coursed through her veins. She felt the heat rising in her face. She clawed at her dress front, felt as if suffocation was imminent.

"Just because he's from Lancaster, you have labeled him already. That's just wrong. He is a perfectly presentable young man, and one I hope to be able to . . ."

Her words were cut short.

"No. The answer is no. We have no intention of having our community tainted with *hochmut* of any kind."

He smacked his lips for emphasis.

If rebellion had a taste, it was steel. Cold, hard, metallic, drying her mouth and choking her breath. Her upbringing pushed to the side, she let the power of her fury blaze into her father's unmoving gaze.

"You can't judge, Dat. You can't look on the outward person and make a decision about his character. You are not God."

"Mary!" her mother gasped, disbelief on her pallid face, a sheen of perspiration above her lips.

Her father shot out of his chair, brought his fist down on the table, rattling utensils, rocking a water glass.

"You will listen to what I have to say. You will not have a partner in a relationship that can only spell trouble. Neither will you return to that place of worldly living. If he comes here once, he'll be a bad influence, and we want to keep our youth simple, free from fashionable impression. God is not pleased with the *hochmut* he will bring. And you, Mary, are already walking a thin line, walking the edge of a cliff, the stone crumbling, enabling you to pitch headlong into the pit of fire and brimstone."

She became very calm then, quiet and still. She went completely numb, her thoughts vacant. She felt her spirit shriveling inside of her, a sort of death. Slowly, her shoulders slumped, and her head bent.

If her father spoke the truth, and she went against his wishes, then yes, there was a fearful place waiting for her. She could feel a stern-faced God, could see Moses holding the stone tablets with the Ten

Commandments pointing an accusing forefinger, the voice of doom coming from his mouth.

"Honor thy father and mother."

And rebellion warred with those words. How could a person truly honor parents whose rules were clearly ridiculous? Who judged anyone according to their dress or where they came from? It was wrong for one person to decide whether another person was living by his or her own conscience, or if they were openly rebellious.

But he was her father, and her mother was beside him, quivering like congealed porridge, knowing only one thing, the path of submission to the Lord of the house.

She could find no words, only her spirit giving in, giving up.

"Alright," she whispered.

WHEN BEN RECEIVED her reply in the mail, he sat for a long moment, his head in his hands, the letter beside him on the couch. He felt his dreams crumple, felt them broken, liquified, carried away by a dark brown torrent of raging unfair expectation. Who could do this to their daughter?

It was not right.

Could he change his ways, his dress, his way of thinking and being?

Could he put aside everything he had always known to take on a severe lifestyle, one portraying a few centuries ago? Was one expected to do this for love? He did love Mary, but was his love strong enough to give up all he had ever known?

He had a long talk with his parents, one he would never forget. Their counsel proved to be his saving grace. A day at a time, saturated with prayer, a spirit willing to be shown, and a faithful father in Heaven who was all seeing, wise, and loving. If his feelings for Mary remained strong in six months, in a year, then perhaps something could be worked out. If time would ease the ardor he felt now, then He would provide another young woman with whom he could share his love.

He felt profound loss, his days without color. The future was an endless wasteland without Mary, but the love of his parents was like the emergence of one small flower along his dismal path.

It required tremendous willpower, to abstain from a letter in reply, but it was what she wanted. He felt the flap of dark wings of hatred, the cawing of an evil crow of rebellion, but took his father's words seriously, and he realized God was a just and loving God, one who took delight in the well-being of His children, and he slowly surrendered.

THE SUMMER WAS hot, torn by rumbling thunderstorms. Jagged lightning ripped through sturdy oaks, sizzled along metal barn roofs, and sliced into huddling cows, felling them like bullets. Amos Glick stood beneath a spreading maple and counted four dead cows. One of his best milkers had gone down.

He felt the curse from a stern God who showed displeasure.

He told Mary the new *coppa schtuft* had to go. If she couldn't use the organdy for her covering they were accustomed to, well then, she'd be expected to leave. *Gott lest sich net schputta* (God is not mocked).

The lightning had killed.

Tighter and tighter, the noose encircled her throat, making breathing difficult. She sucked in the spiritual life she could find, sought refuge in a singing brook, the beauty of a sailing butterfly. She cried.

CHAPTER 8

She yearned for Ben, but wore the organdy covering and waited till peace settled on her shoulders. She feared a God who sent lightning and loss to punish the *ungehorsam*.

School doors opened the end of August. Twenty-one darkly clad children wended their way up the hill, by foot, or pushing scooters, came through the schoolyard gate, and viewed her with suspicious eyes.

They'd heard parents' concerns about Amos Glick's Mary. They half expected to see a short skirt, or perhaps worldly shoes, but she appeared to be a teacher like all the teachers before her, dressed in navy blue, a cape covering her neck, rounded over her shoulders, black shoes and stockings, a large covering showing a bit of red hair.

Her smile was quick, her hips wide, her voice carried well.

She proved to be a competent teacher, one who taught her three first graders well, sending them off to a running start.

One clear September evening, when the sound of the last child had gone down the hill, Mary stood at the door, gazing across the rumpled valley, the ridges and crevices creating waves of color and light. Shadows purpled as trees swayed, the white puffs of racing clouds like blown soapsuds. She was vaguely aware of a restlessness, a wondering if she had acquired everything life had to offer. She had won a slice of her father's stingy approval, although he had told her that morning he felt she needed to tie her covering a bit farther up toward her chin.

Or more cows will be hit by lightning, she thought, bitterness like chewed acorns. She squelched it successfully by the nameless fear she lived by. Was this, then, the highest pinnacle of success? Living by your parents' honor? Pleasing others, serving the community, afraid of anything else, even one's own thoughts?

A vehicle climbed the hill, slowed. The gate was still open. A white two-door Jeep, the wheels wide and black. She felt a moment's unease.

She stepped back and watched as the back of a man's head and shoulders emerged. Tall, wearing a bill cap. Gray shirt. He stepped forward, came around the front of his vehicle, turned toward the view. He took in the white fence, the horse shed and backstop on the ball diamond. He looked toward the white, one-room schoolhouse, the doors both open to the late afternoon light, then moved across the gravel drive to step up on the porch.

"Yoo-hoo," he said softly.

Mary swallowed her fear, stepping out with courage. She found him halfway up the steps, so their gaze was level. He had graying hair along the sides, his facial hair tinged with gray, clipped and shaved into a neat mustache and thin beard. Blue eyes, edged with curiosity.

"Hello," Mary stammered.

"Yes, hello to you. The teacher, I assume?"

"Yes."

He stepped up on the porch, extended a hand. She took it.

"Travis Caster. Photographer."

She said nothing.

He turned his back, his hand making an arc in the air. Long, tapered fingers, brown skin, smooth nails.

"Beautiful. Could I photograph this?"

She hesitated, thought of her father, the lowering of his eyebrows.

"I don't know."

He turned, a half smile on his face. "What?"

"What I mean is, we're against all forms of photography."

"We?"

"Yes. Our people. Old Order Amish."

"Yes, I could tell by your dress. Well, okay."

He drew out the O, a wry smile on his lips.

"So, who do I ask if it's allowed?"

"I suppose the school board."

"I would love a picture of you, standing in the doorway. A one-room schoolhouse Madonna."

Mary blinked, frowned, and said no.

He smiled. "Ok. I'll be on my way."

And he left. Mary hurried straight to the worn 1986 set of encyclopedias, ran her forefinger along the alphabet, found the M, fell into a seat, and found the Madonna.

Seriously. Her heart beat heavily. What had he meant? She closed the heavy book, the picture of a serene face instilled in her mind. Was this what he had seen? Peace and rest. Quiet. Oh, but her soul was often restless, so often unsatisfied, seeking for something she could not name.

She attended every Sunday evening hymn singing, knowing the requirement, knowing the hope of her parents. Find a chappy, settle down, and get married. And she was torn between obedience and rebellion. She could not accept any of the men there—the unwashed hair and large black hats, the purple cotton shirts and ill-fitting trousers, faces with acne scars and yellowed teeth. More than once, she'd been stopped, a clawlike hand on her black shawl, a tug.

Into the shadows, to avoid the shame of being seen.

"May I take you home?"

"May I come see you on Sunday evening?"

Breath like decaying onion. And she thought of Ben's mouth, the taste of . . . what was it? Cleanliness, sweetness. Was she tainted now for the remainder of her life? Did she assume she was better than those around her?

But she could not seem to help herself.

She sat staring into space, her hand on the encyclopedia. Her disobedience, her time in Lancaster was finally catching up to her. Reaping what she had sowed, just the way her father said it would.

She would never marry, never find true love, her spirit circling restlessly all the days of her life. Well, so be it. She would throw herself into the job at hand, teaching the innocent children she loved. Isn't that what most older girls did? And most were content.

She propped up her chin with her hand, her eyes sweeping the walls of the school. Time to take down some of the freehand art. She'd start the colorful pumpkins, the brilliant leaves.

Schoolhouse Madonna. She smiled.

He was back the following week. She was sweeping the porch.

She stopped, frowned. He walked toward her, a camera on a strap around his neck.

"I'm back."

"Obviously."

He grinned. "You never told me who to contact. I still don't have permission."

"I'm sure I can't keep you from photographing the view from here. It's the schoolhouse, the, you know, fence and shed, whatever belongs to us that would be off limits."

"Right."

He stopped, looked at her.

"What about you? Would I be allowed to take your picture?"

"Oh my, no." She gave a small laugh. "Absolutely not. That would be the worst sin of all."

"Yeah. Well."

An awkward silence. She picked up her broom and began to sweep, excusing him. He stayed. She looked up, a question in her eyes.

"You never told me your name."

"You don't really need it."

"But I want to know it."

"Why?"

"I told you mine."

She sighed. "Mary Glick."

"Mary Glick."

He reached out with his right hand. She met his halfway. Strange how soft an English man's hands were.

"Pleased to meet you," he said softly.

She said nothing, mostly because she wasn't pleased to meet him. He brought unwelcome stirrings of emotion, wishing she was not kept here in this cage called Pinedale Valley. Those thoughts were sin.

"So, this is your job? You're an Amish teacher?"

"Yes."

"You've been here all your life?"

"Yes. Well, no. I spent a few years in Lancaster County."

"Hm. The mecca of the Amish."

"What is this? Some sort of interview?" She was becoming irritated.

"No. Just curious. That's the photographer's curse, or his blessing. However you choose to name it."

She smiled. He asked if he could see the classroom. She knew he shouldn't, but she wanted him to see the clean, glossy, wooden floors, the colorful display of art.

She stepped aside, lifted a hand and ushered him in. Surprised, he swept past her, and she caught the scent of cologne. She watched him circle the classroom, his hands behind his back. She guessed he was forty something. Definitely attractive. A wingflap of dark danger.

"This is amazing," he said softly.

She said nothing. He turned.

"You know, I find you inspiring. For one thing, you're highly talented. For another, you know how to stay quiet. So many women overthink everything, come out from left field, the right, chattering, loud, opinionated."

He laughed, a hand on each side of his face.

"Noise, chatter, assault on every side. I can't imagine your life. You're quiet. No cell phone, no television, no computer."

She shrugged.

He looked into her face. "I'd love a photo of you."

She bit her lip, shook her head.

"No, sorry."

"It's alright." He put up a hand.

He went out, sat on the top step. His shoulders were wide, his back bent slightly. He patted the step beside him.

"Come sit. Look at this." He spread a hand. "Just look at this."

She would not sit beside him, but stood, tense, unmoving.

He lifted his camera, hit a few buttons, then walked away. She watched as he circled the playground, noticing his shoes. Expensive leather. She felt the need to hitch up Dolly, get on home. It was getting late, and her mother was prone to worry. He finished his photographing, went to his vehicle, and put the camera on the front seat.

"Need a ride home?" he called.

"No. I have my horse."

She hoped with all her heart he would not ask to see the dilapidated, mud-splattered courting buggy, the aging Dolly, black hair graying around her stomach. Every rib on her sides showed. He'd turn her in to the animal rights activists. A thin horse hauling around her substantial bulk. Terribly embarrassing.

"Can I see the horse and buggy?"

Quickly, "No."

"Okay. I'll be off then."

She was late, mostly on account of Dolly's slow pace, the beauty of the early autumn scenery, and the reliving of his visit. Nothing had occurred that wasn't perfectly *gehorsam*, no exchange of anything that was improper or frowned on. Her mother would have done the same.

But she knew he was an attractive man, a clean, educated man of the world. A temptation. She wouldn't think these thoughts at all if he hadn't told her she was a Madonna. And he wanted a picture of her.

Verboten, but it put a smile on her face.

Her mother was in a sour mood, her propane gas refrigerator on the blink, and no repairman available. There were no funds for a new one to be shipped from the nearest dealership, and this after the loss of four cows. Abner was summoned, the faulty appliance brought out of its enclosed space, cleaned, adjusted, followed by repeated attempts to light it.

Finally Abner got to his feet, dusted his hands, and said there wasn't much anyone could do to save it. Her father's face turned sorrowful.

"Well, we'll have to do without. The tobacco check won't be here for quite a while."

"We can't do without one, Dat."

"Mary."

The word was meant to hush her, but it was laced with so much condescension he may as well have poured gasoline on a red hot coal. Her outburst was quick and emphatic, laced with unrest and the unfairness of life, frustration of being held in a schoolhouse, living with aging parents who lived in the nineteenth century. She was promptly and thoroughly reminded of her dangerous walk, fueled by her elevated sense of self, therefore providing room for the devil. Abner's sad eyes followed her as she left the room.

The deer bologna on her homemade bread was spoiled a few days later, and she flung it across the schoolyard fence with the fury built around her father's simpleminded view. How was anyone expected to live without a refrigerator?

She found herself watching the road, watching for a sign of the white Jeep, all the while telling herself she was not doing it.

The children kept her occupied during the day, the daily challenges a welcome task, keeping her mind on the important aspect of her job.

She loved them, these eager, unspoiled young souls who often delighted her with their antics. No matter how strictly they were raised, each child was capable of expressing their own personality.

There was a chill in the air by the middle of October, the heavy woolen shawl a welcome refuge from the cold on her way to school in the morning. She'd asked her father if she could use the top buggy, or market wagon, with a closed front, but he thought it wouldn't be necessary just yet. She shook numb fingers before she was able to unhitch, wallowed in rebellion, thinking how she would not do this for the remainder of her life on earth.

She thought of Ben, wondered if he'd moved on with his life, and stayed later at the schoolhouse, telling herself she had to prepare extra work for Yoni King's Enos. In second grade, he was reading upper grade books, zipped through his arithmetic and spelling, then sat at his desk pestering his classmates. But she knew her eyes kept going to the road.

Well, he was a traveling photographer, she told herself. Old. He was likely older than her brothers. She tried losing weight, thought perhaps he'd drive through someday, then confronted the reality with self-loathing and disgust. Of all human beings on the face of the earth, she was the lowest.

English men were completely off limits. As remote as an island. Only a major upheaval in a family, a death, an excommunication was parallel to having a relationship with a man of the world. And a photographer at that. She knew all too well the consequences of her thoughts, knew too, her yearning and restless heart were shameful secrets never to be brought out in the open.

Her mother watched her eating habits change. Only an apple for lunch, smaller portions at the supper table. By Thanksgiving she'd dropped twenty pounds. Her sisters commented on her trimmed down figure. Her brothers teased. A chappy. There was a chappy on the horizon. She laughed. Her parents talked about Mary's happiness, how she had finally found peace and contentment.

WHEN A SLOW advance of churning gray clouds were spotted at recess, the children shrieked with delight.

Da schnay! Da schnay iss an komma! (The snow is coming!)

And sure enough, by the time school left out for the day, the snow was falling thick and fast. Those on scooters were allowed to go home early, the roads quickly becoming too treacherous for them.

She breathed a deep sigh after the last little black shawl was pinned securely, the last bonnet tied under wet chins.

She turned to her desk and the stack of correcting.

Her thoughts traveled to last night's supper table, the silent scraping and swallowing of fried potatoes and tomato gravy in the gaslit kitchen. Shadows in the corners, the scent of manure on her father's boots, the snapping of her mother's loose dentures, the way she heaved herself out of her chair to remove them and rinse them in the kitchen sink. Her father's rumbling burps, followed by armpit scratching.

She tried, she really did. She felt genuine affection for both of them. Narrow minded, simple, they thrived in a world of *ordnung*, a stringent existence of black and white, completely content.

She questioned herself and wondered.

She got up to pile wood on the old rusty furnace in the middle of the room before locking the doors for the night. She dreaded going through the fresh snow in her shoes, before the long, cold ride home, her wet feet like blocks of ice before reaching her destination.

She turned to pull down the dark green blinds, and saw the Jeep. Her heart lurched at her chest.

She met him at the door. In the gray light of falling snow, with her weight loss, her eyes were enormous, the freckles in full detail on her face. His smile meant too much.

"Mary Glick," he said.

She could not hide her pleasure. Her smile was genuine.

He stood looking at her without saying anything. She looked away.

"I remembered you."

She bit her lip and said nothing.

"Want to see the pictures?"

"Yes."

They stood close as she shuffled through them, admiring the beauty of the view she took for granted every day. When she had seen them all, she handed them back, then stood waiting, her hands at her sides.

"So how have you been?" he asked.

"Oh well, you know. Not always thrilled to be here."

"I can imagine."

She'd gone too far, she could tell. That was simply unacceptable, a bold invitation of her unrest. She tried to correct her blunder by saying how much she anticipated the snow, and he asked if she was driving home.

"I am," she said.

"I'll take you. It's too cold for you."

"No. I can't leave the horse tied overnight."

"Did you ever ride in a Jeep?"

"No. I can't. I have to get home. My mother worries easily."

He was wearing a brown leather jacket, and no hat. She'd been right, the gray flecks in his brown hair giving away his age. She thought of her silly weight loss, thought of sitting in that vehicle with her black shawl and bonnet, cringed under the weight of her shame. How far out of her comfortable boundaries would her thoughts take her?

Her thoughts of him were so wrong, so terribly sinful. And she was the worst creature, a lowlife giving herself over to despicable thoughts.

But she stayed, listened to an account of his travels to Maine, crossing over to Nova Scotia on the new ferry, the fall scenery.

"My mind couldn't quite let go of you," he said.

Or mine of you, she thought.

But she gathered her papers, quickly crammed them in her briefcase, and faced him decisively.

"Well, it's good to be remembered. But I know you know it's better for you to move on. I mean, not that I'm saying . . . you know. I just don't want you getting ideas."

She paused, thought she may have to take flight, wished instead the floor would open up and swallow her.

"I'm not married," he said.

"That has nothing to do with it. It's a culture. A way of life. It can't be."

"Do you wish it could?"

"No."

There, now she'd done it. She had sent him packing, effectively, and in doing so, had provided her own safety net. It was called denying self, and as of late, she'd become quite adept at this. Taking up the cross wasn't all that hard, really. A bit of self-discipline, a bit of awareness.

"I hate to see you go out on these roads alone. It'll be dark, and a horse on this snow, with these hills." He shook his head.

"Just go. I'll be alright. I've done it a hundred times. Goodbye, and please don't come back."

He got as far as the porch, before turning.

"Can we talk sometime? Like meet at a restaurant and have dinner?"

A flash of transport, away from the hardscrabble existence, but only till she got her balance, thought of her mother's pain, her father's shock. They took up a lot of living space in her head, their voices of disapproval, the cutting admonitions a constant restraint.

"No. You don't really get it," she said firmly.

"But I want to tell you my story. I want to hear yours. Why can't two people who are perfectly responsible have dinner together?"

"Because I'm Amish."

"That has nothing to do with it."

"It has everything to do with it."

"Oh boy," he sighed. "I'll be a gentleman, so my white flag of surrender is up. I'll not be back."

And he walked away and got into his Jeep without looking back.

She cried on the way home, the tears coursing hot on her cold face. She trudged into the barn on feet like blocks of ice, stumbled into the house and threw her briefcase on the kitchen table.

Her mother looked up from her sewing, asked if she was cold.

"Duh," Mary said flatly.

"Stop using that worldly expression. It's so disrespectful. Not quite a swear word, but surely a worldly slang."

"Mam, I'm sick to death of this term 'worldly.' If I hear it one more time I'm going to run away."

She stomped upstairs with her mother looking after her, openmouthed. She had no idea how easily Mary could have just done that. And Mary dug beneath the covers fully clothed, drew up her knees, and shivered till she felt a warm lethargy creep over her, like a soft, comforting mist.

Would it be so awful to tell her mother she was having dinner with an English photographer? But she knew the answer before the thought was complete.

Everything, just every single thing was wrong. Sin was thick as blueberries in a good year. A rolling black cloud enveloped her, filling her with dread for the future. How could she stand fast in Christian duty till the end?

When she awoke, it was dark outside, a thick blackness that crowded in against the window panes. Her throat hurt and her mouth was dry. She heard the deep rumble of her father's voice, the lighter tone from her mother. Likely deciding which sin they'd have to remind her of next.

She went downstairs, to the accusing eyes of her father.

"Mary. Sam Lapp stopped in today to tell me there was a white Jeep parked in the school yard and a man on the porch. He asked if you'd said anything about it to us. I said you didn't, and he asked if I didn't want to question you. What do you have to say for yourself?"

In even tones, she told him it was a photographer on his way to Maine who asked to take pictures of the school and herself, but she had not allowed it. He had, however, taken pictures of the ridges, which she felt was alright.

Her father was satisfied, her mother nodding her approval.

Neither of them would ever need to know the reality of her attraction, the weight loss all due to the traveling photographer, the near romance.

How she watched the road, how she thrilled at the sight of the white Jeep, had said all the right words while she yearned to ride in his vehicle, to be escorted to a fine restaurant, and yes, to be as worldly as she could be.

CHAPTER 9

THE WINTER DRAGGED ON AS SNOW PILED IN DRIFTS. THE CHILdren packed paths through the snow, played Duck, Goose, and Tramp. They rode sleds, made snowmen, ate snowcones, and went ice skating after cleaning the pond with shovels.

The schoolhouse filled up with somber black shawls and bonnets, black hats, and coats. Children sang hymns, recited poems about the birth of the Christ Child, solemn and long. Mary felt as if her whole being was being ironed, flattened, as she compared the somber affair with the lively songs, skits, and poems in Lancaster.

She received a few pinched words of praise for her efforts, a small pat on the arm and a half smile accompanied by, "Keep up the good work, Mary." Teatowels, glass dishes, a small cedar chest, among other small gifts were brought by the glowing children, which warmed her heart. She would likely be content if she had never gone to her aunt's house, but after a taste of freedom, it was hard to regress, to take up the strict bonds, the ties that bind.

How did one decipher the right path?

She knew she lived a lifestyle not true to who she really was, but she lived it for her parents, and wasn't there a blessing in that?

To honor thy father and mother was indeed the highest calling, but was it always this hard?

She questioned the windblown clouds, she asked the racing white gusts of wintertime, and never received an answer. She no longer prayed much about her future, a bit disgruntled at God, the way He never really bothered answering. She had been free, she had. Her decision to come back home had banished the crippling anxiety, the fear that dogged her days after her niece's death. But here she was, chained to a teaching job she did not enjoy, living in a house devoid of beauty, full of serious admonition and threats of tumbling off a precarious pathway.

Sometimes she felt as if she was being eaten slowly by some strange and terrifying virus.

But spring came eventually, bringing mud and frequent rainstorms, slush and budding dandelions poking through. She found moments of joy, if rare. Sometimes the sun burst through dark, muddling clouds, and her mind would respond with appreciation of light and health and wellbeing.

When one of her third graders was stung by a wasp in the wooden privy, she discovered dark bruises on his thin arms. She considered how Elam, with liquid brown eyes, straight black hair, and an impish smile had slowly degenerated to this pale, spindly boy who retreated into himself and often laid down his head on crossed arms and fell asleep.

That evening, with courage and purpose, she turned Dolly to the left and went down the hill and around the curve, her tracks on the macadam road leaving two thin, pale imprints for the steel wheels. She drove through pine woods, by fields too wet to plant, skirted barbed wire fences surrounding pastures containing fat wooly sheep, until she came to the home of Eli and Sarah Allgyer.

She'd been here before, to church services, or singings, so she felt at home, urging Dolly to the hitching rack and tying her. When she reached the *kettlehaus* door, she heard singing, followed by the laughter of children.

"Hello!" she called out.

"Oh, we have a visitor. My oh, Mary. It's such a good thing you came to see us. I was going to write a note this morning, but time simply got away. It's about Elam, yes?"

Mary nodded, gladness filling her up.

"Yes. I debated for a while already, if I wanted to come talk to you. He's not feeling well. He falls asleep so quickly, and the bruises on his arms are a bit alarming."

Mary nodded, listening.

"We've been in denial, Mary. Too long. But he has an appointment now. Bloodwork. And to be honest, I'm anxious. We both know the word we just won't say."

No, there was no use saying the dreaded word.

"Come now, and stay for supper. Eli will be home in a few minutes."

Sarah's kitchen was airy and bright, with three windows facing the south. Plastic pots of red geraniums were assembled on the cloth-covered sewing machine, the linoleum a light beige and brown. Children were playing with Legos in the adjoining playroom, small girls with gleaming dark hair, talking quietly as they played. A few stainless steel kettles bubbled on the stove, and Mary quickly offered to help, tilting the potatoes to drain them before applying the handheld potato masher. Sarah made gravy, stirring rapidly, her smile quick, her brown eyes twinkling as she spied the tall form of her husband unfolding his length from the work truck.

She met him at the door, and although they did not touch, what passed between them seemed more intimate than a touch.

A bright smile from both, a long look between them.

"Come, Eli, we have company. The schoolteacher."

"Why, Mary. Hello. So nice of you to come see us. Is it Elam?"

"Yes."

He nodded soberly. "We'll discuss it later."

The supper was delicious, the fried chicken crispy, the mashed potatoes hot and buttery, lima beans, and spring onions. The children were quiet, but an occasional titter of laughter emerged, bright dark eyes inquisitive.

Elam was draped across his chair, picking at his food, his face as pale and colorless and the tablecloth. Mary asked him questions about school, and he smiled wanly, replied softly. A shadow passed across Sarah's face.

As they did dishes, they talked easily about everyday things, but they sat down when Eli came in, their faces sober. He asked Mary how he performed in school, and Mary was forced to tell the truth.

"He's just very lethargic. So tired out he falls asleep, and doesn't play sports at all anymore."

Eli nodded. "I was afraid of that."

For a long moment, he was quiet, then a smile crossed his face.

"But we don't have to despair in the face of this. God knows what he has in store, and we only have to put our hands in His."

Mary drove Dolly through the warm spring evening, the bright kitchen and gentle ways invading her thoughts. Here was a home where light and love, faith and contentment lived, so every community, no matter where, had sweetness and bitterness. Could it be this? The day you were born, you were given the task of living with a group of people assigned to you, and you were irretrievably stuck there, through blood relation.

Mary sighed. She wanted to take her mother's hand, guide her to this warm bright kitchen with red geraniums glowing on the sewing machine, show her the way to a happier existence. Her father's pinched look, his view of such a kitchen would influence her mother's way of thinking, and together they would call it "worldly." Look at the cost of all those windows.

With the white Jeep and its occupant gone, Ben Stoltzfus efficiently disposed of, Mary took comfort in food. She gained back the twenty she'd lost, and by the end of the school year, she told herself she'd work it off on the farm. She did work hard, her skin turned a golden tan, her hair a coppery red, bleached by the sun.

Little Elam was diagnosed with leukemia, the word they had not spoken of. Acute lymphocytic leukemia.

Mary did all she could to support their family. She stayed with the children while Eli and Sarah spent many days at the hospital in Griffith, New York. She became friends with Sarah's sister, from an Amish settlement in Missouri, a sweet, tall girl who bore a resemblance to Linda. She was outspoken, voiced opinions with confidence, and Mary enjoyed every moment with her.

Mary's long summer took on new purpose as she traveled to Griffith Cancer Center in the city to visit Elam and offer support to his parents. Little Elam was a courageous child, but she hardly recognized the ravaged face, the dark hair all gone. He gave her a wan smile, his thin hands plucking at the white blanket. His skin appeared to be transparent, as if the outer layer of skin was cellophane, revealing the maze of thin blue veins underneath. His head was like a sheep losing its outer layer of wool, patches of bare scalp visible through thinning spots. His collarbone protruded sharply above the line of his oversized hospital gown.

"I'm doing good. Sometimes I have to throw up, but then I feel better," he said, in his soft voice.

Mary smiled, patted his shoulder. "You'll be out of here before you know it."

"I think so, too."

Both parents smiled from their chairs, nodding in approval. Their own faces appeared ravaged, lines of worry creasing their foreheads, fingers plucking nervously at folds of fabric. This strange place, this pulsing metropolis teeming with English people, the world in all its forms.

Here they experienced dyed hair, cut in a fashionable style, earrings dangling from earlobes, skin pierced and decorated with gleaming jewelry.

Tattoos, which they could only glance at before looking away quickly.

"Judge not, that ye be not judged," Sarah told her husband. And out of these mouths came words of kindness, encouragement. Tattooed arms soothed and comforted, encircled their suffering child with a freedom expressing love in an unrestrained way. Elam was their own personal project, they told Eli and Sarah.

A winsome child, with the face of an angel, they said, bringing hope and reassurance, an air of transport from nights of fear and wondering why.

Mary sat with Eli and Sarah, who spoke of their journey. Taught by the many warnings of the Old Testament, Eli wondered what they'd done wrong that God smote their child with cancerous cells.

Sarah twisted a faded handkerchief between nervous fingers, her eyes downcast, nodding in agreement.

Had they dealt unfairly with others? Been given to slanderous gossip? Had they ceased to examine their own hearts, and thus fallen into depraved and unfair thoughts?

Mary was astounded. She watched Elam sigh, turn his head to a side, and saw his eyelids droop over the brown eyes.

"But you were so strong in the beginning," she whispered.

"I guess we were," Eli said softly. "But do you have any idea how hard it is to watch your sweet child suffer the way he has? It's only normal to blame yourself, blame someone, anyone. And yes, I know, we shouldn't do this to ourselves, thinking we did something wrong, that God caused these cancer cells in his young body to punish us."

"It's in us," Mary said. "In our Amish way of thinking."

Silently, they nodded in agreement.

Their reverie was broken by a large nurse walking briskly to the door, tapping, and entering. Her top was stretched tightly across her massive stomach, her legs like tree trunks. She said nothing but walked over to Elam's bedside, lifted the thin white arm, watching the watch on her opposite write. His eyes flew open, then closed again.

She adjusted a few things, checked his temperature, patted his cheek and said, "Go right back to sleep, honey."

She stopped, said hello, then lumbered out the door in a swish of fabric, the sound of rubber soles on the waxed tile.

Sarah said this place contained so many nice people—friendly, caring individuals who went far beyond being here doing a job.

"It's almost as if Elam was their own child. I don't know if I'd be capable of loving someone else's child the way they truly love Elam."

Eli said there was so much good left in the world.

MARY TOLD HER parents about Elam's condition, the kindness of strangers, leaving out the description of their way of dress.

Her father leveled a long, dark look at her.

"You must be careful, Mary. When we are out in the world, we can easily become led astray."

"Meaning?" she retorted quickly.

"Don't give me that sass, Mary. You know what I mean. If a person is worldly, dressed without *ordnung*, we cannot take their kindness as the real thing, and don't you forget it, young lady. These people are there for the money, and that's all they care about. Why, some of them make up to fifty dollars an hour. More than that. No one can fairly make that much money. And you know what the Bible teaches about that. Any money we receive that isn't earned by the sweat of our brow is cursed."

Mary was stiff with rage. Her breath came in short puffs. She left the table slowly, went upstairs, and shivered in her room, sitting on a cane back chair, her elbows on the wide window sill, gazing at the unpainted barn.

She felt choked with unspoken words, questions jamming in her throat like a bacterial infection. Sick of this cloying vanity, this refusal to see in any way except his own. His attitude beyond understanding.

As her father walked behind the plow and the thin mules, he was dressed exactly the way he promised he would the day he was baptized, upholding every important aspect of the church, a truly humble person, invaluable to the community. His children following in his footsteps, his wife nodding constant approval.

And yet he was steeped, marinated in an attitude of harsh judgment of others, thankful he wasn't a worldly person. Thankful to work by the sweat of his brow, thankful to be raised by God-fearing parents with a place reserved in heaven.

Should she be thankful, or more grateful for a godly heritage? The folks in this community did not all believe the views her father upheld.

"Honor thy father and mother." Honor them, even if they weren't honorable themselves? Confusion was a spider web, one she tried swatting away, only to be replaced by a fresh, thicker one.

Whether she understood perfectly or not, one thing stood out to her. She was on a quest, a journey. God had given her this mind, these inquisitive thoughts, had taken her to Lancaster and back again. Robbed of a person she believed was meant to be her friend (husband being too far on the horizon), robbed of anything she truly wanted to be, even the freedom of making her own choices. She had to come back to New York, her anxiety and fear a dictator of her conscience. And here she was, still confused.

She had no one to confide in, no one who would understand.

To her way of thinking, kindness was kindness, no matter from whom. And she was confident that the professionals at Griffith Cancer Center had spent thousands of dollars on schooling to recognize a dream, a goal, and deserved every penny.

They certainly did work by the sweat of their brow.

She felt the steel wedge work its way between her father and her, tasted the bitterness of her disappointment. She was almost frightened to know the resentment she harbored for her mother's lack of courage to think for herself. She shook her head, then lowered her face into her hands.

"Heavenly Father," she whispered. "Help me. I don't want to be a dishonor to my parents, and yet I find it harder and harder to accept their stringent views."

She prayed on and felt a measure of peace. She watched the evening sun break through a smattering of thready clouds, throwing the black barn into a golden light, She knew the photographer, Mr. Caster, would notice and capture this moment for a prizewinning picture had he been there. In spite of herself, her eyes followed the road winding up the slope, through the fir trees.

Cameras, cell phones, any device able to keep an image of what the eye could see, was *verboten* (forbidden).

"Thou shalt have no other gods before me." Photographs were graven images.

She watched the display of golden light, moving clouds creating shadow.

Drawings were allowed up to a point and she had been a good freehand artist in school. Praise was tightfisted, pinched, but she'd remembered the look of amazement on Teacher Rachel's face, before sliding her drawing under the remaining artwork.

Mary turned, got up slowly, uncertainly. She looked out the window, then walked purposefully to the aging kneehole desk against the opposite wall. A small sketchpad, a lead pencil, her box of one hundred pencil colors. Quickly, before the light faded now, her heart audible in her chest, she sat down and began to sketch.

WEEKS WENT BY, the days following a pattern in quick succession after school began. There was some satisfaction in the rhythm of Mary's days—arithmetic after singing class, then reading, listening to the little ones stumble over words, answering raised hands. She nipped whispering in the bud, gave stern reprimands when students forgot to wipe their muddy feet before entering the classroom, but she also tried to instill a love of learning and to see each child as worthy of her time.

Winter blew in and stayed. Public school had snow days off, but the small parochial school on the hill stayed open, parents ferrying in their children to school with sturdy, well shod horses drawing sleighs or closed buggies, Mary's faithful team among them. There was a roaring fire in the old furnace, so even with cold air seeping through cracks below windows and a loose door ushering in finely drifted snow, it was fairly cozy. The children were a hardy lot, shrugging into homemade coats when chills chased up their spines. They raised their hands and asked to be allowed to warm their feet by the furnace where they stuck cold toes against hot steel and recoiled with surprise. Hands to mouths, the students tittered.

Slowly, Mary came to realize how much she loved to teach, though she wished she had access to a better curriculum. So many things could be improved. She taught well. She played in the snow with the children at recess, building snow forts and pummeling the opposing side with loose snowballs.

She brought up the matter of a better curriculum with her father. Her mother lifted worried eyes as her father set down his coffee cup and lifted his hip to reach into his pocket for a handkerchief to wipe his mouth. He coughed. His eyes watered.

"Well, it's a reasonable question. But you know here in Pinedale we don't uphold those worldly books Lancaster County uses. Too much *oppganga* stuff in them. We use leftover books from the libraries. Castoffs we get for nothing. Books from the fifties and sixties."

This was said with a resounding belch, no apology.

"Would you be okay with me bringing it up to the school board?"

"You can try, see what they say."

Her mother's shoulders slumped with relief.

THE SCHOOL MEETING was held at Henry Beiler's, the farm nestled between rolling hills, forested with a thick thatch of pine trees upholding tons of snow on drooping branches. Mary tried to hurry the plodding little horse along, while watching the snow peel off in layers as the cold north wind attacked the laden branches on the hill. Everywhere there was one picturesque scene or another. She tried to keep them in her mind's eye, would get out her sketch pad later.

She brought her request to the table and watched wearily as expressions changed in stoic faces, long vertical lines surrounding grim mouths deepened. Throats were cleared, feet shuffled uncomfortably.

"Well," Henry Beiler said finally.

The teakettle on the Pioneer Maid range whistled. Henry's wife, Mary, rose to her feet to set it back.

"I don't know," Sam Swarey said softly. "Funds being what they are, I just don't know."

"We appreciate your effort to improve the children's learning, but we would be glad if you'd continue in the old way. We don't want to start anything new."

This was voiced by the chairman of the board, who was met with solemn agreement all around.

Mary sensed opportunity slipping away.

"But we can't reasonably expect the children to believe a dozen eggs costs twelve cents," she protested, referencing the old Strayer-Uptom Arithmetic books from the forties.

"It doesn't matter. It's still working with numbers. They know the amount of a dozen eggs."

This came from Davie King, in a mocking tone, which fueled Mary's disappointment to the point that she said rather heatedly, "Sure, but the more relevant we can make their textbooks, the better they will learn. The eggs aren't the only example . . ."

She tried to continue but was met with a rumbled warning from the chairman of the board.

"There is danger in discontentment, Mary. We should always strive to uphold tradition. To walk the way of our forefathers is a privilege worth more than gold. Our children learn enough to grow up to be upstanding members of the community, to make a good living the way their fathers have done before them. There is no need for new books."

And that was the end of that.

Subject to obedience to the men on the board, she seethed her way home in the frigid night. She was cold, hungry, and more than upset. Why couldn't they see how much the children could profit from better workbooks? She was the teacher. They weren't. Every last one of these people in Pinedale were stuck in the same old groove.

She chafed at restrictions everywhere—at home, in church, and at school. Secretly questioning sermons, she often opened her German Bible, read passages, and disagreed with the interpretation she'd heard at church.

Little Elam returned to school, leaving Mary in awe of his healing. His compromised immune system kept him home on many days, but there was an air of optimism about his return, and his grateful parents showed their support. Mary was grateful for his quiet presence, his healing, and through the months of thawing ice and snow liquified by the soft spring sunshine, she felt close to content.

As she drove the chunky little horse through slush and rivulets of melting snow, a satchel of papers to be corrected on the seat beside her, she knew there was no change on the horizon. She would do just this for the remainder of her life, a future of teaching school in the hills of Pinedale, her steps decided for her, by the school board, the ministers, and her parents. How she wore her coverings, how her dresses were made, the books she would use in the classroom, the strength of yes and no according to her father's interpretation of the Scripture.

Many young women found this acceptable, found the boundaries a safety net of peace and stayed content within them. They depended on God to provide a good husband eventually, which He surely did, so why couldn't she find this same happiness?

And yet she could not find her way back to Lancaster with a clean conscience.

The school picnic was the second week in May, a time she'd anticipated, displaying her artwork with that of the pupils. She was quite proud of her ever-improving work done in colored pencils, was thinking of learning watercolor painting. Parents and children noticed her talent, standing in awe as they viewed her drawings of snowy landscapes, barren trees, sunsets over the fields.

She enjoyed the day of the picnic immensely, loved handing out prizes to the winners of footraces and other games. Elam's wan face contained a spot of color on both cheeks, his smile lighting up as he clapped his hands when his friend Samuel won the lower grade's race.

She watched her father's face take on a light of pleasure as he ate the good picnic food, filled his plate to heaping, and visited with the chairman of the board, laughing at his jokes. Her mother was duly pleased, as well. Here was their daughter Mary, the one gone astray, back in the fold, a respected schoolteacher, a leader of the other schools in the valley. Surely *der Herr* had blessed them beyond what they deserved. Surely.

But when Amos overheard a parent praising Mary for her artwork, he pulled her aside to warn her against the sin of pride. She should not be drawing attention to her own self, he said. Why had she chosen to hang her artwork along with the students'? She must learn humility, before it was too late. His stern look was like a rain cloud on an otherwise beautiful day.

CHAPTER 10

Bᴜᴛ ᴜɴʀᴇsᴛ sɪᴍᴍᴇʀᴇᴅ ʙᴇʟᴏᴡ ᴛʜᴇ sᴜʀꜰᴀᴄᴇ ᴏɴ ᴛʜᴇ ꜰɪʀsᴛ ᴡᴇᴇᴋ at home. Everywhere, there was work to be done. Her mother had steadily gained weight though the long, cold winter months, had accumulated a severe dose of hypertension, her blood pressure escalating. A visit to the family doctor found her with a prescription for medication, a rumbling displeasure from her skeletal husband, and no will to keep up with all the work the old farm required. Salt was restricted, as were many of her favorite foods.

Mary bit back words of rebellion, thought bitterly about the interpretation of the words "summer vacation." She pushed the rusted old reel mower through thick, wet grass, raked it up, and used it as mulch between the pea vines. She milked cows, drove horses in the stony soil, hoed flower beds, and did laundry with the smelly old gasoline engine powering the agitator and wringer of the washing machine.

She asked for a better clothesline and did not get it.

And then they received word that her Uncle Leroy had been felled by a massive stroke. Her parents received the message with the stoicism of her people, nodding their heads solemnly, and then going on with their chores.

Mary was affected deeply, though. She wept in the bean rows as she brought her hoe down on thistles and chickweed. Poor Lizzie. Her heart cried for the loneliness, the bewilderment of her beloved aunt.

They prepared themselves for the trip to Lancaster for the funeral. Mary's hands shook as she dressed in her black suit, drew the plain covering up over her hair. She was deeply ashamed to be seen in Lancaster like this. She had been one of them, and now she wasn't.

But she went, feeling caught between one way of life and another.

The teeming hubbub of Lancaster was like a shock to her, but her thoughts stayed on Lizzie as she followed her parents through the friends and neighbors who were preparing the shop for the funeral service, cleaning and cooking for the family, receiving casseroles and baked items, fruit salad, puddings. She found herself numb with grief as she spied Lizzie and her children, dressed in black funeral attire. She bypassed her parents, who were shaking hands with other visitors. She threw herself into Lizzie's arms, taking comfort as she clung to her dear aunt, then hugged her cousins in turn.

"So sudden, so final," Lizzie was murmuring. Then she turned to shake hands with her brother Amos and his wife, Barbara.

Mary was pulled aside by her mother and reminded firmly that she must refrain from such a worldly display of hugging.

Mary found herself stumbling through the lines of benches occupied by relatives in black funeral attire and made her way blindly up the stairs and into the safety of what had been her own room. It was the same as she had left it. The beautiful furniture, the fine quilt, were like a balm of beauty to her starved spirit, although she knew she could not allow herself this luxury for more than a moment. She was from Pinedale, not Lancaster County, and never could belong here.

But oh, how she wanted to live here again. The truth of it washed over her, filling her with a glimpse of what she wanted for her future. But was her will God's will, too? How did one go about deciphering the two?

She stood in the middle of the room and found her image in the mirror. She truly appeared to be a middle-aged minister's wife, the way she dressed, the way she had gained back her weight.

Nothing to be done about it now, she thought grimly. *I am from Pinedale.*

The door opened. She turned to find someone she did not recognize, a young mother holding a tiny baby wrapped in a thin blanket, her face asking if it was alright to come in.

Mary smiled. "Come," she said.

"You sure I'm not interrupting?"

"Certainly not. Sit here."

She waved a hand toward the love seat, the small couch she'd spent so much time on with Linda, building hopes and dreams.

Another world, another time.

"How old is your baby?" she asked politely.

"She's four weeks."

"She's precious," replied Mary. "I'm Lizzie's niece, Mary. I used to live here."

The young mother's eyes widened. Mary could see her mind working.

"You are?" she asked finally. She gave a small laugh.

"I'm Ben Stoltzfus' sister Lavina."

"Ben? The Ben I knew?"

"Yes."

Flustered now, Mary sat down on the bed and turned her face away as if the information was far more than she could comprehend.

"How . . . how is he?" she asked, after an awkward silence.

"He married in February."

Kindness laced her words, but it was a cruel slap in the face. Mary struggled to keep her emotion in check, her face passive.

"May I ask who?"

"You probably wouldn't know her. She's from a neighboring county. Eli Lapp's Hannah. Sam's Davey's Eli?"

Mary shook her head.

"He really liked you, Mary. He was devastated, and sometimes I'm afraid he married Hannah on the rebound. But he seems happy."

"Good. I hope he is. Will be."

"Yes."

Lavina looked down at the infant in her arms, folded the blanket up over her shoulder. Her covering was picture perfect, her hair in heavy rolls, sleek with styling gel. Mary experienced a pang of remembrance, the joy of nice clothes, the company of young men.

"So how have you been?"

"Good. I took a job teaching school."

"That's awesome."

"Yes."

When had she heard the term "awesome" last? It was like coming home to a familiar world, stuffed full of things she had longed for without realizing.

"Do you like it?"

"I do." She paused, then added. "Sometimes it's hard. After being here with Lizzie, it was never easy returning to . . ."

She lifted a hand, waved it in the direction of her covering.

The door was flung open and her friend Linda rushed across the room and into her arms. For a long moment, they stayed in a close embrace, swaying back and forth. Mary thought how she had had no physical touch since returning to Pinedale, a luxury she now appreciated.

"Mary. Mary." Linda cried.

And Mary wept a bit, felt the closeness as if it had always been.

"Don't you cry, or I'm going to start," said Linda. "You are not supposed to be in New York, I guarantee it. You have to come live with Lizzie now. She's going to be all alone, and if I know her, she won't be ready to throw in the towel and get rid of the bakery. You know that."

Mary laughed. She cried. She shook her head, said, "No, no, Linda. I can't do that."

THE VISITATION, THE funeral service, everything passed in a blur of people clad in black, teams trotting along in an orderly procession, the emotional burial and the comfort of friends. Lizzie took her aside after most of the family had left.

"Come live with me, Mary. Please do. The bakery has never been the same without you. I'll tell your parents. Amos can get off his high horse and realize you need to do this."

Mary lifted eyes liquid with longing.

"Lizzie, if you only knew how much I want to. But my parents will never give their blessing. I am trying to do what is right."

"Oh, I know, Mary. I know. Do you want to stay in Pinedale?"

"Of course not. I was reasonably happy till I walked into my old room, and everything came flooding back."

"Mary, I would never want you to go against your conscience, but will you pray about it, at least?"

Mary nodded her head and gave Lizzie another long hug before parting.

Mary climbed into the van, accompanied her parents. On the ride north to Pinedale, she prayed fervently, asking God for wisdom and direction and peace. By the time they arrived home, her mind was settled.

SHE PAID A visit to Henry Beiler from the school board and told him she was needed in Lancaster. Her uncle had died and she needed to go live with her aging aunt. She was wished well and found herself back in the buggy with a song in her heart.

She left a message on Lizzie's answering machine, telling her she'd be back the following Tuesday.

The showdown came later in the evening, when she joined her parents in the living room to tell them of her decision. Her father's face was grim. Her mother was seated beside him, her hands in her lap, her mouth in a prim line.

Mary was given an ultimatum. Stay, and God's blessing will be upon you. Go, and you will reap the consequences. This was followed by a barrage of premonitions for her future. She had expected no less, so her words were few, but respectful. She said with as much humility and love as she could that she understood their position, but the decision was made.

She paid one more visit to Eli and Sarah, presenting Elam with a new sketchpad and pencil colors. She went away with the assurance of receiving a letter from time to time, along with copies of some of his drawings. She drove past the schoolhouse, the dogwood tree in full bloom, sketched it in her mind as she made her way down the hill. She paid another visit to her sisters, where she was met with varying degrees of disapproval, which she had expected as well.

Later, she had a long talk alone with her mother.

"Mary, if you go, you can always hold yourself back. You don't have to be dressed in the latest style. Your background is plain. You can be reasonable."

"You know I will be reasonable."

"Yes, you do have a good head on your shoulders."

"Mom, you know I respect your way of life here, and I wish I could be one of you. But it's not who I am, truly. I would never marry here, this I don't doubt. And perhaps I still have a chance in Lancaster. You do want me to have a chance at marriage, don't you?"

"Only if he's in the *ordnung* and was raised by God-fearing parents."

"Mam." Her voice was laced with despair. "You speak as if *ordnung* defined your Christianity. That you can't believe in Christ unless you dress a certain way."

Shocked, her mother drew back. "Well, this is so."

"No. That isn't right. You can believe in Jesus's sacrifice and follow the Bible without wearing a black dress and an organdy covering."

Round and round they went, the mother and her daughter simply seeing the world through different lenses. They hurled accusations then melted into half apologies, tearful promises, and pledges to love each other in spite of their differences. They agreed to write on a weekly basis, to remember the ties that bind.

THE THROBBING ENGINE of the Greyhound bus lulled her weary soul into a restful slumber. Mary awoke late in the afternoon, aware of being alive, of going toward a long-awaited destination. She felt the tingle of anticipation, the deep-seated happiness of new experiences ahead.

Since moving back home, she had taken up the cross and followed the rules and regulations to the letter. If life was a journey, then she had come far, had followed stepping stones of wisdom and experience in what God had set in her path.

No, she could not go as far as accompanying a very attractive photographer to dinner, but neither could she marry a young man like her father. There was no peace or contentment in a place where you are placed to please men, to uphold the family name. For some individuals, perhaps, but not for her.

Had she felt the fear, experienced the panic attacks, to return to Pinedale to learn these things? She believed so. She bowed her head and thanked the Father of lights, the giver of all good gifts.

Aunt Lizzie met her at the bus station, plans all set to eat at a nice place, a celebration of her return. They ate, wept, talked, reminisced, voiced appreciation, and Mary went to her old room and slept soundly until seven the following morning.

Awakened by the hum of traffic, she rolled over, stretched, and jumped out of bed, eager to try on her colorful dresses that still hung in the closet.

They still fit, and she tied on the black bib apron, did her hair, and pinned her covering to the tune of that song in her heart.

Aunt Lizzie looked up, smiled, and laid down the book she was reading, a devotional for grieving hearts.

"I still need my morning boost, Mary. Grieving is a terrible thing. There are so many things I want to say to him."

But in typical Lizzie fashion, she was up and running ahead. There was a delivery coming from Dutch Valley. Bills to be paid. She was selling the horse and carriage, all the shop equipment.

And Mary went back to the bakery as if she'd never left. She ran to the mixer, rolled dough, and socked it with her fist. She laughed and sang, whistled and drank Pepsi with ice.

The sun shone through the bakery windows, showing the smudges, the grease, and the fly dirt. The floor was dull from less than thorough mopping.

Caitlyn was short with a picky customer, and Mary appeared like magic, asking her to finish the cinnamon rolls, then turned the customer's irritation to pleasure by taking back the questionable sponge cake and supplying her with a fresh one free of charge.

After hours, she washed windows, cleaned floors, threw outdated sacks of walnuts and pecans into the trash, ordered fresh cinnamon and cloves.

Lizzie sat on a rolling office chair and said she could simply prostrate herself on the floor and worship. Mary replied she had better cut that out right now, that she wouldn't tolerate idol worship. They both laughed freely, heartily, and it did them both a world of good. Lizzie said she felt better than she had since the funeral.

But Mary heard her walking the floor far into the night, sometimes blowing her nose. A life together for many years is not easily extinguished, and Lizzie was swept up in a maelstrom of emotions she had no way of controlling.

On long summer evenings, they drank lemonade on the back patio, listened to the chirping of katydids and crickets, saying nothing, drinking in the quiet companionship.

One evening, Lizzie told her what she missed most about Leroy is how he put on his socks, leaning forward from his recliner, rolling down his pantlegs just so. And Mary told her she felt a sense of guilt, leaving her mother with the farm and her blood pressure so high, her lack of energy.

Lizzie snorted audibly, said it was high time those two got off the farm, for pity's sake. High time Amos quit stumbling over that rocky soil, dragged by his ugly old mules. He was born bull-headed. That had been determined when he was two years old, screaming and yelling and rattling the yard gate to get his own way. Yes, he had done that. She still remembered.

Marcus and Linda were engaged to be married in the fall, but she took Mary along to the suppers and singings in her new black suit, which was definitely slimming. Mary found a sense of confidence, greeted old friends.

She enjoyed her time immensely, making plans for the following weekend with some of the other young people. She felt comfortable, relaxed, for the first time in ages.

LIZZIE'S DAUGHTERS ARRIVED on a Monday morning to have coffee, make waffles, and go through their father's belongings. They sorted, organized, and reminisced. And Mary truly felt a part of the family dynamic, even more than she felt at home with her own siblings.

LIZZIE ACCOMPANIED MARY to the Lancaster General for an MRI of her stomach, never quite having the nerve to tell her it was likely the churning up of acid, caused by stress. Nothing showed up on the report, so she put her on green herbal pills and a vile, evil smelling protein shake that turned her teeth green, until she returned to the swallowing of a tablespoon of organic vinegar in a glass of warm water every single morning without fail.

She went to the beach with Linda and a group of girls. Five of them stayed in a house on the edge of the sand dunes. Mary stood on the porch, her hands clenching the wooden railing, speechless. She had often read about the ocean, the sea, salt water, and sailing ships of old, oil tankers and fancy yachts slicing through the heaving waves. But never in her wildest moments could she have imagined the vast, untamed power of tons of water crashing on sand in huge curling foam-tipped waves. She gazed at the rolls of water, coming toward the house in a perfect line, then receding again.

The other girls weren't aware of Mary's disbelief, but ran around putting sheets on beds, storing food in the refrigerator, turning on the television, opening windows to let in the sea breeze.

They shrieked and yelled, pounded pillow cases.

Linda regretted this would be her last trip with the girls. She would be a married woman next summer. So would Susie. Ruth said they were lucky; her Mark hadn't joined church when he was supposed to, so it was two more years before marriage for her.

"Where's Mary?" they asked each other.

Relieved to find her on the back deck, they returned to the house, leaving her to drink in the wonders of the sea. She felt as small as a pinhead, a feather in the vast universe. Mary felt the draw of the ocean's power, the wonder of God's design. How could the sea be contained in its place? What kept it from crashing farther inland, to spread out and out, way past the house, carrying it along the current without a Master?

She went down the steps, across the wooden walkway, and through the sand. She stopped to touch the grass. Tough and wiry. She poked her toes in the sand, felt sharp edges. She bent to retrieve the object and came up with a broken shell. In awe, she turned it over and over, amazed to find a black color, the grooves spreading out in perfect symmetry. It was so beautiful, this broken piece of the sea.

Gulls wheeled above her, their cries thrilling, a part of the spray of salt water. She looked up to find a dozen of them, two dozen. Then she saw a man bending over his small son as he threw pieces of food to the gulls. His wife stood nearby, scantily clad, one arm up to protect her sun hat from the strong ocean breeze.

Oh my, she thought. *What would her parents say?*

The old awareness of guilt, of disobedience and its repercussions, came roaring back. The ocean turned dark, ominous. The sun lost its warmth.

With every ounce of willpower, she emptied her mind, took long cleansing breaths, and slowly gained her equilibrium. She let the waves soothe her spirit, calmed the roiling thoughts by reciting Bible verses about God's unfailing love.

She began to walk. She found the wet sand to be more solid, easier to navigate, so she walked along the water's edge, delighting in the cooling wavelets dashing over the tops of her feet. She breathed in deeply, smiled greetings at friendly vacationers. She received curious glances, saw a woman mouth the word "Amish" to her partner.

Nothing bothered her, absolutely nothing.

It was beyond words, this newfound world of saltwater in crashing motion, wet sand, dry sand, shells and gulls and spindly sandpipers.

She wanted to fling her arms wide, to launch herself into the waves the way the English children did. Amazed, she watched them dive through the waves and ride them on some sort of Styrofoam board.

She watched for a long time, saw how it was done, and resolved to learn.

She learned how to eat steamed shrimp, how to peel them and dip them in cocktail sauce. She ate blue crabs, found them delicious. She tasted fish tacos with blackened grouper, learned to appreciate the taste of lime juice dribbled on spicy, coarsely grated cabbage.

And she did learn how to swim in the ocean. Caught by giant waves and tumbling about like a cork, she received brush burns on her arms and legs, swallowed salt water, and thought she might drown after all. Still, she loved it.

All the girls agreed. Mary was something else. The other girls had often experienced the ocean, but this was her first time, and she wasn't afraid of anything. Oh, she was a trip.

She lost all sense of shame, sat on the back deck in her swimming suit, put her feet on the rail and unwrapped a grape popsicle, told the girls one week wasn't nearly enough.

They had long serious talks about boys, marriage, and parents. Susan's sister and her husband had visited their parents one evening, told them they were sorry to break their hearts, but they saw no sense in remaining Old Order, choosing to drive a car and join a more liberal church. Mary listened, thinking of her father.

The condemnation would be total, coming down like a hammer on an anvil. Would the same thing happen if he saw her now?

Oh, but what an experience. What a satisfying taste of the wonders of God's earth. She wanted to drink in the rising sun and the setting of it as it slid into the choppy sea. She wanted to carry the wonderful scent of saltwater with her forever.

She thanked the girls for asking her to go and knew for sure she had never experienced anything like this before.

A close bond was formed among them, a friendship born of secrets and shared soul talks. They laughed, they cried, they were amazed at Mary's stories of being raised in Pinedale, New York. No one made fun of her upbringing, only listened, incredulous, nodding in agreement when Mary mentioned the irony of all of them being Old Older Amish, yet all so different. The diversity of *ordnung*, the striving to keep the balance.

After her return, Mary felt as if she had finally put both feet on solid ground. No longer allowing fear or anxiety to drive her, she became confident inside, finding a sense of calm.

She wrote letters to her mother, sharing only the details she would want to hear. She was never dishonest, but there was no sense upsetting her with descriptions of her clothing or adventures. Her mother wrote back in pitiful prose, telling of the weeds in the garden taking over, the peaches overripe in the baskets and no time to can them. She had sent word to Mary's sister Lydia, who was always ahead of her work, but she was down with a miscarriage. "Miss," her mother wrote. The accepted, subtle term for the early loss of a baby. Amos had to let the hay go, and offered his help, but then the hay was rained on, costing them thousands of dollars.

More like hundreds, Mary thought, knowing their thin hay didn't bring a good price.

Of course, her mother's words pierced her heart and brought a sense of having abandoned her parents, leaving them to scrabble a living from the unforgiving soil, while she was experiencing the world, reveling in sights and sounds hardly imagined. She wrestled with guilt, wrestled with the thought of all the good she could do at home in New York.

She wrote back, told them it was time to sell the farm. Let one of the boys have it. Build a *daudy haus* (in-law suite). They had done their share, now it was time to rest.

The letter was met with resistance from her father, who wrote on lined tablet paper in his cramped, sparse words. They leaped from the page, assaulted her with condemnation.

"If you were here, there would be no reason to consider selling this home your mother and I have worked so hard for."

CHAPTER 11

HER STOMACH ROARED. GIGANTIC, UNSETTLING BELCHES ERUPTED from her throat. She upped the dosage of vinegar, wrinkled her nose, and fought nausea, but continued the only remedy for acid reflux that worked.

Lizzie knocked on her door, hovered like a worried hen, told her she was making an appointment for her. A specialist for her stomach. "No, no." Mary shook her head. "Yes, yes," was Lizzie's reply.

They took the bus into the city of Lancaster, a bustling metropolis. Mary thought of her parents' disapproval everywhere she looked. Men in business suits, men wearing sleeveless t-shirts, exposing hideous tattoos. Women in running shorts and ponytails.

Mary's breath came in short, rapid gasps, her lips dry and cracked, her eyes wild. The tall building appeared to totter, leaning in toward the sidewalk, ready to topple, to crush, to maim.

"Lizzie?" she breathed.

"Yes, Mary?"

"I . . . I can't do this. I can't see a doctor. We did the MRI and there was nothing wrong. He'll laugh at me for coming to see him."

Lizzie looked into Mary's frightened eyes, assured her the doctor would not laugh, and calmly steered her in the right direction. They went through a glass door, read a few names, and stepped into the proper waiting area.

The doctor prodded and poked, sent her for an ultrasound, which turned up nothing. He put her on anxiety medication, which she disposed of the minute she was home. These pills were absolutely dangerous to her health and well-being. Absolutely not.

She took to carrying a small jar of organic vinegar in her purse, simply having it with her a source of comfort.

A while later, back for a check-up, she was sitting alone on the bus, staring out the window, thinking how she had been accosted by these symptoms after she'd been at the beach. Yes. She had sinned and God in his mercy was bringing her to task. Her thoughts roiled, her guilt piled up like windblown sand, creating dunes on which she tumbled and rolled.

She sniffed. Someone or something reeked of vinegar. She looked around. People sitting in various positions, bored, half asleep, a young mother with her hands firmly on an unruly son's shoulders.

She breathed deeply and was hit by the realization of where the odor was coming from. Her purse. In dismay, she bent over, found the slow leak from the loosened cap, her purse smelling to high heaven.

There was nothing to be done but tighten the cap, swab with the lone tissue, and hope for the best. Heads swiveled, noses wrinkled.

She was being observed, glares from disconcerted passengers. She tried to meet the inquisitive stares with bright smiles, her face flaming.

Finally, the young woman with the active son turned and asked if anyone knew where that smell was coming from. Mary pretended not to hear, kept her eyes averted, and got off the bus with her head held high, before finding the first restroom and washing everything, pouring the vinegar down the drain.

She lied to the doctor, simply said an outright lie, and told him the anxiety pills were doing the job. He was pleased and wondered at the smell coming from her, but he thought perhaps she hadn't washed in a while. She was let go without an appointment to return, went home, and cringed alone in her bedroom that night, the lie vibrating like the rattles on a snake's tail.

Forgive me, Father, for I have sinned.

The phrase came into her head. She'd read it many times, these words of contrition the Catholic Church used at their confessionals.

Well, whoever and wherever they were used, they surely were necessary in her case.

A letter arrived, the envelope thick with many pages written on lined paper torn from an old composition book, yellowed along the edges.

Dear, Mary,

Greetings of love in Jesus's Holy Name.

How are you? I have returned from the doctor with a severe reprimand. Overweight, high blood pressure, with orders to rest. What am I to do? My heart is giving out, Mary. I have no one to carry the load.

The remainder of two pages were filled with lamentations, of life on the farm with Amos, the children with lives of their own, bills to pay, and no one to help.

Mary took a deep breath and opened the page from her father. Accusations and dire threats leaped from the page, circled and attacked, her conscience taken down like a wildebeest in the jaws of a lioness.

She felt the life flow out of her, felt the flame of her interest in things around her slowly dwindle. She put her head in her hands, thought of being bashed back and forth like a baseball.

When Lizzie saw the letter, she was furious. She went to her desk and opened her tablet. She stopped, leaned back in her chair.

"What am I expected to do without you, Mary? They can't do this to you. He needs to get off that farm. And Barbara could fix all her health problems with a bit of self-control. She needs to stop eating that everlasting fried mush."

Mary sat in the recliner, her covering crushed into the headrest, her hands busily locking and unlocking in her lap. Her stomach groaned. She went to the kitchen for a bit of vinegar water, opened the refrigerator door.

Ah, yes. That sweet pepper dip with pretzels. A diet Pepsi to bring up the burps. She opened the freezer door, put ice cubes in a glass, then slowly poured the carbonated liquid over them. She arranged the dip on a plate with a few handfuls of pretzels, listened to Lizzie without comment.

"You're not going back," Lizzie said firmly.

She searched her own soul that night, lying awake as the white full moon moved across the clear night sky.

Was it so wrong to find pleasure while you were here on earth, or were you truly expected to take up the cross of self-denial in everything? Was it a sin to experience the ocean, to taste delicious food, to wear a swimsuit and have a whole troupe of loving friends?

She groaned inwardly, felt truly agitated, unsure.

She'd given up Ben. She'd been tempted by the attractive photographer in the white Jeep, but had successfully evacuated herself from the grip of romance.

She longed for freedom from nagging doubts, doubts about everything.

She finally reasoned that she would never be able to please her siblings or her parents. Even when she had given it her best effort, she had never quite reached the height of the bar they had set for her.

She simply hated the very plain lifestyle. She needed beauty. She wanted freedom to indulge in the joy of nice things, furniture, light-infused rooms without dark green blinds, the purchase of pretty items in which she would find delight.

Was that so wrong?

She knew now that she would like to be married one day, but the path to love and marriage in New York was simply not possible. If she returned, would she be expected to live the life of a nun?

Or might it be enough to find pleasure in small patches of spring violets, a bluebird's flight, the cry of the tenth newborn?

Could she be simple enough, reduced to the world of the very plain?

Questions became tiresome, answers elusive. She knew the riddle was complicated, the answers never set in stone.

LIZZIE CALLED AN emergency coffee meeting and invited Linda, Suz, and Ruth. She prepared a breakfast pizza and made homemade waffles with fresh peaches and whipped cream. They considered every angle of Mary's decision. Children ran and yelled, voices rose as opinions were hammered out, as cup after cup of coffee was consumed, fueling the already steadfast beliefs of what should happen to Mary.

"I don't care what anyone says," Suze fairly shouted. "You don't have to go back. They can move off the farm. Where are all the rest of your siblings?"

"They're busy."

"Busy doing what? Having more babies?"

Mary winced. This was, after all, her family. The mocking tone hurt.

Lizzie insisted the reason Barbara was suffering was on account of her brother Amos's refusal to move off the farm, so why put all this undue responsibility in Mary's lap? It wasn't fair to her.

The breakfast pizza was so good, made with a homemade crust, fried hash browns, scrambled eggs, crumbled sausage and bacon, cheese melted on every slice. Mary ate three slices doused with homemade ketchup. She listened as they whacked her life around like a soccer ball, smiled, frowned, but mostly ate a copious amount of food.

Linda held forth that Mary was needed at the bakery, and Mary felt a decided responsibility. Yes, she would stay. She would. Then Ruth mentioned she did feel badly for Mary's poor mother, and then Mary knew she must go.

But finally, Lizzie persuaded her to stay. She reminded her that even if she returned, she could not solve Barbara's health problems. But she could be a real help to Lizzie at the bakery as Lizzie continued to navigate her grief.

As SUMMER WANED, she grew increasingly aware of something being amiss. Anxiety mounted, rising to alarming heights. She drank glass after glass of vinegar water, took to chewing antacid tablets like candy, added papaya enzyme pills to her daily list, and still the sense of unease persisted.

She found her weekends empty. Two of her friends began dating, both attractive young men she would have accepted without a second thought. But she realized she probably wouldn't qualify, given how much weight she'd gained.

On Saturday night, she left the house early, went to the library to return a few books, and was soon immersed in the serious task of finding a few self-help books. How did one go about sorting the good from the bad? How did one maneuver the twists and turns of life without making mistakes? She flipped through several copies, before settling on one, and was turning to go, when she found herself face to face with Ben Stoltzfus, his face framed by a neatly trimmed black beard, his eyes alight with recognition.

"Why, Mary!" he said.

"Hello," she answered, and blushed to the roots of her hair, hatefully, despairingly.

Gladly, she would have dropped to the basement of the library, if only the floor would have been kind enough to open up and swallow her.

"It's good to see you. You're back?"

He allowed himself to check her out, up and down, a smile on his face.

"Yes. Uncle Leroy passed away and Lizzie needed me."

"I heard he had passed. I'm so sorry."

An awkward silence hung between them, a solid wall of remembering a time when things might have turned out completely different.

"What did your family say about you coming back?"

Was there a mocking note in his voice, or was it only her imagination? For a moment, she felt the urge to protect them, to stand up to his assessment of their conservative lifestyle. But what could she say?

"They weren't thrilled."

"This I can imagine."

"Yes. So, how is life treating you? Is your wife with you?"

"No, she's with her family. I'm spending time looking for a certain book. Haven't found it yet. Should be in this section somewhere. It's the talk of our circle. A book on marriage. Christian leadership."

"Oh."

Another uncomfortable silence, before Mary said she must be going, the evening was moving along.

She went home on her scooter, climbed the stairs to her room, and read the book she had chosen. But she soon became bored with it and called a few of her friends to see if there was anything going on. There was nothing much planned, but she was invited to go along to Sara Ann's married sister's place. She said she needed to rest before church in the morning, which was a half truth. Really, she had begun to feel that no one really wanted to include her in their plans.

She tried to rid herself of these negative thoughts, knowing she belonged to a tight knit group of girls only a short time ago.

Of course she still did, there was simply nothing planned for this Saturday night, she told herself.

She sat uneasily in church, unsure of her plans for the afternoon, something highly unusual. She had dressed with care, had taken extra pains to appear as neat and proper as everyone else, but felt a sense of incompetence, of being large and a bit unkempt.

When the Scripture was being read, she hurried to the bathroom and made an attempt to fix her hair, thinking she should have used more hairspray. She saw Lizzie's smile on her return, which was heartening, and she settled in for the second sermon with confidence. She noticed him, then.

How had she missed him when the young men filed in?

A stranger for this district. Quite nondescript, really. He would never stand out in a crowd as unusually attractive, but there was an arresting quality about him. He sat above the rest, his face giving away his age. A prominent nose, nice mouth, with ordinary, smallish eyes. A deeply tanned face. Thinning hair, she noticed.

She kept her eyes on the minister, concentrated on the eloquent words he spoke, but her attention repeatedly shifted to the new face.

Her curiosity was rampant, as usual, but as the last song was sung, she told herself she was becoming desperate. She forced herself to forget about him and went to the youth's supper and hymn singing and had a great time with her friends. The evening dispelled every negative thought in her head, and she went home and was immensely thankful for the choice she had made. Here in Lancaster was where she truly belonged.

THEN, HER MOTHER had a stroke, the blood clot leaving her paralyzed on the left side, her face misshapen, unable to speak a single phrase. The outlook was bleak, and Mary found herself on the Greyhound bus, traveling through the afternoon countryside, crying silently.

Why, oh why was her life constantly in a tailspin? Her whole being rebelled against the direction the bus was taking her. She knew if she lived to be a hundred she would never forget the profound reluctance, every fiber of her being straining back toward Lancaster County.

This was almost more than she could bear, these frightening days that stretched before her, knowing she had no experience as a nurse, knowing all too well she did not want to be her mother's caregiver.

Her own mother. The person who went through her days doing the best she knew, comforting herself with bowls of milk soup and slabs of buttered homemade bread. Who knew nothing of earthly pleasure, sights and sounds of the universe hidden away from her in the hills of New York, and was perfectly content to remain in this state.

I must gather courage, Mary told herself.

But the first sight of the farm was almost more than she could bear, the growth of weeds around the buildings, the rusted steel roof in disrepair, tall, seeded grasses hanging from either side of the long, stoney driveway, like the unkempt beard of a slovenly man. As the driver drew up to the house, anger surged. There was a goat tied in the front yard, thin cats laying in a pile by a filthy rug, a scrawny dog slinking beneath the broken floorboards of the porch.

She noticed the flower beds choked with weeds, the garden a solid mass of them. Flies dotted the car door before she had paid the driver, gnats buzzed around her head as she lifted the back door of the minivan.

Her heart sank, and sank again. The goat eyed her balefully, stamped a hoof in the uneven grass, and resumed his mad chewing.

The screen door was polluted with flies, rising in a buzzing clump as she drew back on the handle. The house was shaded in the dull evening light, so she found no one, and no one called out.

Her father made an appearance eventually, long, lean, his gray tresses matted to his head, a gleaming ring where his hat had pressed the unwashed hair against his scalp.

"Mary."

"Yes. It's me. How is she?"

"She's home."

"Yes, I heard she would be."

She was propped up on pillows, unrecognizable, the way half her face seemed to be sliding away. Her eyes were closed, but when Mary stepped up to say hello, she opened one eye, tried to smile, but it was a pathetic lopsided attempt.

Mary's hand went to her mother's face, her heart swelling with pity and compassion.

"Mam," she said softly.

Tears rolled down her mother's face, and Mary wiped them away as tenderly as possible.

Her father cleared his throat.

"Mary. I expect you to change out of those clothes. We do not need to have such *hochmut* around a sick bed."

Mary refused a reply, refused to look at him.

"Mary."

"No, Dat. No. I live in Lancaster, and this is the accepted *ordnung*."

"Not in my house."

"Then I will leave you to care for her."

She could see the battle on his face, see the refusal accepted, then relinquished, the anger at his daughter's rebellion mounting. She saw his eyes slide toward his wife, evaluating their position, balancing the seesaw of good and evil. He finally rested his eyes on her, in disbelief.

"You must change your clothing."

"I will not."

Again, the same conflict.

A stench rose from the sickbed. Fright rose in her father's eyes. Mary realized he was terrified of the task before him, felt helpless and untrained. She could not deny the same sense of inexperience, but someone had to step up and do it.

Embarrassed, ashamed for his wife, he slunk out of the room, until Mary called him back. She told him he had no choice, she needed assistance.

It was then she knew she would have to take charge. No one else was capable. She made a list, walked to the neighborhood telephone, called in home nursing care to give her mother physical therapy once a week, sent a driver to summon the married siblings, and sent her father for supplies.

The first day was one of the most traumatic of her life. Dressed in a pale blue dress and black bib apron, her hair rolled well past the accepted criteria, she barked orders. She told her siblings they would rotate shifts, each taking twelve hours at a time. She would do the bulk of the work around the house and farm, but she could not also care for their mother around the clock.

Every day, every night, someone had to be here. Dat would take a turn, too.

No cloth diapers, she announced. It would be Depends. Prescription costs would be shared by each family. A new recliner would be brought in.

She worked for a month, hoed weeds and mowed grass, loosened the rope of the despicable goat and led him to the cow pasture. Her father said no, but she ignored him. She washed porches, gave the cats to the animal shelter, sprayed for flies, dug potatoes, edged flower beds, trimmed shrubs, painted the kitchen, took down greasy, torn window blinds and replaced them.

Her sisters-in-law feared her, gave her wide berth, but also gave her due respect during the frenzy of hard work. Her mother was clean, rested, allowed the nurses to do therapy without complaint, and ate only the light, healthy food set before her.

By late October, her mother was getting around in a chair, able to speak in slurred sentences, had lost forty-five pounds, and was seemingly grateful for all the effort the children put into her wellbeing.

Mary and her father, however, ran a silent war of wills. He begged and pleaded on the grounds of her salvation, she lifted her chin and refused to change, telling him her clothes were perfectly acceptable, and would he please, for once in his life, let it go.

He rumbled on about lust of the eyes and the pleasures of this world, and she turned a deaf ear. The siblings stayed out of it, except Abner, who was always his father's staunchest ally.

She swung her hips and tossed her head, told him to raise his own brood and stop sticking his nose into other people's business.

This brought a dark anger to his face, but she didn't care. She was well past the accepted age of being an adult, and this time, she wasn't giving in.

As her mother got stronger, Mary longed to return to Lancaster, and finally brought up the subject with her father, who cleared his throat and looked at her with sad eyes.

"I don't know how we can manage without you," he said.

"You could if you'd get off the farm," she retorted.

"Mary, I'm not ready."

"You need to face reality, Dat. I don't want to stay here. You and Mam cannot manage on your own. She won't be able to, ever again. Why can't you give up?"

"That's not my place. I am the head of the house. What I say needs to be respected. I'm not moving off the farm till it's paid for."

"How many more years?"

"Two. Well, one and eleven months."

"And you expect me to stay until then?"

"I do."

Her mother nodded from the recliner, her eyes shining. Her gray-ing hair was neat and soft with cleanliness, her body so much thinner, freshly bathed and dressed in a clean, cotton dress. She lifted her left arm up and down, over and over, working tirelessly on her therapy. And she had come a long way.

Sometimes the work had been overwhelming, the sleepless nights putting her into a state of despair, arguments with her father cropping up like unwelcome spring dandelions. The intimacy of washing her mother's helpless body was uncomfortable, and at first her mother had resisted, too. But what other option did they have? The giving up of her own will to allow Mary to see her nakedness had slowly taken off the rough edges, the severity of her judgment.

Sometimes she would clasp Mary's hand and allow her eyes to tell her how grateful she was, and Mary would nod, say, *Ya, Mam, ich case.* I know, Mam. I know.

Two years sounded like an eternity, two years of work without pay.

Her savings account had already dwindled from paying the sup-plies for her mother, until she called another family meeting and made everyone contribute their fair share. When Lizzie came for a visit, she approved of everything, and when she was told about the two years, her kind eyes bored into Mary's, extracting the truth about her feelings.

Silently, they exchanged words.

I have to. And Lizzie answered with her eyes, *I know you do.*

CHAPTER 12

How would she fully explain the long New York winter that year? Chills chased continuously up her spine as she stuffed wood into the inefficient range in the kitchen, shivering her way to the barn in the frosty starlight to milk cows with her father, always aware of his disapproval of her dress.

And she determined to be who she was. She had learned how to dress in a decent, becoming manner in Lancaster County, and her beliefs were firmly entrenched. Clothes weren't that important, no matter what anyone else thought.

The long winter evenings with the gaslight humming away were the hardest times. The work of caring for her mother and the house kept her busy, but her mind was starved for intellectual conversation, for ideas, for beauty. She didn't bother going to the Sunday evening singings since she had no interest in these young men, and also knew she'd be looked on as a dangerous influence.

It angered her father when she told him this, and she was bombarded with the whole artillery of warnings, dire prophecies coupled with frustrated threats. Sometimes, resentment toward both of her parents drove her to a corner of the room, curled up in a chair, pouting like a spoiled schoolgirl.

After a fresh snowfall, when the wind packed the drifts and the temperature dropped, she asked Dat what had ever happened with the big runner sled.

"In the woodshed," he said from behind his paper.

"Mam, will you be alright with Dat if I go out?"

"Sled riding?" she slurred, her words still garbled.

"Yes. I think the snow will be perfect."

Dat lowered the paper.

"Those runners will be rusty. Better use paraffin wax."

She was trudging through the deep snow when she had to hurry across the road to avoid being caught in an avalanche of hurled snow from the passing snowplow. She waved a mitted hand, before stepping out into the freshly plowed roadway.

She evaluated the length of this hill, the one they'd dared each other to sled down as children, and thought, yes, it was fine. She could do this. She'd wait till the plow scraped the opposite side.

She stood, shaking her mittened hands to restore feeling and stamped her feet to keep them from going completely numb. Her nose hurt from the cold, her hair tore loose from the restraint of the black scarf around it.

She sensed more than she heard the dull thwock, thwock of hooves on packed snow, and stepped back, looking both ways, to find a team of black work horses pulling a heavy bobsled, the wooden runners silently gliding across fresh snow. It was a rare portrait, the eager horses, gigantic, windblown manes and tails, heads held high with ears pricked forward.

They'd spied her.

She stepped back into the deep snow, hoped she wouldn't spook the horses. The driver waved, his black hat covering most of his face. She lifted a hand. Soon enough, she heard the roar of the snowplow returning, so she scrambled to the opposite side, allowing him to deposit the wall of snow on the bank. She waited till the blinking lights disappeared through the fir trees before trailing her sled behind her on up the hill. Breathing hard, she turned and stood in awe.

Absolutely breathtaking. The most beautiful winter scene she could imagine. The downhill road was scraped smoothly, white banks of snow on either side, fir trees with snow like vanilla frosting, and far below, the old homestead tucked among rolling hills, patches of forest, smoke curling up from the chimney in the homiest way.

If someone, anyone, could buy the farm and had money to renovate the buildings, it could be a perfectly lovely home. But as long as her father owned it, it would remain in disrepair.

She felt the beginning of possibility and hardly knew how to explain to herself the opening up, the flowering of a very dim and distant idea.

She told herself it was only the powerful emotion of experiencing the vista before her, but the feeling of it left a fluttering in her chest.

What it was, she reasoned, was being alone with crotchety old parents.

She considered the length of the hill, remembered the reckless descent of years past. Her heart thudded in her chest. Before caution could overtake her, she flung herself on the sled and shoved off.

She had forgotten the speed, the flying particles. She couldn't see a thing. Between squeezed eyelids, her whole world was a blur of whizzing snowbanks, everything white and glittering and downhill.

She sensed dark movement, heard a distant shout, pulled back hard on the right handle guiding the sled, hit the snowbank at a glance, veered across the road, and socked into the snow-filled ditch, finally slamming into a fence post. She lay on her back as pain pounded behind her eyes. Flexing muscles, turning her head, she tried sitting up, but fell back immediately.

A dark form above her.

"Are you alright?"

Suddenly furious, she shouted, "Of course not. I almost killed myself coming down that hill."

"Here. Give me your hand."

She did, and felt herself being pulled to a sitting position. She glared at a lowered face, the eyes concerned, a black beanie surrounding it.

"Why didn't you stop when you saw me coming down?"

"I couldn't handle the horses. You spooked them."

"I did not."

"Course you did. You were going about ninety miles an hour."

She looked at him, shook her head no.

"Can you get up? Make sure you're alright. You slammed into that fence post pretty good."

He extended a hand. She gripped it with both of hers and got to her feet. She swayed, would have fallen if he hadn't caught her by the waist.

"I don't think you're okay. Where do you live?"

She pointed toward the farm.

"Come on."

He took her sled, held her mittened hand, walked slowly through the deep snow, then out on the scraped road.

"Careful there."

"I'm dizzy."

With that, she moaned and slid to the ground as the world disappeared from her eyesight. Alarmed, he slammed the sled into the back of the bobsled, then went back to the still form crumpled on the roadway. He had never experienced anyone fainting, but figured she'd come around soon enough, which is exactly what she did. The moment she realized what had occurred, she became angry again, yelled at him to go away, that she was going to be sick.

After she'd been sick, she thoroughly wiped her mouth with snow, then rolled over and held still.

"You might have a concussion," he offered.

She closed her eyes and said nothing. He looked at her red hair, the bulk of her, the fashionable snow boots trimmed in brown fur, and thought he might have seen her before. She wasn't from around here, that was sure.

"You okay?"

"Stop asking the same question. Of course not."

"Well, you can't just lay there. You'll get too cold."

"I can do whatever I want."

"Then I'll drive off and leave you, if that would suit you better."

"Don't."

It was the feeble "don't" that made him stay. Eventually, she felt well enough to be seated in the bobsled, but since there was no place to turn around, they had to go back up the hill, then find a place to turn before heading back down the hill. Mary was weak, cold, and humiliated beyond words, so she said nothing.

"This driveway?"

She nodded.

He looked at the farm, at her, and back to the farm. A mystery. When he stopped at the porch, he offered to help her to the house, but she shook her head.

"Let me at least introduce myself. Sam Riehl. I'm originally from Lancaster but am helping my uncle get started building sheds."

She softened then, giving him a more careful look. "Mary Glick. This is my home, but I lived in Lancaster. Is there a possibility of you having been to Dan Dienners' to church? Newport Road?"

The last word trailed off in a whisper, and he realized she was feeling sick again.

"I was, in fact."

"I thought so."

"Look, let's get you to the house. You don't look good."

"I will be capable of sagging my way to my own front door, thank you very much."

He laughed aloud, liking her choice of words. She gave him a small smile and walked slowly to the front door, turned, and waved. He drove off with the runner sled on the back of the bobsled without thinking of it once.

SHE RECOGNIZED SAM Riehl in church, but a relationship with him or anyone else was the farthest thing from her mind. She'd made a fool of herself in front of him, fainted dead away, deposited her dinner, lay on the road like a dead elephant, then had him deliver her to the decrepit old farm. He probably still pitied her.

Every evening after chores, she played Scrabble with her mother, making sure she picked up the small wooden tiles with her left hand, for therapy. She cooked and cleaned, did laundry, and milked cows with her father. Week after week, her mother showed a small improvement.

She received cards and letters from her friends in Lancaster, but as the winter wore on, they became less and less. *I may as well be dead*, she thought to herself. *That's how quickly a person is forgotten.* She felt strung between two bases, like a hammock, with no security on either end. In spite of remaining "fancy," she felt a certain sense of home here in New York, but could not imagine a future in these hills or with these people. Especially her siblings.

She had no ill effects from slamming into the fencepost, which was surprising, the way she may have experienced a serious injury. Sometimes she wondered if Sam Riehl would ever bring back the sled.

IT ALL STARTED with doughnut making on a cold, dreary day in January. One of those upstate New York days when another snowstorm was imminent, arthritis flared up, babies were cranky, and the sky had the distinct illusion of falling on your head, Chicken Little style.

Mary found herself at wit's end, facing another boring winter day. Her father really got on her nerves, walking around with a cough, a cloth diaper slathered with some rancid garlic or onion salve for a sore throat, and rheumy eyes sprouting tears all day.

Her mother suggested doughnuts. Her father, who was in a mood, said doughnuts wouldn't rise for Mary, as grouchy as she was.

She mixed them to spite him, and they turned out beautifully.

Plump and pale, laid out carefully in hot lard, sizzling their way to a golden perfection, then glazed with a thick homemade concoction of milk and confectionary sugar.

As the snow began to spray against the window above the sink, there was a knock on the door, and Mary opened it to one of the seed salesmen who was a friend of her father's.

"Yes, come in. My dad is here."

His name was Walter Brown, around her father's age, and he sniffed the rich aroma of frying doughnuts and almost cried with happiness.

He went home with half a dozen for him and his wife, who shared them with her sister-in-law, and word got around about Amos Glick's daughter making doughnuts.

By the end of February, she was in business.

She made glazed doughnuts, cream-filled doughnuts, and cream sticks, an oblong doughnut with a cut on top, filled with vanilla icing and frosted caramel on top.

The old kitchen was too small, too cramped, the kettlehouse damp and insufficiently heated, but there was nothing to do about any of that. When she was sold out, there was nothing to do but turn customers away.

Mary charged two dollars apiece, twenty dollars a dozen. The doughnuts were huge, delicious, and no one complained. She began dreaming of her own bakery, but said nothing to her father, who would certainly disapprove. She hinted to her mother, who frowned and waved a hand in dismissal.

She sighed, wished she could be released from these suffocating bills, but she kept making doughnuts, buying supplies, and counting her money.

The time spent on her mother's care dwindled as she regained the use of her left side, and increasingly, she could wash dishes or help put icing on the cream sticks. Her siblings no longer needed to spend their days with her and her mother, so that was a huge bonus, especially to have Abner and Lydia gone. Sometimes she felt bad for the lack of love for a few of her brothers, but that was understandable, the way they were so much like her father.

By the time spring breezes began to melt the piles of blackened snow, she had replenished her savings account but realized she could not keep the yard and garden, do spring house cleaning, milk cows, and keep on making doughnuts. Customers whined and begged, but Mary refused, knowing her limits.

With the arrival of soft spring rain, grasses grew and flourished. Crocus and violets poked through the wet soil. The air took on a lovely scent of melting snow, new plant life, and blossoming trees. Mary woke at four-thirty every morning, milked cows, made breakfast, did dishes, then returned to the milkhouse to wash milkers before taking on the day's work. Her mother was almost to her usual self, although she would never be strong enough to work more than a few hours at a time. Her parents no longer harassed her about her way of dress, which caused a rift in the family, some passing harsh judgment while others shrugged, saying no one dressed the way they had twenty years ago. Her father made rumbling sounds in his throat, which meant he was hatching a volley of words which never came forth.

She planted seeds in the garden, mowed grass, and tore down the old yard fence singlehandedly. She rode the seat of the harrow with four mules hitched side by side, felt the sun on her back and the breeze in her hair. Her face turned a rich shade of honey, the freckles splattered like small copper pennies. She viewed the blue mountains turning green with buds, sniffed at the rich scent of rocky soil, and wondered if she had never realized these things before.

Perhaps New York was not as dull and colorless as she'd always thought. Although this thought was infused with question marks.

Who was Mary Glick?

Not like other girls, who would be married with a few children by this time. Was she a fancy Lancaster girl, running the bakery and taking vacations at the beach? Or a farmer, working her hands at the plow and learning to love the land?

She chuckled, bouncing around on her harrow, the ears on the mules flapping like solemn amens to the ring of hooves on small rocks.

She couldn't admit to liking it here, not yet. But could it be that true happiness was found in the least likely places?

And what happened to the anxious stomach? Was there rest from anxiety when you forgot about trying to obtain what you knew deep down was not yours to have?

She took a deep breath, straightened her back. Perhaps she was a true hillbilly, who loved the stony soil and the rolling hills, but needed a bit more from life than her conservative father thought was acceptable?

Oh, who knew? At this point in time, who cared?

THEY FOUND HER mother lying on the floor, her large form helpless, her mouth opening and closing like a poor fish out of water, her eyes large with fear. Her father tried everything, rolling her over and putting wet cloths on her forehead, but sent Mary to the neighborhood telephone to summon an ambulance. Out of breath, she could barely respond to the voice of the dispatcher, but she managed to get the situation across before running and walking alternatively, back to the scene of her mother's pitiful attack.

She stood by, wringing her hands as the trained professionals bent over her and asked questions in caring tones, her father answering to the best of his ability. Was she still taking her meds after her stroke? He looked to Mary for assistance, who was ashamed to admit she really didn't know, but thought she would be, of course. At first she had kept track carefully, but as her mother became stronger, she'd paid less attention. She couldn't remember the last time they'd refilled the prescription.

As the ambulance moved swiftly down the rutted gravel driveway, both parents inside, Mary had never felt so alone. It was milking time, and she should go to the telephone again, call a driver to be with her father, but she decided to take care of the cows first. She could never do all the chores properly, but there was no one else to see to it, so she removed her covering, tied a *dichly* around her head, and set off to the barn.

As she let the cows in, each one going to her own stanchion, she prayed for her mother. As she assembled the milkers, started the diesel, she wondered who her mother really was.

Would she die? Would today be the final moment she had ever spoken to her? Her thoughts went back over the years, wound down the many lanes of growing up with her mother. So many children, scrabbling along through the years doing the best she knew with what she had.

Had she always given herself fully to the role of wife and mother, lived in submission to the will of her husband always? Or had she once been a young girl with dreams and plans, bright-eyed and rosy-cheeked, smiling tremulous smiles?

MARY'S PARENTS WERE both raised in Lancaster County, had been married there. She supposed he'd been conservative back then, dissatisfied with the fast-paced life, the encroaching arms of the world increasingly reaching into the church, bringing new and "better" ways. When he realized he simply could not live in unity with those who were more liberal, he packed up his two children and his reluctant wife and set off for a place more suited to his beliefs.

Pinedale Valley suited him to a T, the reasonable land prices, the seclusion of each farm scattered throughout the splendid countryside.

Two Amish families had gone ahead of him by a few months, both of them concerned about the headlong dash of the Amish in Lancaster, and where would it all end if no one held the reins back?

Her mother had never been enthused about Pinedale Valley, but went willingly enough, set up housekeeping in the rundown farmhouse, painted the cracked plaster, hung up green roll down shades, and made a go of it. She birthed nine more children, ran her house on a shoestring, stretched the groceries, and made do with a minimum amount of clothing for herself and the children, patched and sewed and handed down.

By the time her youngest daughter came screeching into the world with that mop of red hair and as plump as a ripe peach, she'd lost most of her youthful beauty and all of her good-humored outlook.

Seeing through the eyes of her husband had soured her eternal optimism, unknowingly creating the same brittle conservatism in her mind and her heart. Only occasionally would she catch glimpses of herself and remember a time when she delighted in a brilliant purple dress, a new pair of black Sunday shoes with only a very small wedge heel, just a fraction above her sisters'. She'd laughed back then, laughed and sang, whistled while she worked, and noticed tall, dark Amos Glick.

Over the years she'd learned to keep so much inside, to cut the wires of gaiety and frivolous thoughts. Life was serious, raising children a gloomy responsibility. He must admonish them when they rose from their beds, while they worked, and before they went to bed. Grace did not reach the *ungehorsam*, the disobedient.

And so she meted out punishments for small misdeeds, the wooden paddle brought from the pantry for slight disruptions of the smooth cogs of the household, her husband's hand on the lever running the entire operation.

She displeased him often, until his rumbling words of admonishment brought her into quiet subjection, and she became his helpmeet in raising a brood of likeminded young men and women who labored over the old Dutch Bible and gleaned the same dire predictions of fire and brimstone for the slightest misdemeanor, saved only by sincere repentance, the spiritual picture of sackcloth and ashes.

Her mother had relinquished her hold on all worldly pleasures and instead took pleasure in pleasing her husband and in the work of her hands. At quiltings and the get-togethers of her life, she held her tongue, watched the goings on through narrowed eyes, judging others through the eyes of her husband. Life was serious, *ordnung* and behavior important, so she kept an eagle eye intent on separating the good from the signs of impending evil.

Then, when her body was tired, her spirit waning, Mary was born, yelling her indignancies to the plaster walls, refusing to nurse properly, raised on goat milk and blackstrap molasses to keep her bowels moving. By the time Mary was six months old, she was crawling, inch by inch on fat little knees, still screeching out her displeasure when the slightest thing upset her. She was spanked soundly and often, the lack of response worrisome.

AND NOW MARY stood, an elbow propped on the jutting hip of a cow, listening to the chugging of the diesel, the hissing of the milking machines, and pondered her mother's life. Had she always been sober, frugal, quiet? Had her shoulders always been stooped with care, rounded arms fleshy from eating inexpensive homemade bread and fried mush?

Did she know who her mother was?

Her first memory was of her face being held against her rounded chest as she washed her neck and ears before her Saturday night bath in the tub upstairs. She said after a week, there were too many cracks and crevices filled with dirt, and so proceeded to take care of the problem efficiently. She could hear her mother breathing, feel the movement of her chest as she swabbed at her neck and ears before sending her upstairs with Annie and Becky.

She remembered her mother pulling dreadfully on her thick red hair as she rolled it severely on each side of her head and being sent to school with the sense of having had her hair pulled out by the roots. She always had a cheese sandwich on homemade bread, a sugar cookie, an apple, and a jar of milk in her tin lunchbox, which was never quite enough to get her through the day without being so hungry by late afternoon, and she was denied a snack till suppertime.

Her mother always kept a flock of chickens, a mixture of brown, white, and black speckled ones, the one thing she was proud of. She guarded the henhouse with a fierce concentration, put the hens in at night, sealed any slight crevice a marten or a mink could squeeze through. She washed and boxed the large brown eggs and sold whatever she could, feeding the children oatmeal instead of eggs, so she could make a few dollars for other groceries.

The sound of her laughter was rare. Did she even remember a time of audible, unabashed mirth? A smile, a twinkle in her eye, but very seldom, a genuine laugh.

But Mary wondered if sometimes, in the deepest chamber of her heart, there was a woman who laughed aloud, who loved pretty colors, who gathered flowers into bouquets, who heard a harmonica being played and nodded her head, tapped her feet, and felt an elevating sensation. One that was not wrong, but lifted her spirits to the skies, made her feel as if the world was full of a beauty so rare and bright, it created an ache in her heart.

CHAPTER 13

THE FUNERAL PROCESSION WAS A LONG, SNAKING STRING OF GRAY and black carriages drawn by a variety of horses. The first one in line was of extra length, carrying her mother's body in a wooden casket, followed by her father and her, then her siblings and their children, followed by her siblings from Lancaster County, and her father's family, aunts and uncles all dressed in black, faces sober and severe.

Barbara had lived her life according to the *Schrift*, had kept the *ordnung*, and for her, there was a good hope for her soul. The funeral was a large one, with extended family all present, the service conducted in the solemn manner, which was fitting.

Mary was seated last, behind the brothers and sisters, their spouses and children. She did not appear in the same uniform manner as the rest of them, her hair rolled higher, her covering smaller, her black suit fashioned after the latest style. She kept her eyes downcast and wept quietly at the soft sing-song voice of the minister who spoke of her life. She was hit by the ringing hammer of finality, the end of her mother's life. She was keenly aware of having disappointed her in so many ways, never quite achieving her expectations of coming into the *ordnung*, of giving herself to a young man like all her sisters.

But it was done. Her mother's life was over, and nothing could be changed. She bowed her head by the grave as nephews shoveled the dirt on the lowered casket, listened to the drone of the German *leid* being read, before praying silently with the huddled mass of mourners. As the men replaced their black hats, the crowd slowly dispersed, some drifting off to visit loved one's graves, others climbing into buggies as horses were loosened.

Aunt Lizzie caught up to her after the funeral meal was served and eaten.

"Mary."

"Yes?"

"Now, I told Amos you can't be expected to stay here. He has to find himself a *maud*. I still need you as much as I always did. Let him take care of himself."

Mary kept her head bowed, did not know how to answer. Was there lasting happiness in the fast-paced world in which she had not been born and raised?

She raised her eyes to the concerned gaze of her aunt.

"I don't know, Lizzie. I'm confused, I suppose. I need a bit of time to sort out my feelings."

"Of course. Losing your mother is a shock. But don't go telling me you like it here. I do not believe a word of it."

"I didn't say that."

"Well, then."

Lizzie gave her a hug and made her promise to write as soon as she came to her senses. She shook hands with her brother Amos and reminded him that he could not keep Mary here, in a place she could never be herself.

Amos cleared his throat and gave her a withering stare, then gathered his children around himself and took solace in their company. He tried not to display emotion, but a few tears came to his eyes. He said he could not see his way through life without Barbara.

All the children stayed by his side, a foundation of support. Finally, they said it all came down to Mary. Would she stay? Would she care for her father in his time of need? She could be a big help to him in his sorrow. The blessing would rest on her head if she took her duties seriously.

Oh, Mary knew how the conservative souls in Pinedale saw it. Of course the single daughter would be the sole support to a mourning parent.

Could she accomplish this huge task? Could she keep her own identity while being overshadowed by his strong presence, the everlasting rumblings of calamities hovering on the near horizon?

She told her siblings she would stay for the time being, which was met with quiet approval.

SPRINGTIME ON THE farm held its own form of charm. If the house was devoid of beauty, the barn and outbuildings in disrepair, there were budding trees, flowering lilac bushes spreading their scent among tulips and lilies long past their prime, apple blossoms coating freshly mowed grass like a lace shawl. New calves and baby chicks, nests of yellow and white kittens, a gangly foal in the pasture—all meant new life.

As her mother's body lay beneath the fresh soil, Mary pondered life and death, wondered at God's timing. She wept often, the shadow of her mother in every section of the house, by the stove, on the chair by the window, out in the henhouse, and in the garden.

How could she have known how much she would miss her mother? Could anyone prepare themselves for the loss of a parent?

Her sisters arrived, left the children with willing husbands, the work at hand a sacred task, not one that needed distraction. They placed high value in going through their mother's possessions, placing all things dear in neat piles to be distributed evenly.

Annie, Becky, Mattie, Miriam, and Susie. All patterned after the same mold. Of medium height, neither overweight nor too thin, dressed in large coverings and plain dresses, gray aprons pinned around their waists, bare feet and quiet words. Mary did not feel close to any of them, with her substantial frame and glowing red hair, her knowledge of Lancaster County and the world beyond, the world of vacations and Saturday night movies, flip-flops and bib aprons, and music and cellphones.

There was an invisible divide, a wariness in the way they circled around each other, never revealing their innermost feelings. So many things were simply not spoken of, so much of past lives hidden. But as the day wore on, when they brought casseroles and desserts from the kettlehouse, she felt an ease, a certain kinship.

They read excerpts of their mother's diaries, chuckled quietly about her description of various happenings. They cried together, ate a delicious dinner with their father.

They helped Mary clean out the attic, keeping some of the stored items for themselves. They asked Mary about a "chappy," or if she would always remain single.

Mary smiled, sat down on the attic floor, and shook her head.

"I had a boyfriend, but Mam and Dat forbid the relationship."

"What happened to him?" Mattie asked.

"He's married."

"Wasn't meant to be," Susie said, closing a box and shoving it under the eaves.

Mary said nothing. Wasn't it?

How could one tell? Could a parent's judgment sever a relationship efficiently and call it the will of God? Rebellion sprang up.

"Well, I still feel bitter sometimes. He was a good man. Mam and Dat would have liked him if they'd given him a chance. I still feel bitter about it sometimes."

"Oh, don't do that. Life is too short. And now our dear Mam is in her grave, and you can continue through life knowing she only wanted what was best for you. There is always blessing in honoring your parent's wishes."

Mary said nothing, but searched her sisters' faces for honesty. One by one, their gazes fell, one by one they busied themselves without further words. They left that day having acquired a certain bond with Mary, but all acknowledged the unseen rift between them.

THE HEAT OF summer brought an abundance of vegetables from the garden, leaving Mary with her days crammed full, no time for romantic wonderings about what might have been. She canned string beans and tomatoes, made spaghetti sauce and pickles. She cut corn from the cob, and her father took it to town to the Cold Storage Company.

Mary snorted inwardly, thinking of solar powered freezers in basements, and why in the world would you go through all that unhandy bother of hitching up your horse and driving that corn to town? Why couldn't Pinedale move along a bit?

One evening, when she was feeling especially tired and disillusioned with the workload, she found it increasingly hard to find a blessing in the way of obedience she had chosen. Restless with the old ways her father kept in high esteem, she questioned him about some of his practices.

"Why do we have to wash clothes with that smelly gas engine?"

He looked at her, asked why not, in that superior way of his, setting her teeth on edge.

"You could bring air power into the house," she ground out.

"It costs money."

That irked her to the core.

"If you can't afford some improvements, why don't you just get off this farm and let me go back to Lancaster to help Lizzie at the bakery?"

"If I let go of the farm, I won't live long. I would have nothing to live for, since Barbara is gone."

"Well then, at least fix the exhaust on that horrible gas engine. I'll die of carbon monoxide poisoning," she said sharply.

Her father was not accustomed to anyone standing up to him in such a way, so he gave her the benefit of his disapproval, nailing her with a withering glance, which did nothing to remedy the situation.

But that was only at the worst of times. She cooked and cleaned and kept the house well, earned high praise from the community, and decided to stay as long as her father needed her.

Then, taking a letter to the mailbox, she found a single white envelope propped against the inside wall. Her father's handwriting sprang out. Incredulous, she picked it up.

"Jemima Peachey," it read.

For a long moment, she held the envelope, unseeing. Bitterness coursed through her veins, filling up every atom of her being. Her mother was barely settled in her grave and he was writing to someone?

She felt betrayed, stomped on. He had quickly and efficiently rid her of Ben Stoltzfus, so now it was her turn. She marched up the drive with her head held high, her eyes blazing righteous fury, and wasted no time in approaching him.

He told her calmly that yes, he had sought God's leading, and felt this was His will, and since he was the head of the house and she his subordinate, she had no say in the matter. She also needed to know the ways of God were not to be questioned and she would do well to read the passage in the *Schrift* where it pointed out how women were the weaker vessel, not someone who would make wise choices.

"But what about our mother? How can you do this to us?" she cried out.

"I told you, God's ways are not to be questioned."

"Oh, so now you're God?"

Her anger threw all caution to the wind. She felt as if her dedication, all the hard work and the sacrifice she'd made, were for nothing. No reward, no appreciation. She threw in his refusal to accept Ben Stoltzfus and the fact she had every right to her own refusal of Jemima Peachey. When he heard the name on her daughter's tongue, spoken with such a tone of derision, he rose up and threatened to put her out.

After that, they circled each other warily without speaking.

WEEKS WENT BY, a month. Then there was a letter, written in black letters, too well-crafted to be a man's handwriting. And when her father had a spring in his step the following day, she swallowed her anger and carried on. She told her sisters, who gasped in disbelief, hands pressed to their moths, eyes round in consternation. Opinions varied, but all agreed, it was too soon. Who would have thought it possible? Their own father.

But one by one, acceptance settled in. Even well wishes. He was, after all, their father, and this required respect.

But Mary struggled. She wanted to hurt him, wanted revenge, which she knew was wrong, but her sense of being wronged overrode her obedience. She told him if he wanted to bring a girlfriend to the house, he'd do well to fix it up a bit.

He winced at the term "girlfriend," told her to stop using that worldly term, and she smirked, said what else would you call her?

And then, one day, she showed up on the porch, when the mountains were shrouded in wisps of fog from a cold rain the night before, the maple leaves were transformed into a fluorescent orange, pumpkins grew fat on depleted vines, and squirrels heeded the instinct to frantically store acorns and hickory nuts.

She was tall and wide in her hips. Her face was plain, her gray hair frizzy, a thatch of it visible beneath her large white covering. Beneath her chin a large bow was tied, her black cap and apron spotless.

"Hello."

A deep melodious voice, like velvet.

When Mary didn't answer immediately, she said, "He said he'd be here."

"Hello. I'm Mary. I suppose you're Jemima."

"I am. Call me Mima."

I'm not calling you anything, Mary thought.

She stepped aside. "You may as well come in."

She was fixed with a level stare, an accompanying sniff.

Mary sniffed back.

"You sure he knows you're coming?"

"He knows."

Her father appeared, freshly washed and shaven, his eyes twinkling, a wide smile on his angular face. Gone were the vertical lines, the severity of his outlook, the hangdog look of having been wronged.

"So, Mima. You're here."

He reached for her hand and shook. She blushed a deep shade of red, the thatch of frizzy gray hair like leaves on an apple.

"Yes, Amos. I am."

Her words rang through the house, bounced from cracked plaster ceiling to peeled paint on the walls, lurked in cupboard doors, and trailed down hallways. Mary had a clear sense of her father openly defying convention, of being *ungehorsam*, of being caught in adultery. Her mother's round, tired form, moving slowly from tasks too overwhelming to be performed properly, but doing the best she could, always searching for his approval.

How much had he even loved her?

A sense of unfaithfulness invaded her. This could not be the Lord's will, six months after her mother was buried.

Her father, so quick to judge others, so terribly conventional in all his views.

Quietly, she let herself out of the house, away from the sight of both of them standing there in her mother's living room, an invasion of all that was good and right.

How was she expected to cope? She needed to come up with a way of escape. Surely he would not expect her to stay on till they were married? Or even afterward? She walked blindly, her sneakers crunching on gravel, the splendor of leaves beyond the aura of black anger.

The truth was, she simply wanted no one else taking her mother's place. She did not want this odd Jemima Peachey to inhabit her father's bed. The thought was sickening. Disgusting. In his eyes, everything was wrong. Couldn't he see that this was wrong, too? She ground her teeth in frustration.

Why could she not be married herself, safely harbored in her own home, far away from the sight of her own aging father meeting his new girlfriend? All the disappointments in her life bunched together, becoming like a cold stone in her chest, suffocating her. She turned off the main road, followed an old logging trail beneath an arbor of wild grapes, tried to rein in her churning thoughts, cleanse her mind in purity, so she could pray.

But it was simply not possible. The hurt was too raw. She brought up one knee, clasped it with both hands, sat back on the log, and looked up through the thinning branches of the pine tree above.

At first, she thought it was a black bear, then realized it was too small. An eagle? A giant hawk?

Or nothing, she supposed.

A pine cone fell, an object scraped against bark. Loosened sections of it skittered down, landed a short distance away. She looked up, found someone, a human being, perched on a branch, stirring.

Should she be frightened? She decided to wait, see who would appear, before getting to her feet, watching the figure's descent through the thin branches.

"You messed up my hunting good and proper."

The voice from above was as unfriendly as acid, accusing her of something completely unfair.

"I didn't know you were up there. Besides, how do you know you're allowed to hunt here on our property?"

He dropped to the ground, faced her. Hatless, a headful of thick brown hair, she did not recognize him. Not at first. Slowly, recognition dawned.

"You're Mary."

"And you are Sam."

He gave a slight bow. "Sam I am."

"Oh, come on. Really?"

He laughed, his eyes filled with it, squeezed shut, producing laugh lines.

"We have met, I believe."

"We have."

And they laughed again, together this time, the pleasure startling and immediate.

"You're still here, in New York?"

"Yes. Although, not sure what will be from here on out."

He lifted his compound bow, fiddled with the arrows, then set it against the base of the tree, before turning to her.

"Well, since you frightened all the deer away, we may as well sit down and talk a while. I have a driver coming to pick me up at sundown."

"I'll go. Then you can resume your hunting."

"No, stay. What were you doing? Out for a walk?"

She shook her head, avoided his eyes.

"You won't believe it if I told you."

"Go ahead."

She started with her mother's stroke.

He drew back. "That was your mother? Seriously. I heard about it in the neighborhood district, but never put two and two together. Back in April, or was it May?"

"Last week in April."

"I'm sorry. You must still be grieving."

"I am. But that's not the worst of the story."

He waited without saying anything.

The whole story tumbled out, and it was a relief to share it with someone. She realized the weight of it, pressing down on her shoulders, wearing her out.

"It wouldn't be half as bad if he wasn't so strict with everyone else."

He nodded. "I can see that."

"And there's just something about your own father courting someone. Romancing. Ew. And my poor dead mother. She was so completely overtaken by him. Monopolized. She had no will of her own. Simply thought and did and said what he wanted her to. It's just . . ."

"Yes. I can see how hard this is."

She paused. "I shouldn't be saying these things to you. You're a stranger. I don't know why I keep blathering on."

"It's not blather. It's perfectly understandable. For you, this is very real. Hard to comprehend. Everyone needs someone."

She nodded, then sighed.

"Ah well. It is what it is. I'll probably move to Lancaster to help my Aunt Lizzie again.

He raised his eyebrow. "You won't stay?"

"Probably not. Lancaster is okay, it's fine, actually. Just a bit fast-paced if you were born and raised here. I'm sort of caught between two extremes, if you know what I mean."

"Yeah."

For a long moment, silence was sandwiched between them. She searched for something to say, then realized it was not necessary, the way silence was comfortably absorbed. The spicy scent of pine bark and needles was heavy, the dry odor of autumn grass mingling with other forest smells. The wind sighed through the branches, sifted the needles.

"Everyone in the English world lumps us all together, and it's much more complicated in real life. Our *ordnung* is varied. Kept so differently, in so many places."

"How do you feel about Pinedale?" he asked.

"It's home. But I spent a few years in Lancaster, widened my horizons, and now I find it stifling."

"You don't dress like the rest of the women here."

"Not that anyone approves."

"I'm not very stylish," he offered.

She laughed. She almost told him what she thought, then remembered how dangerously close she came to Old Maid status, at her age.

"How come you never married?" he asked. "I'm guessing you're at least twenty-five, maybe older."

"I would be, if my parents would have allowed it." She gave a short laugh.

He looked at her, saw the darkness portraying her sarcasm.

"I didn't know that was still done."

"Here it is."

He gave a low whistle. "Wow."

She told him of the return to Lancaster, her mother's stroke, and how glad she was she had been there to help out when she wasn't well. And how she had found the letter in the mailbox, followed by Jemima's appearance much too soon.

"The thing is, lots of men don't do well on their own. He's lonely. He needs a companion to share his days," he suggested.

When she gave a sound of disgust, he told her he was only trying to be fair, to help her see her father's viewpoint.

"I'm not ready for that. He could have been nicer to Mam. She was merely a pawn on his chessboard of life. She dressed, cooked, ate, thought, and did what he required of her. Six months down the road, and he's off prancing around with Jemima Peachey."

He tried to keep a straight face but failed, bursting into a roar of laughter that sent a pair of doves into startled flight. She looked at him in astonishment, shook her head and said, "I mean it."

"Uh my," he finished, wiping his eyes. "No doubt, you will be no one's pawn on their chessboard."

"Don't plan to be."

"It might be interesting to see what happens when you get married. Maybe I'll be around to see it."

CHAPTER 14

WHEN SHE RETURNED, HER FATHER SAT ALONE AT THE KITCHEN table, without a trace of Jemima. She tried to sneak past him, but he called out. She froze, willing him away.

"Mary, where were you? You weren't here to help with the milking."

"I was on a walk."

She moved past the kitchen quickly.

"Mary, come. We need to talk."

"No. I have nothing to say to you."

"That makes me very sad."

"Good. You should be sad."

"Ach, Mary."

Using his best form of pitiful martyrdom, the tone of voice that would have sent her mother into sincere servant mode.

"Mary," he begged, but she was on her way upstairs and had no intention of changing her course. *Don't Mary me*, she thought. *Sit there at the kitchen table and think about what you're doing.*

The conversation, the unexpected meeting with Sam Riehl, was the only small bright spot in her life. She would not allow herself to think he would ever want her. It was odd the way he'd said he might be around to see her marriage.

She thought then of Jemima Puddle Duck. If she knew what was good for her, she'd hightail it right out of here.

In the shower, she scratched her head beneath the shampoo so hard her head felt raw, but at least she'd vented some of her anger.

She did not want to stay. Knew eventually she couldn't do it.

Her father packed an old overnight bag and disappeared with a driver on a cool fall Saturday, without a word to her. She knew where he was going, though. She built a good hot fire in the kitchen range, made a batch of pumpkin cupcakes with caramel icing and a whole popperful of buttery popcorn, poured a glass of ice cold cider, and nested on her mother's recliner with one of her favorite books.

She ate three cupcakes and over half the popcorn, burped, looked at the clock, and knew it was only an hour till milking time.

The neighbor boy, Danny Fisher, was coming to help with chores, according to a note her father had left. Danny was a spindly little thing, only thirteen years old, but if he could feed calves and the horses, it was a big help. She had no problem with milking the cows, the small herd of nineteen or twenty.

She sighed as she stood at the mirror putting on her dichly. Would she always be here, even with a stepmother named Jemima? She thought her reflection promised no turn of events. Who would want the red hair and freckles, the hefty bulk beneath? She needed to watch her weight, stop baking cupcakes and eating them.

Danny came pounding in the drive on a long-legged pony, half wild and almost sliding to a stop at the barn door, her head in danger of being scraped off.

"Hi, Mary! Whoa there. Hold it," he yelled, all in one sentence.

"Hey, Danny. You better be careful up there."

"He's alright. Just full of pep."

"Glad you're helping me."

He helped her finish milking, told her his dreams of training wild horses, then asked if she'd heard about the pack of wild dogs running loose between here and Parkersburg. Feral dogs. Worse than wolves after they had a taste of blood. Killed Abie Zook's sheep, a whole bunch of them.

When he threw himself on his pony and pounded haphazardly down the drive, Mary shook her head, held her breath, and thought how you were only thirteen years old once. Everything, just everything was fun back then. Did she ever have fun now? She was turning into a sour, world-weary singleton, with bundles of disappointments beneath her belt. The only bright spot was the pumpkin cupcakes she ate, which had to come to a halt, immediately.

Perhaps she could go to the Sunday evening hymn singings again, see if she could still have fun. Fun. What was it, even?

She gave a small laugh, then took a shower and watched the early darkness fold the old farm in its shroud. She lit the gas lamp, thought of the quick, easy access to light in Aunt Lizzie's house. But she kind of liked the humming, the soft buzz, of gaslight.

She read a while, then stoked the woodfire and made her way upstairs to bed. She heard the barking of a dog, thought of Danny's words, but felt no fear, with solid walls and sturdy doors, the cows in the pasture, capable of protecting their own.

Danny was there in the morning, riding his pony even more recklessly in the dark, a flashlight's small signal to ward off traffic. He went off to feed calves but appeared soon after, his face pale, his eyes bulging, clearly frightened out of his wits.

"Mary, come quick!"

In the pale stream of light from his flashlight, she saw that a calf had been horribly mutilated during the night, the small enclosure successfully scaled by what they both believed to be the feral dogs. It was very sobering, and Mary's thoughts went to the young foal, capable of running, but could she outrun an entire pack?

She kept the horses in the barn, barricaded doors, made a pen for the calves out of metal gates, then made sure every barn door was latched properly. To take her mind off the horror of what had happened to the poor calf, she made a big breakfast of pancakes and bacon, a pot of coffee, and tried to settle into a long, peaceful Sunday.

She fought off a network of thoughts about her father, wondering if he'd be bold enough to be introduced to her family.

Surely he wouldn't do that.

Who was this woman, and where on earth did she live? With whom? By lunchtime she was thoroughly bored, restless, pacing the floor, wishing someone would come for a visit or she'd have somewhere to go.

She decided to walk the two miles to her friend Anna's house, just to get her mind off herself and the circling thoughts about her father.

THE DAY WAS pleasant enough, the wind sharp through her cable knit sweater, but the sun held a leftover warmth from the sleepy days of September.

She breathed deeply, expanded her chest, her eyes roving the fields and ridges of Pinedale. Bare black branches were interwoven with fir trees, and whispy clouds drifted along the pure blue above. The air was rich with the scent of pine, wet bark, and decaying grass, the cornfields harvested, fodder laying thick and heavy above the soil.

Their corn harvest had been thin, the silage less than the neighbors. She'd cooked for the silage crew, listened to yields, and knew her own father's was below average. Much too frugal to spend on fertilizer, he reaped in smaller quantities. The men were kind, knew Amos Glick, and never commented on the difference.

As she swung along, her shoes crunching on gravel roads, she wondered why God seemed so far away, as if the hills of Pinedale were eliminating the easy access to Him through prayer. She no longer communed with Him, the way she had in the past, but hardly knew the remedy to correct it. She felt as if it was all her father's fault, the way he created the coiling sarcasm in her, the hurt about Jemima.

She was lost in thought, sifting through the unhealthy anger toward him, wondering if any rebellion was a good thing, ever, and whether it was okay with Him to blame someone else when bitterness and hatred sprang up. Her father simply expected too much of her. He did whatever he wanted with no thought of his grown children, leaving them to search, to scrabble desperately for the ability to give up their own will, to acknowledge his superiority.

And she thought perhaps she needed distraction, needed some-thing, anything to keep her from sliding into a state of resentment, a sticky mire of despondency she could never fully get rid of. Perhaps her entire problem was one of her own making—first and foremost, her inability to give up her own will.

Why couldn't she be happy for her father? Resentment toward him was blossoming into a poisonous growth, threatening to gnaw at her relationship with God, filling her healthy spiritual cells like a cancerous growth. She was an adult, capable of making her own choices, which were obviously directed by the simmering indignation she carried.

As she swung along, she felt the pull of muscles behind her knee, her feet beginning to feel the weight of the miles behind her.

She came to an incline, the gravel road dipping into a hollow, a small bridge spanning a wide creek, the water tumbling over stones, lined with grasses drooping at the end of summer. "Picturesque," was the word that came to her mind. That was the thing about New York. The unexpected beauty springing out at you, like a rare glimpse of something so much greater than yourself. She thought of Lancaster and how every square foot was used up in the development of houses, farms, businesses, or crops. The manicured lawns and tourist attractions left little room for natural beauty.

She thought about how she'd felt the need to climb the ladder at the bakery, first manager, then owner, her own shop. She wanted to build and build and build, ever upward. And for what?

For money. For the riches she knew she could heap together. She was weighing these matters as she strode down the gravel road toward the creek.

At first, she saw them, that pack of dogs, but it didn't register immediately.

Two of them were drinking from the creek, a few milling through ferns.

Adrenaline rode on fright, directing her footsteps in the opposite direction, but mind numbing panic kept her rooted to the spot. She felt the dull hammering in her chest, felt the same sensation in her chest.

A large yellow dog, a mixed breed with the wide flat head of a pit bull, spied her first, immediately opened its mouth, and bayed with a high pitch undulating howl of surprise. Another one, a pitch black dog with the thin, coiled body of a serpent, raised his head, pierced her with a look, and emitted one short, violent bark, followed by the sound of the others.

Her first thought was, *No. No, not now. Not yet. I'm not ready.* As the dogs gathered their feet beneath them, the black one hitting the water, she turned and ran. But it was uphill, and she knew she wasn't a fast runner.

A weapon. She needed something, anything to protect herself from the slavering jowls of these animals.

Blindly, she ran on, her steps falling hard on gravel, her legs churning.

Oh please, please.

She looked back, and what she saw covered her in cold chills. A sob tore at her throat. A bobbling, weaving, flapping, howling pack of feral dogs, mouths open, tongues lolling, flying in the wind.

That was when she felt herself giving up. Her spirit was handed over, a delicate wisp of her soul in God's Hands. The only thought was of how young she was, a life cut off too soon.

Have mercy on my soul, she cried silently.

She heard them behind her, coming closer. When she reached the top of the incline, her steps increased, the speed picked up. She was gasping, her lungs exploding, but she demanded more from her burning legs.

The howling and yipping was unbearable, like demons, horrible creatures from an unearthly void.

When she felt the hot breathing on her flying skirt, she let out a long scream of agony, before she stumbled to her knees as the dog's fangs tore into the calf of her leg. She kicked, beat her fist blindly on the yellow skull, twisted and grunted as she tried desperately to regain her freedom. A ripping, blinding pain tore through her leg, and she screamed again.

"No, no!" she cried out.

After that, they were all on her, pulling her down, razor-like incisions cut through her sweater. She felt the crunch of jaws, the shattering of bone in her forearm. She remembered throwing an arm over her face, instinctively trying to protect it.

They were so heavy. Hot, stinking breath. Yellow, fiery eyes. She tasted blood, cried, and moaned, then realized her end was here. This was how she would die.

She was choking, a vile, burning taste in her mouth. Her tongue felt twice the normal size, and as dry as a piece of cardboard. She struggled to breathe, but had no idea how this could be possible. She faded into oblivion.

The lights were too bright. They bored a hole in her skull, attacked her eyelids with a dull pounding. She closed her eyes.

She saw all of her siblings, plus their spouses. White coverings tied neatly, capes pinned on shoulders. Long dark beards.

They left, went through the walls and ceilings, the black Sunday shoes leaving ragged holes.

A beeping sound. Stars in the night sky, framed by a window. Her mother called to her. She had to go.

"Mam," she whispered brokenly.

But her mother was too far away.

She tried calling out, opened her mouth wide, but no sound was possible. She begged and pleaded for her mother.

A face above her. A black beard. Abner.

Her mother was back. A joy rushed through her, but the joy had a color. It was pink, then changed to gold, silver, and back to pink.

She tried to hold onto this color, but as she watched, it turned into a large set of wings, and slowly lifted away.

She cried for the return of beauty, the celestial shades unlike anything she'd ever seen.

Green walls. The odor of Spic-and-Span.

Mam! There she was. Her own mother. Dressed in the dark colors she always wore. Mam, I'm coming. Wait.

A long time passed, so long she couldn't count minutes, or hours, or days.

"Mam, you have to listen to me. Don't you know that?"
     Her mother shook her head, smiled, lifted a hand goodbye.
     "No, Mam, don't go." But she went.

"I believe she's awake," she heard a man's voice say.

Rolling mountains of pain, mountains that walked and ran, then stopped and began to fall on her, squeezing out the breath of life.
     A deep rumbling voice said, "It's touch and go."

A cotton swab in her mouth, a sweetish taste. She shook her head. A buzzer rang. The room was full of too many people. She didn't want to see any of them.

There she was again.
     "Mam?"
     "Mary, you must go back. You have work to do. Mine is finished."
     Her dark clothes turned white, her face youthful, glowing with the light of a thousand candles.

WHEN SHE BECAME fully awake, she was alone. It was nighttime. There was a white ceiling, beeps and clicks, and a large plastic hose in her mouth.
     She turned her head, saw a white rail, tubes, lines, narrow hoses.

She wanted someone, anyone to remove this plastic from her mouth. She turned her head.

There was a blue, vinyl chair with a shroud-covered person. Where was she?

The still form moved, sat up, then quickly lowered the footrest and came toward her. In the dim light, Mary did not recognize her, but felt grateful when the long, bony hand crept along the rail and pressed the buzzer, which brought a woman immediately, an English one.

"She's awake," the low, rough voice said.

Lights overhead, a wait, then the room was filled. Mary recognized them as nurses and doctors.

"Mary?"

Mary nodded, focused her eyes on the face. A man, gray beard cut short, dark rimmed-glasses.

"If you hear me, move a forefinger."

She tried to, but it was far too heavy.

"Mary?"

She nodded, very slight.

"How about your toes?"

She managed to wiggle a toe.

THE PLASTIC HOSE was removed, but not without pain, nausea, nurses over the rail on both sides, swabbing her mouth. Someone was putting ointment on her cracked and bleeding lips. It was Jemima. Mima. She was crying softly.

"Can you tell us your name?"

The doctor spoke softly.

Mary opened her mouth, but there was no voice. Her throat was rough, dry, and painful.

She nodded, formed "Mary" with her lips.

"Where are you?"

It took a few attempts, but she mouthed, "Hospital."

"Yes. Mary, you are in a large hospital in a city far from your home. You were flown here in a helicopter. What they call a Life Lion."

She drew her eyebrows down. Did he mean those pink, silver, and gold wings? She was confused. A helicopter?

Then the comprehension flowed. Yes, a helicopter. One of those choppers that made the funny sound in the sky, gave you the shivers knowing it was often an emergency, someone's life in the balance.

Had hers been?

"Do you remember anything?"

It was too hard, the effort too tiring, so she shook her head.

WHEN SHE AWOKE, there was sunshine through the window, flowers on her bedside table. Her nose was stuffy, her mouth dry. Her right shoulder burned like fire.

She took inventory of her own body, rolled her eyes to take in the heavy plaster cast on her right arm. Her hand was bandaged. Both hands. There was no cast on either leg. She wanted to lift the covers, but wasn't capable.

All that day, Herculean effort was required of her. To focus, to hear and comprehend, to answer questions and recognize members of the family, was like climbing a steep mountain. She struggled to remember, but could not fully bring back anything of the Sunday they said she started out on a long walk to visit Anna.

Mima stayed at her side, offering encouragement, bringing her water, taking notes when the nurses shared information. Mary was annoyed at first, but soon found herself grateful for the company. Mima never interfered, was extremely polite and kind to everyone, and helped Mary when her stitches itched, or she experienced muscle spasms. She would calmly apply Doterra oils and massage lightly between healing cuts, massage her sore neck and the back of her head, saying nothing.

When her sisters came, they cried, sniffed, blew their noses and turned away. They comforted each other. Her brothers blinked, their mouths wobbled with emotions. But it was Mima who stayed, who sat by her bedside and told her the story in a soft, low voice, like a man's.

The five dogs had tried to kill her. To drag her down like a deer, and would have accomplished this but for the appearance of two

Harley-Davidson motorcycles, both men stouthearted, the terrible sight bringing righteous anger and no thought for themselves.

They'd come to a sliding halt, left their bikes, and ran toward the snarling, savage pack. Yelling, waving their arms, they'd distracted them long enough to keep her alive. Both were secretly armed and produced small handguns that they quickly used in self-defense, as the bloodthirsty animals' sights were trained on them.

Heroes. Heroes with cellphones, covered in tattoos, wearing bandanas and leather jackets adorned with chains and the Harley logo. Their picture was in the paper, the story remarkable.

She'd been given nine pints of blood in the coming days, pint after pint of life dripping into her veins. Her right shoulder had been torn from the socket, the skin mauled, both legs mutilated, lacerations so deep and so many, the stitches too numerous to count.

A large part of her side had been ripped and torn, ribs exposed.

Mima said they were angels in disguise, and disguised well, according to Amos. She'd shaken her head, said it was high time this family had a good and proper shake-up with their moldy attitudes.

Another long-needed shake-up was the township, the county deputies. They'd known about the dogs, farmers all up and down the valley had tried to do something for months.

Mary watched Mima's face and thought long and weary thoughts. It was too much, this second goodbye to her mother, when she longed to be with her, to experience the joy that was a color, to be free of everything that troubled her.

There was a place somewhere so much better than here.

CHAPTER 15

SHE WANTED OUT.

She hurt all over and was sick of being confined to this narrow bed. She was short with the nurses, told everyone to go home. There was no use hovering over her. The day finally came when they got her out of bed and moved her to a room with less intensive care but more doctors trained to help her get strength back.

She walked with a walker, every step excruciating, but bit down hard on her lower lip and kept going. Sweat broke out on her forehead, she gripped the handles hard, and kept walking the halls. She became a celebrity, of sorts. The nurses called her "Mary Max" for maxing out her strength and determination, and Mary laughed. She said at least she'd lost weight.

And her rescuers came to see her.

She was seated in her bed, her hair freshly washed, a hospital gown covering bandages, reading a few lines from a book a nurse had brought her.

Two men, with two ladies beside them. Ordinary English men. They knocked, then moved shyly to her bedside, leaving the scent of women's fragrance, chewing gum, and cigarette smoke.

"Darling," the one woman said softly, and wept.

"Hey, miracle girl," said the other, and promptly made all kinds of strange facial expressions to keep from crying.

The men took her bandaged hand, touched her shoulder. Both were of average height, powerfully built, and they sported long hair tied with a ponytail, neatly trimmed beards, and kind eyes.

"Honey, you were all but gone," the one said huskily.

"I understand that," she said quietly, and thanked them for saving her life.

Introductions were made. Dennis and Stew, short for Stewart. Bonnie and Tanya. They lived in Parkersburg. The men were out for a Sunday ride while the women shopped.

"The worst sight of my life," Dennis began. "I don't want to give you nightmares, but it was unreal. We simply did what anyone else would have done. Guess it made the news. Our pictures were in the papers. They're doing a story in *People*."

Mary's eyes opened wide. She shook her head.

"It likely won't go down well with my people," she said.

"We didn't think so."

"See, Tanya, I told you Amish don't like this kind of thing."

They all talked at once, then, embarrassed.

"Excuse us, we shouldn't be doing this. Tell us how you're feeling."

"It's up and down. I'm just sick of this place, and want out. I want to go home and relax, heal," Mary said, smiling.

"You know how lucky you are, though?" Stew asked.

"Yes, I do."

"I know it's not luck. Me and Denny were guided that day. We actually stopped at the end of Chestnut Road, deciding if we wanted to go into Parkersburg, or if we wanted to run the scenic route. Both of us thought there was no hurry, why not take the road you were on? That's not luck. That's God talking to your spirit."

Mary nodded. "I don't know how to thank you. I will never be able to pay you back."

Her voice was shaking with emotion, and both men sniffed back tears. A bond was created that day, with Mary rejoicing at the fact they were believers. Their appearance may not suit the Amish ideal, and certainly not her father's ideals, but all that was beside the point at a time like this.

She was given a small wooden box inscribed with the Harley logo, and upon opening it, a gold medal on a chain was imprinted with her name and both of theirs, the date of her near death, and the inscription, "In God's Hands."

She was deeply touched.

They described the dogs in detail. Mary winced.

"I don't remember anything, but as time goes on, I sort of recall the moment I began walking. Dreams were mixed in with a blurred sense of reality for a long time."

"No doubt about it, girl, you were close to Heaven's gates, let me tell you," Dennis said, very seriously.

IT WAS A windy, rainy day when she was finally released. One of those late autumn days that herald colder temperatures and flurries of snow mixed with rain, the harbinger of a long New York winter. Her father and Annie came to take her home, their faces soft with love and caring. Her father offered to get her a hamburger, going through the drive through at McDonald's, which was unbelievable.

But she shook her head. Her left knee did not appreciate the lack of space in the car and throbbed painfully. She asked for Tylenol twice before Annie relented. Mary told her now was not the time for the deeply ingrained fear of medical pills, but Annie set her mouth in a straight line and said she'd need to go on a colon cleanse to rid her body of all the toxins.

LIZZIE HELD A longstanding grudge against her brother Amos, and so did not visit until a cold day in November, her girls in tow, as usual. Mary had made progress in a month's time, but was still going to therapy in town twice a week, mostly for her right arm. She was blessed by a thin little man named Tom Luck, who had been a therapist all his life, skilled in his profession.

Lizzie marched right up to the porch, wearing the required black with Barbara in her grave, knocked on the door, and let herself in.

"Yoo-hoo!"

Mary came to the door with halting steps, gladness written all over her face.

"Lizzie! Oh, Aunt Lizzie, it's so good to see you."

"Mary. Ach, Mary. We heard the horrid story. Is it all true?"

"Probably not all of it. Why haven't you come?"

"You know why."

One by one, the girls nodded soberly, their expressions grave.

"What that Amos thinks he's doing is beyond me. I guarantee you one thing, this horrible thing that happened to you was a wake-up call for him. A girlfriend! Really?"

She almost hissed at the idea.

"Come, Lizzie. Everybody come to the kitchen. We'll sit by the table and talk. Coffee is ready. We have plenty of food. Everyone has been wonderful, bringing meals every single day. Even now, when I'd probably be ready to make Dat's supper."

"Where's Amos?" she asked sharply, her roving eyes taking in the green window blinds, the old cabinets and outdated glossy paint on the cracked walls.

"He'll be in."

Lizzie ran a nervous hand over her stomach and reached up to tug her covering over her ears. She asked Mary to tell them her story, which Mary did, pouring coffee and bringing it to the table.

Lizzie listened as the words tumbled from Mary's mouth, stopped her often with questions, but was sympathetic and so kind. Lizzie's eyes kept going to the door, nervously waiting for her nemesis, her own brother, whom she judged with what she presumed was a righteous judgment.

When he did make an appearance, she sat up straight, tugged at her covering, and answered his hello with a cold version of her own.

"So, Amos, I guess you've really been through something with Mary here."

"Yes, Lizzie, we have. Indeed."

"Who is going to pay that hospital bill?"

"Oh, now Lizzie, we don't talk of these things. We're just so glad we still have Mary."

Lizzie's eyes rolled.

Mary caught the mockery and felt hurt.

Her father looked old and rumpled, his nose red from the cold, almost afraid of Lizzie. He poured himself a cup of coffee, carried it to the table, and sat self-consciously.

And Lizzie had him in her crosshairs immediately.

"So, when's the wedding?"

"Not yet."

"You may as well go ahead and tie the knot if you're going to. What's the difference, dating or getting married? One's as bad as the next if your wife is barely cold in the grave."

Amos lowered his face, tugged at his Adam's apple, opened his collar as color spread across his cheeks. Mary felt the beginning of pity.

"A man gets lonely, Lizzie."

"A woman does, too. Do you see me gallivanting all over the countryside with a new man?"

"No. I don't. And that is commendable."

Lizzie sniffed, sat up straight.

There was an uncomfortable silence, with Susie clearing her throat and Ruthann getting up to use the bathroom.

"Well, Amos. I guess if you choose this route, you'll consider letting Mary go. You won't need her when the new bride arrives."

"That decision is hers, not mine."

"Pooh. Expect me to believe that."

But Mary felt a rising panic. Her body was no longer the perfectly capable one it had been. She couldn't imagine putting in the long hard hours at the bakery.

"You influence her so heavily she doesn't even think for herself. Amos, you can't subject her to a stepmother. You know that's not fair."

Her father offered very little information, simply answered basic questions and ignored the rest, which made Lizzie hopping mad. Both exercised common good manners, however, her father extending the invitation to stay for lunch, and Lizzie accepting.

They heated casseroles in the oven and set out leftover lettuce salad, an orange jello ring with pineapple, and dinner rolls. Amos became quite affable as Lizzie praised the food.

Mary talked and laughed, although she soon tired out and went to sleep on the recliner for a short time, waking to the tune of a serious conversation between her father and her aunt, discussing her future.

As usual, the air between them was muddled by the disturbance, and Mary suddenly found it extremely rude. Torn between love for her aunt and dedication to her father, she felt a lump form in her throat.

"Lizzie," she called out.

"Yes, Mary?"

"Don't you think we should wait a while to come to a decision?"

"Why?"

"I need time to get healthy, stronger."

"Yes, I suppose that's true."

So she left on a good solid note of understanding, which gave Mary a restful night, in spite of having to get up twice to take her pain medication.

Recuperating was simply not a walk in the park.

On Saturday, Jemima arrived, her fresh white covering tied beneath her chin, her face alight at the sight of her father, breezing past him after the customary handshake, a cardboard box carried in sturdy hands.

She brought loaves of fresh whole wheat bread, homemade butter and strawberry jam, an apple spiced cake, and two pumpkin pies. Everything was perfect, especially the spice cake, frosted with brown butter icing, moist and tender, melting in her mouth.

She cleaned, did laundry, then sat by Mary's chair and massaged her feet, her shoulders, and her aching head. Her touch was strong, firm, and gentle at the same time, her low voice soothing as she told her the ordinary things about her life. Her childhood, sisters and brothers, the leading of God's Hand in her relationship with Amos.

THEY WERE MARRIED only a week after the first anniversary of her mother's death. It was a plain ceremony, with few guests, but the service carried out as usual, the marriage license signed, well wishes received, and she became Amos Glick sie Mima, mother to Mary, who was still at home.

Lizzie attended the wedding, which was a bit of a surprise, but Mary was glad. Mary knew a big part of showing up for the wedding was her curiosity about this Jemima Peachey, but she still enjoyed having her there.

Mary was not back to her usual robust state of health, but was improving every week, helping around the house, although Danny was now her father's full-time worker, doing chores, baling corn fodder, repairing loose boards in the machine shed, anything to make life easier. Her life took on a new rhythm, a slow pace complete with winter landscapes and a certain tone of gratefulness at the miracle of being alive.

It was hard at times, watching her father and Mima's love evolve into a state of contentment. Where he would have set boundaries for her mother, applied rules and disapproval, there was a respect for her view, her voice a serious admonishment in his own life.

And she pondered this, wondering at the difference. Mima was not afraid to assert herself, and did it wholeheartedly. She was unabashedly herself, and no one was going to tell her differently. Time after time, if her father's rumbling voice smacked of the ultra-conservative, or became unfair in his severe judgment of others, Mima's strident disapproval rang out.

SPRING'S WEEPING ARRIVAL was made up of dark skies, high winds, and endless rain. Mary was almost back to her usual self, except for the constant ache in her shoulder. The doctor contemplated a complete replacement, but Mima put her on an arsenal of pills, including an herbal capsule that set her gut roaring, taking her back to her days in Lancaster. She wondered what God wanted of her, what He had in mind, felt restless, disillusioned, and weary of Pinedale, but didn't want to go back to Lancaster, having been dropped off the map by all her friends the minute she returned to her father's farm.

Where was Sam Riehl? She wished she could have another conversation with him, but thought if he would have found her entertaining or attractive, he could have written or got in touch somehow. And to be very truthful, if nothing happened, was it so terribly wrong to live in her father's house with Mima?

They were very careful of Mary's feelings, showing no affection for each other when she was around, always including her in conversations and decisions.

And Mima quilted, the gaslight above her hissing softly, the wood in the stove cracking and popping, the rich aroma of baked corn and apple goodie lingering in the house after the dishes were washed. There was a certain coziness now, a mother's care, with gleaming floors and dusted furniture, shining lamp chimneys, and fresh baked bread.

One day, when the rain beat against the north windows, the wind rattled the downspout and moaned through cracks in the wooden siding, and Mima shoved more wood on the fire and rubbed her hands up and down her forearms.

"Chilly in here, Mary."

Mary looked up from her book, nodded her head. That was the way it was with Mima, easy comfort, fitting in like a lost puzzle piece. She could say and do whatever she pleased, and could always know it was alright. Mima simply wove it into her tapestry of life.

"Doesn't it ever bother your day, these tumbledown buildings?"

Mary looked up, bent down the page of her book, and set it aside. She rubbed her shoulder.

"You know, Mima, I honestly don't think it does anymore."

"You should call me Mam."

"I know. But it's hard."

"I understand."

She continued. "First, when I came here, I could barely believe it. Very few Amish homes look as, well, run down and neglected as these. It seems as if it's not a priority. He doesn't even see it."

She sighed.

"We never had enough money. When I returned from Lancaster, it was very hard, but since I was in the hospital it seems that stuff doesn't matter anymore. I'm just grateful for each new day."

"You should be. But, Mary. I would love to fix up the barn, maybe tear down this house. Build a new one, small, but airy, with lots of windows."

Mary thought of Eli and Sarah Allgyer, and little Elam who had been in remission from his leukemia. Their bright, sunny kitchen, the first sign of a possibility of staying here in Pinedale.

She wondered if Elam was still in good health.

"I'm sure Dat would never."

"How do you know?"

"He wouldn't allow my mother as much as a gallon of paint."

"Are you serious? Well, maybe I had better shelve that idea."

She sat down at her quilt, picked up her needle and shoved a thimble on the opposite middle finger, bent over, and began to quilt again.

The wind howled and loose siding shivered as nails screeched. Rain sluiced down the old window panes.

After a bit, she said, "I have money."

"What?"

"I have money. A sizable inheritance from my parents."

"Why did you get all their money?"

"I didn't. It was split four ways. They had a lot."

"Goodness."

"Yes. But would it be wise to upgrade this old farm, if we could sell it and keep a nice spot and build a *daudy haus*? I mean, of course not till you get married. I certainly don't want to chase you out."

"I may never marry."

"And what would be wrong with that? I had a good life, completely unattached. Taught school, which I loved. Worked in a dry goods store, worked in a chicken plant, saved my money, and went on a riverboat down the Saint Lawrence Seaway. You talk about a fish out of water. Ei-ya-yi, the people were some fancy. The music was loud, the people ate and drank. They danced. Oh, it was worldly. I enjoyed every second of it. The only reason I got away with it was because no one really knew what I was doing or where I went, just that I went on a trip. Huh. What a trip. But it was between God and me, and I don't think He's as strict as Amos thinks He is. My goodness, if He was, we'd all miss the entry into the pearly gates."

Mary looked up, aghast.

"I'm speechless."

Mima stopped quilting, turned her swivel chair and asked why.

"You? With that big covering? You're so plain."

"I am plain. I like being plain. It gives me a good feeling, sitting in church. But from time to time, I kick up my heels a bit. You should try it, Mary. Take a friend. My sister, who was single at the time, went with me. We watched television and everything."

"I went to the beach."

"Did you? Now that is something I would love to experience."

And Mary told her all of her observances, while Mima listened attentively. As the rain pattered on the window panes, Mary had a sense of togetherness with this woman who was her stepmother, something she could never have imagined. She'd taken an instant dislike to her, which she now saw was completely unfair.

At the supper table, she mentioned the loose siding to her husband, who responded in the way Mary knew he would.

"It isn't leaking, is it?"

"I don't believe it is."

"Well then. Why fix it if it isn't broken?"

Mima gave him a cold, hard stare when he bent his head to his spoonful of gravy, then swallowed, cleared his throat, and sat back.

"Now that was good gravy bread, Mima."

"Thank you, sir."

Her father's eyes shone at her words, and his mouth softened and wobbled a bit. Mary looked from one to the other.

"I think this old house needs some TLC."

"How do you mean that?"

"It's falling apart."

"It takes money. Money I don't have."

Mima winked at Mary, her small brown eyes like a sparrow's, and Mary gave a small smile in return.

THE RAIN FINALLY stopped.

Creeks ran full. Ponds dripped over their banks, overflow pipes gushed cold water into ditches, filling them to capacity. Bridges were off limits, with orange cones set along roadways, signs warning motorists to turn around, go back.

Children walked past on their way to school, stamped black rubber boots into deep puddles as ducks quacked and waddled their way to the great flooded expanse of pastureland. Mary sat on the front porch, taking in all the newly washed scenery, the clouds above rain-washed and new.

New life sprang up everywhere, the draw of the sunlight expanding small seeds buried in cold, winter soil. Dandelion, crocus, chickweed, wild carrot, and violets grew lush and green, but gardening was still not possible, the soil saturated, footprints leaving indentations in mud.

Mima was impatient. She rolled up her quilt, stored the frame in the attic under the eaves, then began housecleaning the spare bedroom. Mary helped left-handedly, but found she couldn't wash walls with her right shoulder. And she still tired out easily.

She was discouraged, felt old, beat up, and left by the wayside. She counted her get well cards and letters, noticed the absence of friends in Lancaster, felt freshly cast aside.

She cut fabric, sat at the treadle sewing machine, and began to push on the cast iron treadle, up and down, reaching a satisfying speed as the needle flew along with a clicking sound. She was pleased at her effort, felt another wave of contentment. Mima examined her work and praised her, said it was a real accomplishment.

She tried not to think about it, but the thought gained entry. When had her own mother ever praised her sewing? To be truthful, never. Always, it wasn't good enough. Too fancy, too sloppy, too much in a hurry, until she hated the idea of sitting at a sewing machine and trying to pass inspection.

Her heart grew warm toward Mima. She wouldn't have believed it possible a year ago, but she could not deny the fact. She was intrigued by her. There was something about her that seemed to infiltrate her father's thick, dull skin, and for this, she was grateful.

CHAPTER 16

THE TOWNSHIP FINALLY TOOK THE PACK OF DOGS SERIOUSLY, GATH-
ered a posse of able-bodied hunters, and made an effort at eradicating
them all. Amish men were included, doing justice for Mary, but her
stoic brothers were against the effort, saying what right did plain folk
have to rub shoulders with the *ausry* (outsiders)? Her father cleared
his throat, his voice rumbling across the breakfast table, saying how
appreciative he was, his staunch sons taking a stand against incorpo-
ration with the world. It would take stout-hearted views to keep the
Old Order operating the way it had for hundreds of years.

His views were expressed with a certain amount of pride, his voice
grating as he held himself and his sons above the struggles of his lesser
counterparts. As he spoke, Mima became increasingly agitated, fid-
dling with her fork, then her knife. She choked on a mouthful of coffee, which seemed to bring two bright spots of color to her cheeks. Her
brown eyes were sharp as a ferret's.

"You'd fit right in with the Scribes and Pharisees, Amos."

"Well, now, Mima. That's . . ."

She cut him off. Words smacked against words. Mary squirmed
in her chair. So, this was what it was like for a woman to stand up for
herself when married to someone like her father, one unaccustomed to
having his authority bucked. Her mother had never resisted, her will
folded beneath her husband's, and all the children following in that
order.

Was this, then, God's way? Mary mulled over this question, knowing it had worked in her family by all outward appearances as one by one the children followed the law of their father, held his views and opinions, supported all he had taught them. Was that the blessing God gave to these repressed women like her poor long-suffering mother and all her sisters and sisters-in-law?

And here she was, taking her own way, her life a never-ending carousel of loose ends, unanswered questions, bits and pieces, starts and dead ends. Was it because she could not give her life fully to Christ, always resisting the way of the cross? What really was the way of the cross?

All these thoughts roiled in her head as Mima's rough voice cut off her father's rumbles of disapproval. Strident, absolutely certain of her views, they clashed, the sound of their voices so alien, so out of place in a home where every trouble had been quickly and efficiently disposed of, swept under the rug of traditional admonishment.

Mima rose from her chair, gathered dishes, the china ringing out as it was knocked on top of each other. Silverware was tossed, hard footsteps carried them to the sink. Only for a moment, Mary caught her father's eye and glimpsed his bewilderment.

When he let himself out the door, Jemima flashed Mary an outraged look, ran hot water and added a dash of Dawn dish soap, and set to scrubbing dishes with a vengeance.

"It makes me sick," she spat, wiping her mouth with the back of her hand.

Mary said nothing, both fascinated and repulsed by this marital strife. She watched Mima wash dishes with fury, thought of her father's ruined confidence. She rubbed her shoulder, grimaced.

After a while Mima seemed to calm down a bit and Mary took the opportunity to change the subject.

"I need to get away, Mima, find a job."

"Oh, do you now? I hope you know you're not even close to being able to do hard physical labor."

But she turned and smiled as she wiped the oilcloth table covering.

"Just be content here with me for a while yet. There's plenty to do on this old farm."

The yard was so different now, the garden thriving in neat rows, flowers and bushes planted along the foundation of the old house, borders dug in straight precision along the edge of any growing plant.

Floors gleamed, windows shone with weekly polishing.

Yet, there was always plenty of work, which ordinarily, would have flown beneath her capable hands. Mima's and hers. She knew working for Aunt Lizzie had taught her all she needed to know of managing duties, how to clean rapidly and thoroughly, the art of baking and cooking, how to wash and iron, how to plan her time so each minute was productive.

She had learned so much in her young life. *Maud*, schoolteacher, pastry chef. She grinned at her own fancy version of "baking." She'd had a nice romance with Ben Stoltzfus, albeit a forbidden one. She'd learned of juvenile cancer and the ways of a good hospital, had flirted with the idea of leaving the Amish to find a future with the handsome photographer. She'd been nearly killed by wild dogs.

Mercy. She shook her head.

Evidently her time here on earth was incomplete, but for what reason?

She had so much time on her hands, too much time to sit and contemplate her past, to dig deeper into her thoughts and emotions. She truly believed everything God sent into her life was for a purpose.

MIMA DIPPED HER window cloth in steaming vinegar water, her hands red from the heat, before applying it to a window that was already clean.

"Mary, you need to start *rumschpringing* again. This is no way for a single girl in her twenties to live."

"Uh."

"Is that all you have to say?" Mima stopped, both hands on her hips, the cloth dangling from a hand.

"I don't want to. The girls are really silly, and Pinedale is devoid of any attractive men. I mean it."

"What keeps you from going back to Lancaster?"

"Dat forbids it."

Mima gave a little snort.

But the truth was, she had grown to love the beauty of scenic New York and found herself dreaming of a quiet home there with a sunny kitchen and a view of forested ridges and mountains with rolling fields and winding roads.

She loved her Aunt Lizzie, loved the liberty of choosing who she wanted to be, but why did it leave her with a mountain of anxiety? She had not been raised that way. She could never judge any other person for the freedom they allowed themselves, and she had nothing against advancing to more modern ways, but she wasn't completely comfortable with them, either. Here in Pinedale, the restrictions were too harsh, but as time went on, she soon realized her family was the most extreme.

"I suppose this valley is my home," Mary told Mima. "My roots are pretty deep. I find the *ordnung* extreme, depressing, but I've also realized, not everyone holds the same views. And, I'm finding my own way. There are pockets of happiness, times I experience joy in the scenery, the fresh air, and way of life."

Mima nodded.

"I believe I understand, Mary. You're smart, brilliant, really, and so often, someone like you, raised in extreme conservative ways, will break loose, which you did."

Mary nodded. "It wasn't right, some of the attitudes of this community."

"They still aren't," Mima snorted.

Mary grinned. "True, but you've started quite the war with Dat."

Mima stopped washing windows, aghast.

"What? Is it that bad?"

"Compared to my mother's timid ways, yes."

"Well, your mother didn't have a nice life. It was her own fault."

"But not everyone has the courage you possess," Mary said.

"It's not courage. It's common sense. We are made to be our husband's helpmeet, which includes seeing if he's sliding off the right track, which he is. I have never in my life seen anyone with a worse attitude about those around him. Everyone, just everyone is flawed, except himself. He doesn't realize how dangerous a view like that is."

Mary nodded, watched the bony hands swipe at the glass, over and over, polishing, cleaning, then stepping back to view the glass from a different angle to look for streaks. She thought of her overworked, overweight mother, the will to work hard crushed beneath the weight of her downtrodden spirit.

"Why do you think I should be running around on the weekends?" she asked suddenly.

"How will you ever get a man, otherwise?" Mima asked.

"That's straight to the point."

"It sure is. No use going the roundabout way. You're not getting any younger. And let me tell you, Mary, it's really nice to have a man. To feel his arms around me at night. A warm human being to touch and to love. I regret all the wasted years of my youth, when I was still capable of having babies."

Mary felt a slow blush spread over her face. Well. She couldn't think of it, her father and Mima.

"I love him. It makes me sad, this so-called piety that is nothing but pride with a glossy cover. It's a trap for Christians everywhere, but boy, has he really fallen into it. But I don't plan to let him stay there."

"Good luck," Mary said dryly.

She thought about Mima's words, of joining the Sunday evening hymn singings again, to seek a possible suitor, to have a companion throughout the course of her life. Yes, she wanted a husband, wanted children, but not in the way she had experienced far too often. The endless cycle of pregnancies, breastfeeding, whining babies and screaming children, mountains of washing, mountains of cooking and cleaning, sewing clothes for all of them, a huge garden and mountains of canning fruits and vegetables. Bright-eyed newlyweds with new furniture and a light-filled future turned into torn cushions, scratched surfaces, bills to be paid, and barely enough for clothing and other necessities.

Where was the joy in that? Or was there a deeper joy, a content heart that delighted in the ways of running a household, of loving a husband and children to the extent of the workload being a joy in itself?

As THE SUMMERTIME arrived, her strength seemed to be gaining. She spent hours in the sun, sitting on a low stool, between the rows of peas, picking the tender green pods. She often popped one open, scraped out the succulent peas, and threw them into her mouth. Mima didn't help her with the pea picking, saying she had other things to do, but Mary knew it was a way of testing her strength.

They were shelling peas on the back porch, the sun's warmth overhead, the heavy scent of peach-colored tea roses climbing the arbor, when her father came across the yard, his stride hurried.

"Abie Zook's barn burned. Wet hay," he said standing with his thumbs hooked in his suspenders.

"Well. My oh."

Jemima got to her feet, dumped an apronful of peas back into the bushel basket.

"I'll get some stuff together. You get the horse ready, Amos."

"Alright."

They gathered quarts of green beans, canned beef, noodles and cheese. Two shoofly pies and leftover chocolate cake were put in a cardboard box. Her apron changed, a clean white covering, and they were on their way, leaving Mary to shell peas by herself. She had volunteered, but Mima shook her head. Better for her to stay, until they knew the plan of rebuilding.

She breathed deeply, relaxed, allowed herself to experience the gratification of simply being alive. Sunwashed, the air heady with roses, a fat bumblebee droning between blossoms, a blue butterfly dizzy with nectar, bluebirds atop the homemade box, twittering as they fed the babies. Across the yard, the view before her was of blue green ridges, and beyond that, the Adirondack mountain range, a beautiful sight on any given day.

She was blessed, among the fortunate, and foremost among the many gifts of life was Mima. How rare, this friendship. She was hilarious, really, with her beaked nose and tiny brown eyes, her complete lack of inhibition. She said what was on her mind, and that was that.

The stainless-steel bowl on Mary's leg was almost full of shelled peas, so she finished the pods in her lap and got up, stretched her back, winced as she raised her right arm. This thing wasn't right yet, but hopefully, would continue to heal. She rubbed a hand across her shoulder, as she often did, to ease the discomfort.

She poured a glass of fresh meadow tea with ice, grabbed the pretzel bag, and returned to her chair. She still had almost a bushel to shell, which would take up most of the afternoon. She enjoyed shelling peas, but it was always best with another person to talk to. Well, Dat and Mima certainly wasted no time in getting over there. But then, that was ordinary. Death, accidents, a community emergency, was always met with a hasty gathering of friends and neighbors. Offering help and support during time of suffering was a time-honored tradition.

Mary shelled peas, sipped her tea, ate too many pretzels, wished Mima would return. Her eyelids were heavy, a stupor clouding her vision. Sleep, blessed sleep, was exactly what she needed. She was leaning forward to shake the peapods back into the bushel basket when she heard the crunch of still rimmed wheels on gravel, the dull thud of hooves.

She looked up, frowned.

A young man, hatless, was driving a nondescript brown horse hitched to a spring wagon. He came to a stop, threw the reins, and leaped off, missing the step entirely. He turned, reached under the seat for a tie rope, then tied the horse to the hitching rail, dusted off the legs of his trousers, and looked at her, seated on the back porch.

He came toward her in long strides, his work shoes as big as small boats. Everything about him seemed to be oversized, even the wide black suspender he wore. Clean shaven. No beard meant a single young man.

"Hello."

Mary watched without answering.

"Um, someone, not sure who it was, sent me over here for some of your father's tools."

"Oh? Well, I don't know much about the whereabouts of any of them, but I can show you where the shop is located."

She stood to her feet, dumped the peapods, smoothed her apron, and looked up at him. Brown eyes, dark hair, wide face. Ordinary features, not handsome, but certainly not homely. Not close to ugly. Rather attractive.

"I'm John. Johnny King."

"Mary."

He extended a hand. "Hi, Mary."

She smiled, then ducked her head. She came down the steps, winced as her ankle hit the top step. Sometimes, she stepped at the wrong angle, resulting in a painful stretch of harmed tendon not healed completely. She gasped, waited.

"Sorry. Guess I was sitting too long. Bum ankle."

"What happened?"

She waved a hand. "Nothing much."

She willed herself to lead him to her father's shop, felt embarrassment at the state of his tools, thrown haphazardly, rusted, in disrepair.

She waved a hand. His eyes took in the array of hammers, screwdrivers, rusted handsaws, rakes, pitchforks, everything showing years of use.

"Help yourself."

"Thanks."

She watched as he chose a few hammers, thrust a shovel in her direction, picked up a chainsaw before looking at her.

"Can you carry another shovel?"

"Afraid not."

He looked at her questioningly. "Okay. I'll come back for the second load."

"I . . . I was in an accident and my shoulder got wrecked. Hopefully, soon I'll be able to carry things again."

"What kind of accident?"

"Wild dogs."

He stopped, looked at her. "You're that girl?"

"I am."

He whistled low. He kept staring at her. Finally, he resumed walking. "That was quite a story. I often wondered what I would have done in a situation like that. They say dogs gone feral are worse than wolves."

"I knew they were in the area. Just never gave it a thought that Sunday as I walked to a friend's house. My father was away for the weekend, a neighbor helped with chores, and we found a mauled calf that morning. Very simple-minded of me."

"But who would have thought, in broad daylight?" he asked.

"Not me, evidently."

When they reached the spring wagon, he tossed the tools in the back, then walked back to retrieve the second shovel. She watched him go. His shirt was sweat-stained. A nice, even gait, one covering a great distance with minimal effort.

She felt ashamed of her interest in him. There was pobably a girlfriend waiting for him, back home in some Pennsylvania Amish settlement. Besides, she was bordering on desperate, at her age, which she had to admit after Mima's frank appraisal.

When he returned, he was still thinking of the dogs, saying immediately, "Did you see them before they saw you?"

"I remember very little. Some of it returns in bits and pieces occasionally, but I do remember hearing them behind me. The leader was ferocious."

He kept staring at her.

"Your face has no scars. That's good."

"Yes. I covered my face, instinctively, I suppose. My right shoulder and my side, my legs . . ."

She blushed, lowered her eyes.

"Wow. A story like that is almost unbelievable. Wasn't it some motorcycle guys who came to the rescue?"

"Yes."

He shook his head in wonder. "Wow," he said again.

He untied his horse, turned to climb aboard the spring wagon, but looked at her again.

"You coming over sometime?"

"I'm not sure."

He scuffed at the gravel with the toe of his shoe, then looked at her again. He saw the golden tan dotted with freckles, the gleaming red hair, the sheer comeliness. It was unexpected, this chance meeting, and he was reluctant to end it, but told himself she was probably dating. The attractive ones always seemed to be taken.

"Well, I'll see you soon, then. Thanks for the tools."

"Sure."

She turned and made her way to the porch, reaching for her right shoulder.

When Mima asked if she wanted to help at the raising on Thursday, she tried to hide her eagerness and answered slowly, unsure if she wanted to.

"You should, Mary. It would do you good to get out, be among people. A barn raising is fascinating, and there's always plenty of work for the women."

"Do I have to wear a cape?"

"No. You're a single girl."

Mary smiled. "That's a nice way of saying I'm approaching spinsterhood."

"Is that even a word? It sounds so stupid. For some reason, I imagine a spider weaving a web every time I hear it."

Mary laughed, a genuine sound of humor, something Mima had not heard from her in a while.

Should she go? Would he be there? A wave of despair crashed over her. The human experience was so cruel so much of the time. Yes, he was attractive. Even more than Ben Stoltzfus or the English photographer or Sam Riehl. And she was less than ordinary, a chunk of a girl, red-haired and spattered with freckles most men would find repelling. Why bother thinking about it?

Besides the freckles and extra weight, she was crosshatched with white scars, purple, deep red, discolored, raised line and bumps, revolting any normal man. Yes, she must remember who she was, without allowing herself the luxury of becoming attracted, to feel the stumbling heartbeat, the knowing there was something better than being alone.

She dressed carefully, wore the color she loved, the color that brought out the olive tones of her skin, thankful for her deep tan. She was careful to keep her expectations low, but it wouldn't hurt to be careful of her looks. Mima loaded the buggy with pies and cakes, a large tupperware bowl of shredded potato salad, a square pan of baked spaghetti. There were jars of applesauce and pickles, pounds of butter and jars of raspberry jelly.

Her father was clearly uncomfortable with this excess and told her quietly she didn't need to provide for the entire barn raising. They weren't as well off as many others in the community.

Mima sniffed, then told him in clipped tones it was all the more reason to give. Hadn't he read the passage in the Bible about casting your bread upon the waters? Give and it shall be given unto you, packed down and running over. Amos, didn't you know that?

Her father was proud of his extensive knowledge of the Scripture, so Mary knew this display of Mima's words was irritating. She tried to imagine her own mother accosting her husband with Scripture.

Mima sniffed again, shrugged her shoulders, and sat with her wealth of salads and pies, later justified completely when two bull calves brought them a check for a whopping eight hundred and forty dollars, which she shoved under his nose and said, "Look at this, Amos."

Mary sat in the back, biting her lip, trying to get rid of the butterflies in her stomach. She wanted to see him again, and yet she didn't.

She reminded herself that there was a very real chance she would not catch sight of him all day among hundreds of others.

She listened half-heartedly as her father spoke of the busload from Salt Valley, and he believed there would be one from Romeo.

CHAPTER 17

JOHN (CHONNY) KING WAS GETTING ON IN AGE, OF THIS HE WAS aware. It bothered other people more than it bothered him, certainly. His siblings were all married, with children, scattered through the hills and valleys of southern Lancaster County, where life seemed to move along at a slower pace, some of the old ways kept at a more respectful level.

He had been born and raised on a dairy farm, but took no interest in long days with no significant return, especially the past five years, and turned to carpentry instead. As an early summer vacation, he decided to visit his cousin, Abie, who had always been like a brother, perhaps even more so than many blood brothers. They hunted wild game together, spent three weeks in Montana fly fishing, went to the wilds of British Columbia moose hunting, completely at ease with bachelorhood, until Abie spied Janie, a girl from Ohio, at a singing in Montana, and that was that.

After that, Abie went out on a limb and moved his family out to this plain area, for whatever reason he never had figured out yet. But he still missed his company at times, and came to visit.

His single status was largely on account of having his heart broken at a young age. So terribly wounded in spirit, the ensuing years were filled with thoughts of her, and the pain deepened when she began dating Sylvan Lapp, and again when she married him. He vowed a life of celibacy, lived at home with his parents, and looked forward to his forays into the wilderness of different states, hunting and fishing, his sole source of leisure time.

A companion simply was not in his stars, and this realization did not come easily, although with resignation came peace, and with peace came contentment. Finding someone was no longer on his agenda, so when he drove into the long driveway that day, it was the farthest thing from his mind.

She looked like a painting, one of those old paintings on castle walls. Far from slender, she was certainly the most arresting sight, her red hair topping an interesting face. Actually, he thought later, probably most men would not find her attractive, but there was something about her, something magnetic, the strong pull of his eyes to her face. She was golden, colorful, somehow damaged, hurt, yet a survivor. She was his dream. He'd never been attracted to thin girls, had always liked a heavier build, so here he was, attacked from every angle, bowled over by an onslaught of Cupid's arrows.

The day of the barn raising found him calmed down, telling himself she wouldn't show up, she had no reason to come help with the enormous amount of food a raising required. She was, after all, recuperating from a near death experience, so he told himself if she showed up, it was a sign from God. Did he want her to be here? After all this time, would it be possible to feel a warm human being beside him?

It was all in God's hands.

THE SUN ROSE hot, a round orange ball of pulsing heat, but in typical New York style, the wind sprang up and a cloud cover pushed away the heat, turning it into a comfortable summer day. Buses and vans, buggies drawn by sweating horses, brought swarms of straw-hatted men with suspenders crossed over light colored, short sleeved shirts.

Blueprints were held, surveyed by capable foremen, and the work began. Hammering rang out, saws buzzed, a dinner bell signaled coffee break. There were mounds of homemade doughnuts, sugar cookies, iced whoopie pies wrapped in cellophane, pans of cinnamon rolls with walnuts thick as a graveled driveway.

The men helped themselves eagerly, then returned to work shored up by sugar and caffeine, high spirits and camaraderie. The last one to return to work was none other than John King, a silly grin turning up both sides of his mouth.

She'd been there. Right there in full view, putting chocolate whoopie pies on a tray, dressed in an olive green color reflecting her eyes.

He went straight to her like a magnet.

"Good morning, Mary."

She looked up. Her smile was glad and so were her eyes.

She nodded. He asked how she was and she said fine. He went back to work and thanked God for an answer. But he had known before, had known the moment he saw her on the porch.

Although knowing could come prematurely, so he kept calm and tried to show no feeling.

Long tables covered in white cloth contained over a hundred men at a time. He was not able to be seated the first time, but was among the last, always seated according to age, as was the Amish custom at most functions. But she was there, serving coffee, hoisting water pitchers with her left hand. When she came to him, she asked if he wanted coffee, and he said yes, took the cup from her hand, felt the nearness to her, the warmth radiating from her sleeve.

And he honestly hadn't thought he would ever feel this way again. Every pounding of his hammer was a song, every whine of battery-operated saws a shout of joy. The skies were a brilliant blue, the puffy white clouds spun gold, the green mountains and ridges a treasure trove of praise.

She washed dishes, dried them, helped count them as they were packed back into the wooden chests. They were wedding dishes for the community, but served the purpose of feeding hundreds of people at funerals or barn raisings, anytime a large group of people needed to be fed.

Her friend Anna worked with her, noticed her high spirits and commented on it.

"Yes. I do feel good. Every day that goes by is an improvement. It's also good to be out among everyone."

"Of course it is. I cannot imagine being housebound the way you have been for so long."

"It's not so bad. My shoulder is by far the worst. I'm not sure if it will ever be okay."

"I hope so, Mary."

Mary didn't answer, her eyes going to the window repeatedly. A skeletal frame had taken shape, rising into the sky like bare bones needing flesh and skin, till the long white strips of metal roofing went on, screwed into place with the high, quick whine of screw guns.

"Mary, who do you keep watching?"

"It's amazing, just unbelievable, the amount of work done in a day. How can the foremen keep up?"

Her answer seemed to plug her friend's curiosity, although Mary found Anna's eyes on her face with a frank question in them. She gave her a quick, bright smile, and the subject was closed.

She rode home in the back of the buggy with hope and wonder, coupled with despair. How or when, if ever, would she see him again? She thought of Mima's words, asking when she'd be going to the singings again, and wished she would have gone regularly as soon as she was able.

She had no idea if he would attend any youth gathering at all, but there was one thing sure, if she didn't go, there was a one hundred percent chance of never seeing him again, which was beyond comprehension.

She told Mima she decided to take her advice and go to the singing, if she knew where it was. Oh yes, she did know. It had been at Abie Zook's, or supposed to be, but with the loss of their barn, Abner Stoltzfuses were taking their turn.

"Oh good. Only a few miles. I'll walk."

"Mary. I'm surprised at you. Have you forgotten the dogs?"

"No, not at all. Getting back in the saddle and all that. And most of them were taken care of, anyway."

"I wish you'd take the buggy."

"No, not this time."

Smiling to herself, she knew this was the reason for walking. A girl could hatch a plan, devise a way when no other opportunity presented itself.

The singing itself was only a blur of color and sound, of shaking hands with visiting parents and being seated at a long table to sing, watching the young men slide onto the benches beside them.

He came in late, after the table was full, so he sat back against the wall where he had a perfect view of her without being seen. In blue, her cape pinned neatly, her covering so different than the other girls', her gorgeous red hair.

She stood out like one brilliant flower among plain leaves. His heart thumped in his chest, and he vowed to see her, talk to her somehow.

After the goodbye song, they were served coffee and cookies, which Mary did not want. Her eyes constantly roamed the room, searching and never finding. She was heartsick, reeling with disappointment, but put on a brave face, and no one could guess the letdown feelings inside. She should have stayed home from the barn raising, should have followed common sense she knew she possessed. Here she went yet again, creating another loose end, another frayed thread that could never be woven into the tapestry of her life.

She decided to leave early, her strong LED flashlight in hand, conquer her fear by striding alone through the dark night. She knew the feral dogs were gone, or at least most of them, but there was always the residue of her nightmarish experience to battle.

She stood on the lowest porch step, took a deep breath, and started out. The moon was almost full, if not entirely, so its light and warmth would be a real blessing. She knew the moon had no actual warmth, but it seemed cozy, the pale white orb in the velvety night sky.

"Mary."

Had she imagined her name being called?

She stopped.

"Wait, Mary."

And he was there, close behind her.

"I almost missed you. Listen, can I walk you home? Or didn't you walk?"

"I walked. It's only a few miles."

"Do you mind if I join you?"

"No, certainly not. I'm relieved, actually."

"Facing down your fears?"

"Yes. I guess you could say that."

"I can imagine it would be terrifying after an experience like that. I'm surprised you'd even consider going alone."

Together, they started out, with no one to interrupt them, no one to call out or tease them as they melted into the darkness together.

The first mile was spent with small talk, nervous laughing, unimportant words, both wondering if the other found him or her boring, but as the distance was covered, they became at ease. They described their childhoods and upbringings, getting to know each other as quickly as possible.

She was sorry to see the old farm at the end of the long drive. Their steps slowed. Sometimes they stopped, turning toward each other to elaborate on a sentence.

At the sidewalk, things turned awkward quickly. He did not want to leave, but thought it quite bold to ask if it was okay to come in. She wanted him to stay but didn't have the nerve to ask him in.

So they stood, shifting their weight from one foot to the other, talking, answering, savoring all the words.

"Well, Mary, I should get along home now."

She said nothing, then became unwilling to see him walk away without the promise of ever seeing him again. It was too hard, holding this unexpected joy, this taste of something promising and brand new, only to have it shattered beneath the sound of his feet as he walked out the drive.

"Would you like to come in for a cup of coffee?" she asked quietly.

A skipped heartbeat, and he said, "Sure. I didn't think you were ever going to ask."

"Isn't that your responsibility?" she quipped, bold now.

"I guess it is. But I'm only a pitiful old bachelor, and I don't know how."

She laughed.

"Not so old, and hardly pitiful. Our house isn't much, so don't look around," she whispered, as they tiptoed into the kitchen. She put water in the coffee pot and turned the burner on high, told him to sit anywhere.

She lit a kerosene lamp, and he asked where the DeWalt was.

"Dat doesn't believe it's a good idea to incorporate battery lamps into our lives. He's ultra conservative."

"Hmm. Really?"

"Yes. You may as well know that if you meet him you'll be scrutinized under the harsh light of his expectation. He . . . he broke up my first relationship. I'm not telling you this for any reason other than to speak the truth if you're thinking of coming back."

He found her large green eyes holding his. There was nothing in her voice but honesty, her eyes clear and truthful, the mature gaze of one who has endured disappointment and knew the adversity.

He gave a low laugh.

"Mary, I appreciate your honesty. You're making this very easy for me. Of course I want to come back. Of course I want to know you better. I also don't want your father's refusal to allow it."

"I'm just telling you. Our . . . my family isn't the same as I am. They have very exacting standards of *ordnung*. Dat would have a real problem with you driving without a hat."

"You're not kidding."

"No, oh no."

"But how does he expect you to learn to make your own decisions?"

"He doesn't. Everyone is inferior, including his own children, and he makes all the decisions."

He said nothing.

"Since he married Jemima, he's mellowed a bit. She thinks he needs to rethink some of his attitudes. Oh, you should hear it."

The coffee was finished, so she brought him a cup, asked if he used cream or sugar, to which he said yes to both.

"The ideal is French Vanilla."

"Oh my, not in this house," Mary said.

"So tell me, do you ever want to get away? Like, move out and get a place of your own, away from his . . . whatever you call it?"

She shook her head.

"No. I couldn't make enough money. And I like Mima, my stepmother. She's nicer to me than my own mother was. Although, the bond was very strong between my mother and I. She just felt that she had to stand with Dat's position on everything."

"Does he act that way with the other children?"

"They're exactly like him."

"Well, we'll cross that bridge when we get there. So, will I be welcome to bring you home every Sunday evening?"

"I believe you will be welcome where I am concerned, sir. You may also pick me up to go to the singing, although I strongly recommend a hat."

"I hardly ever wear one. Do I actually have to?"

"Not if you want to see what happens."

"I'll wear a hat. That requirement isn't hard."

It was after twelve o'clock when he left, so the next morning the breakfast table was awash in rigid disapproval.

"You have kept company with an outsider."

Mary bit her lower lip, bent her head, and waited for the onslaught. Mima looked at him sharply, lowered her coffee cup, and asked outright what that was supposed to mean.

"There was a young man in the kitchen, and it was after midnight when he finally took his leave. And I don't believe there was a horse and buggy at all. How did he arrive?"

"We walked from the singing. And he is not an 'outsider.'"

"And who, may I ask, is this young fellow?"

"His name is John King, from southern Lancaster County. He's here at Abie Zook's. A cousin."

"Lancaster? And he's after you already? You make an easy target with those worldly clothes."

Mary swallowed her retort.

"I know who he is. The one without a hat at the barn raising. He was bragging about his Western hunting trips, which bodes no good for the health of his soul."

Mary bit her lip.

Mima's eyes flashed. She cleared her throat, shuffled her knife and fork.

"Mary, I'm sorry to hear this," he continued. "You have always been misled easily. This fellow of which you speak is the same one who regaled onlookers and listeners with enticing stories of fishing and hunting in remote areas. I can only list the evil of money spent on personal pleasure. I cannot give my approval to such a young man, his head bare as he works."

Mima sniffed, resembling a balloon about to pop.

"As you know, your youth is the best time to serve God in purity, which you have not done in days past. I feel this young man was sent for a test to you, to see whether you are strong enough in spirit to withstand the wiles of the devil. Do this, and God will send you a personable young man who takes the *ordnung* seriously, as I do."

Mary kept her face lowered.

"So, I cannot, in free conscience, give my note of approval," he finished.

That was the slap on Mima's back that expelled the first words.

"And who cares if you approve of this chap or not?" she spat.

Mary looked up, shocked. No one spoke to her father that way, not when he entered his lecture mode, his truth a rumbling, assertive righteousness towering over anyone who might inject a lesser opinion.

"Mima."

The word was spoken with so much sadness, the words awash in sorrow.

"Don't 'Mima' me. I have never heard of anything so unfair. Mary is most certainly old enough to make her own choices. And who cares whether or not the man wears a hat?"

"And now you are taking the way of the heathen, taking up for the children against the parent, a worldly act of the woman of the house being far out of her rightful place."

"Well, that isn't true," Mima said, more quietly this time.

"But you are, Mima. My first wife, Barbara, would never have spoken to me in such a manner."

"Is that right?" Sarcasm thick as fleas, which escaped her father entirely, on a rolling philosophical rant of his own devising.

"Yes, that is right. Mary, you must know you have always been the wayward child, the one needing a firm hand and a parental finger pointing you in the right direction."

"Amos," Mima said evenly. "She is beyond the age where she is considered an adult, one capable of making her own choices. She isn't marrying this fellow, she merely kept company one evening. Don't you think if he proves to be an unsavory character, she would be able to sort it out on her own?"

"No. His works follow him. Western trips, even farther, are *verboten*, and you know this. He's putting his own interest in the sport of hunting far above the *ordnung*, which tells me he will do the same with a wife and children."

Mary's anger boiled, the lid she tried to attach rattling as she watched her father's eyes, the light of righteous anger gleaming at Mima, who met them squarely with the same gleam.

"Your judgment is too harsh, Amos," Mima said evenly.

"You, Mima, would do well to take up the *Schrift* and read about submission. You are meant to be beneath me, your will is my will. At your age, you do not understand the role of a wife, seeing how you were an old maid for quite some time."

He pronounced the "old maid" with force, as if by demeaning her he would be able to stuff her beneath his own will, completely.

"Hm. That's interesting," she responded evenly. "Being an 'old maid,' as you put it, looks very nice about now. But since I promised to marry you, take care of you in sickness and in health, this is what I will proceed to do. Your attitude is not healthy, neither is your judgment of those you consider to be below yourself. And I'm telling you now, you are wrong to speak to your grown daughter in such a manner."

There was not one ounce of defeat, no white flag of submission, merely a strident statement of the way she viewed the situation, which was that he was not walking in truth with his harsh appraisal.

After her voice rang out, he remained quiet and left the table with sad, watering eyes, and the set look around his mouth. Mima noticed his loose trousers held up by his plain black suspenders, the old, patched shirt stuffed loosely into them. She felt a pang of sympathy, but had no intention of backing down.

HE WENT TO help Abie Zook the following Thursday where he cornered John King and stood close, shifting his weight from one foot to the next, his eyes like wet coal beneath a shelf of thick eyebrows, long strands of hair below his earlobes.

He cleared his throat and introduced himself to John, before starting his procession of sentences that pinned him to the ground. John felt accosted, brutally assaulted by words surrounded by fire and brimstone.

No grace for those who seek their own amusement? Gluttony? Imbibing the world? Faster and faster, the words pounded against his understanding, a litany of perceived righteousness.

"My daughter Mary is not of sound judgment. She never has been. She will never submit to your will the way she should. So it's double-sided here. You do not pass the maturity test by your hatless appearance, and I cannot stand by as you stir up unrest among the brethren, allowing dreams of trips out west to upset their Godly thought. I would appreciate your willingness to return to Lancaster County, leaving thoughts of Mary here."

John King was taken by surprise, albeit a thoroughly unpleasant one. He had no idea an Amish man could be quite like this, completely wrapped up in his own opinion of right and wrong, asserting himself without a single misgiving. Harsh. Exacting.

"Well, I have plans to see her on Sunday evening. She asked if I would take her to the singing, which I will do. She seems to be a very nice girl, and I wanted to pursue a relationship with her. But if this is your honest opinion of me, then I see very little chance of ever meeting your approval."

He felt Mary slip away from him, already the beauty of her shrouded in the confusion of her father's words. Perhaps they had moved too quickly, had been too sure. Wearing a hat could never undo all the Western hunting and fishing trips, the source of his ammunition, firing accusations like bullets.

He walked away, his mind churning with justification. What was wrong with hunting and fishing? He had never felt closer to God than standing in an unbelievably clear creek, the sky an immensity of azure blue, fish like God-given gifts of perfection, all of nature a wealth of wonder, a feast for his senses. Since he'd met Mary, he had an ultimate goal of allowing her to see and experience the wonders of creation.

Would it ever happen?

He worked in a daze of bewilderment. He had been so sure.

He glanced over by the barn door, saw Amos Glick with his feet spread wide, his pelvis thrust forward, thumbs hooked in his suspenders, face lifted to the sky as he laughed at his fellowman's joke.

Pure hatred coursed through John's veins. He turned away. A course of action rose up in him. He would use Abie's team, would pick her up as planned, and would not wear a hat, the way he was comfortable. He would talk all of this over with her.

But first, he would pray to the One who would guide him and ask if there was truth in her father's words.

CHAPTER 18

THE PAIN OF BEING REJECTED AGAIN FOR SOMETHING AS INSIGNIFI-
cant as talking to a man who wasn't wearing a hat was even worse
than the pricking of her conscience in Lancaster.

He had accepted her, liked her. He would never love his children the
way some fathers did. He would never show affection, but she thought
they had made progress—he had even accepted the new fabric of her
white head covering.

She felt raw betrayal, a casting out which she could not have anticipated. The pain was searing, deep, spreading like a cancerous growth.

To please her father was far more important than she had ever
thought possible, but now she felt as if she had almost reached the top
of a glass mountain, only to be dashed down to the pit of hopelessness.

Impossible.

She felt the blades of anger against her heart. Was anger the fortify-
ing element she would need? It had served its purpose before, sustaining
her as she created a life in Lancaster, one in which he would not find an
ounce of approval. Rebellion had been sufficient fuel to carry her on,
but she didn't want to return to the power of its grip.

To meet his demand, she would have to tell John King about the
conversation with her father, the following consequences unknown.

She took a deep breath.

SUNDAY EVENING WAS bathed in a golden glow, a perfect sunset promised, laced with lavender, yellow, orange. A perfect summer evening.

She was ready and waiting, breathless in her green dress, the cape pinned to perfection, her black belt apron loose around her waist.

Unknown to her, her father was stationed in the barn, awaiting the arrival of the *ungehorsam* (disobedient), the young man he had expressly forbidden to date his daughter.

She heard the ringing of hooves on macadam, the grind of the steel-rimmed wheels. Her heart leaped. Her eyes searched the windows of the house, hoping her Dat would not make an appearance and humiliate her at the last moment.

It was him, driving Abie's powerful black horse, the buggy gleaming with cleanliness. He seemed to fill the entire window, his light blue shirt and black vest. No hat. Her heart leapt, the beating resumed.

"Whoa."

He stopped the buggy by the hitching rack, slid the door back, and was standing by the horse's head as she walked across the drive. His eyes took in the wonder of her. He had never seen a more attractive person.

She fitted every description of his dreams. The beauty of those unusual eyes. Her freckled skin. He would fight to the bitter end.

"Good evening, John."

"Mary!"

He could not keep the joy to himself. He smiled broadly and allowed his eyes to travel over the freckles, the wonder of her burnt orange hair, the neatness of her large figure.

"Ahem."

They both turned, their eyes wide with surprise. There he stood, glowering at them both.

"This is a flagrant act of disobedience. You have not heeded my words."

For a long moment, the only sound was the busy chirping of sparrows in the spouting, the occasional snort from a horse's nostrils. The large black horse hitched to the buggy lifted his head and shook the neck rein, reminding John of the fact he was attached to the shoulder pad. He walked over to loosen it.

"You must stop seeing Mary. It's not what you want. It's what I want. You can't see farther than your own pleasure, so how can God lead you? You are expressly verboten to take her away with you."

Incredulous, they both stood in silence.

"But Dat . . ." Mary began.

"Can't you see he's not wearing a hat? What does that tell you about his character?"

He had worked himself into a frenzy, spittle at the corners of his mouth.

"Your judgment of me is unfair, I'm sorry to say," said John as calmly as he could. "I feel Mary and I are old enough to choose who we want to see, don't you think?"

"Age has nothing to do with it. It's the fact that she has always been a handful, unwise in her own choices. She is different. And you, you . . ." He pointed a trembling finger. "You have unknowingly displayed your character for all to see at the barn raising. Bragging about your superiority at hunting and fishing, a sport you blew way out of proportion. It speaks ill of your character."

"I'm sorry if you feel that way."

"Sorry will not change my opinion."

John looked at Mary, found her eyes on his face, a message he could not fathom.

"Mary, what do you want me to do?" he asked.

Amos stepped up. "It's not what she wants, it's what I want."

"Dat, please. May I speak to him, alone?" she asked.

"Certainly not."

He walked to the horse's head, hooked the neck rein. Mary followed, stood close. "Meet me at ten. By the woods."

That was all he said. She nodded.

He got in the buggy, picked up the reins, and chirped to the horse. Buggy wheels ground on gravel. She turned, her head lowered, and without a glance at her pale-faced father, she walked to the house.

Mima looked up, her face white, pinched.

"He didn't allow it."

"No."

"*Ach*, Mary."

She paused, her hands curled around the arm of her rocking chair as she got to her feet. She came to Mary, an arthritic hand to her arm. Her eyes bored into hers.

"Believe me, this isn't over."

"He will see that it is."

"Not this time."

Mary spent the rest of the evening in her room, trying repeatedly to rise above the pain of having lost, of knowing she had been hurled into the void of her father's criticism. Again, after all this time, when she felt his approval, his "like," as close to love as he would ever be. She felt the black waters rise over her waist, her chest, her neck. Would she be able to rise above this time?

At nine o'clock, her stomach roared. She threw up, wiped her mouth, and looked in the mirror at her pale, tormented visage. At nine-thirty there was a rectangle of light on the lawn below, and she knew he was waiting. Ten o'clock, and she was too sick to her stomach to leave the vicinity of the bathroom, too weak to withstand his demands, not enough courage. He would restrain her bodily, she knew he would.

There were no tears.

She lay awake, her eyes open wide, trying to keep her head above the ever-increasing tide of depression. He would leave, go back to Lancaster, and forget about her, which was all he could do. And she would submit, would try to find herself in a state of grace, again.

She couldn't go back to her old life of disobedience, could not live with Aunt Lizzie and take control of her own life. She was too old to join the crowd of giggling girls and trips to the beach. Likely many of them were married by now, and she had not received so much as one invitation.

The confusion of a life lived without answers piled on top of her head, smashed her into the deadly waters that now closed over her face, extinguishing her breath. She had to fight, but how? With what?

She felt herself sinking, her spirit drying, her will to live melting away. She cried to God, sought His will with every ounce of courage she had left.

It was then, she heard a ping. Then another.

"Mary!"

Silently, she rose, crept to the window, her eyes going to the dresser. 1:20. There was no rectangle of light. He had gone to bed.

Her face was at the window.

"Can you come down?"

"I'm afraid to try."

"You can."

She did try, but every floorboard, every wooden step squeaked, grated. Door hinges squawked like noisy ducks on a pond. She felt sick. She was on the porch, down the steps, her bare feet whispering through wet dewy grass.

Where was he?

She stopped, frightened. She imagined her father's face in the frame of their bedroom window.

"Over here, Mary."

And he was there, behind the orchard fence. She climbed over, quickly, felt his presence. He had walked back, stayed since ten o'clock.

He needed to talk. She was too distraught, too weakened by her father's force, to tell him of the dark regions of her spirit. She pleaded with him to go back to Lancaster and forget he ever met her.

"Mary, please. You don't mean it."

"John, I lived outside the realm of his approval. I can't do it again. I deal with terrible anxiety, hopeless feelings of being lost. I can never go back to that. I need his approval to be normal. He's powerful in my conscience."

"Mary, you don't realize how abnormal this situation is. It's so extreme. So uncalled for. I don't believe one other Amish father would ever do this to a daughter your age."

"But you don't understand. All my siblings are like him. They live a life of obedience to strict rules, and are all peaceful and happy."

"Are they?"

"Well, the men are. The women have a lot of babies and a heavy workload, but Dat says they're fulfilling God's requirements. Maybe they are, I don't know."

He sighed.

"Well, I'm going back to Lancaster this week, but I can't go until I have a way of contacting you. May I write? Can I call?"

"The only telephone is a neighborhood one in a booth. Dat gets all the voicemails. A letter would be questionable."

"Do you want me to write?"

"I don't know. I don't know if I have the courage to fight. I'm afraid of being overwhelmed with anxiety. I actually become ill with it. Physically ill. I cannot return to that state. I just can't. If I can keep my sanity by obeying, I will, even if I have to stay single my whole life. Anything to avoid that horrible abyss of foreboding, that feeling of being cast into hell."

"Mary," he gasped.

"It's true."

He took a deep breath. "You need a good Christian counselor. This is so unhealthy."

It was very dark beneath the shadows of the aging apple trees, the quarter moon providing very little light. The stars hung like twinkling diamonds, suspended on strings from the dark dome of the night sky.

Crickets chirped without ceasing, katydids rasped their bumpy tune.

They heard animal hooves as the cows moved from one clump of grass to another.

"I wasn't always like this. I grasped rebellion and anger, floated happily along on it. I went to movies and the beach with my girlfriends.

Had a boyfriend who kissed me. I lived my life according to my own terms. I thought that was who I truly was. Me. My conscience was different from everyone else. It was, for a while. Then I became sick with stomach pains, followed by crippling anxiety, which disappeared when I came back. How can I return? I can't."

For a long moment, he was quiet.

"All your siblings are the same? Every last one?" he asked slowly.

"Yes. They are the light of my father's life. I long to be like them, so confident in his delight, in his approval."

"So the only way you will ever be truly happy is to marry the person he chooses, to dress according to his rules, to act exactly the way he demands?"

"Something like that. I suppose."

He sighed, a ragged sound of defeat.

"I think what we need to do is stay in touch. You said your stepmother isn't like your father, so we'll correspond through her. I'll address my letters to her, and my return address will be my cousin Rachel in Westport, Pennsylvania."

She said nothing.

"Do you want to, Mary?"

"I do. But is it wrong?"

"Mary, you are free to serve your own conscience at this point in your life."

"How am I free? 'Honor thy father and mother.'"

When he melted away into the darkness, after nothing was resolved except the promise to write, she stumbled back into bed, caring about nothing, not even the rasping hinges on the door, the loud groan of wooden steps, her father's awakening. She lay in bed, the demons of her past taunting her. All the misdeeds equaled the dog attack, her body riddled, crosshatched with scars, her mind never free of what she had done, of the disappointment she was to her father.

But when he openly taunted her at the breakfast table, making fun of John, being without a hat, laughing, saying he looked like a porcupine with all that unruly hair, a hot wave of anger wiped out all reason.

It was one thing to be denied this chance at love, but to be openly mocked was quite another.

She got to her feet, her hands splayed on the table. The surge of adrenaline gave her sudden clarity. Her voice was strong, did not tremble.

"You will not mock John King, Dat. Neither will you hold me here. I will return to Lancaster, and there I will stay. To be told who I may date and who I may not at my age is not necessary. So, this is a goodbye."

Jemima rose to her feet, her eyes wide. She looked at Amos, willing him to say something.

There was no response from her father except a wave of his hand.

MARY WAS ALMOST unrecognizable, having gained weight, dressed in the most fashionable way possible. Her hair was rolled on top of her head, a too small covering on back of it, mascara on thick lashes, puzzling her Aunt Lizzie, who was trying her best to decipher what had gone wrong in New York.

She had arrived without warning, showed up on her doorstep with dark eyes that sent a chill through her. She seemed a bit off center, her laugh too loud, never giving a legitimate reason for her return. Lizzie asked about her stepmother. Mary waved a hand, said she was the greatest, everyone was doing well, her father was happy in his second marriage.

She threw herself into bakery work, made friends with the fanciest girls, went out almost every night, causing Lizzie's alarm to reach a crescendo of concern.

By late autumn, Lizzie recognized the searing truth. Something was wrong with Mary. She felt responsibility and kept her at the breakfast table one Saturday morning after a very long night, her eyes bloodshot, her visage angry.

"Another cup of coffee, Mary?"

"Yeah. May as well. Head hurts a lot."

"Mary."

"Don't start, Lizzie."

"Start what?"

"Start bothering me."

"Mary, please tell me what's wrong? Tell me what you're trying to do?"

"Nothing. Living my life."

"Mary, there is alcohol on your breath. I don't think you should continue with the crowd you're with. I wish you would be honest with me, tell me why you're here."

Mary picked up her coffee mug, took a sip, wrinkled her nose, laughed, and said she was drying up in New York, needed to come here to experience life again.

"But are you sure you need to be like this?"

"Like what?"

"You're a bit out of line. I'm concerned about you. The company you keep. I can only imagine. I know you needed freedom from your father, but I think you've swung too far the other way."

Lizzie sat quietly when there was no response, watched as Mary's fingers went around and around the rim of her coffee mug.

Finally she said, "Kevin likes me."

"And who, may I ask, is Kevin?"

"You'll flip out when I tell you."

"Mary."

Lizzie was crying inside. Her mouth was dry with fear. Responsibility weighed on her shoulders, the weight of being an outlet for something gone desperately wrong. The Mary she knew was in there somewhere, hushed and subdued by the clamor of anger and rebellion.

"Kevin isn't Amish. He runs with our group, though. I think he likes me quite a lot. So that will be my choice, if he asks me to go out, right? You won't try to stop me, will you?"

She waved a hand airily. "You can't."

She washed large jeans, T-shirts, hung them on the line. Lizzie took them down before neighbors would see, deeply ashamed. She caught her smoking in the barn, loose hay scattered everywhere, and when she was scolded, ground out her cigarette and tossed her head, laughing in her face. When two well-meaning friends spoke to her about Mary's behavior, she burst into tears, said she was at her wit's end.

Something had to be done.

Susie and Linda came, leaving children with babysitters. They begged Mary to tell what had happened, why she was being this way.

People were talking, being concerned.

Mary ate three cinnamon rolls, her blackened lashes giving a macabre look. She told them she was fine, simply enjoying life on her own terms, away from that dried up New York.

No, it wasn't her father. She loved her stepmother, would go back for a visit any day now. She had everything under control, really.

They had nothing to worry about.

But at night, after she was dropped off, she would stumble to her room, dizzy, disoriented, overweight, and reeling with exhaustion. Her vices, the excess in which she lived, taking their toll. It was then the faces and voices were present, taunting her, until she felt she might drown in black waters of despair. She resisted help in all forms, made up lies to herself, was grateful for the mind-numbing effect of alcohol, her crutch to get through each week.

Her dreams turned into nightmares, clear pictures of stalking monsters, waking her with their presence, finding her soaked with perspiration, her screams muffled in her pillow. Her heart rate increased, her blood pressure elevated, she lay awake, unable to sleep, unable to bear being awake.

Kevin introduced her to an array of pills, capsules that kept her energized or put her to sleep. Long after the effects of alcohol wore off, the pills were a lifesaver.

She began to lose weight, had no interest in food. Dark circles appeared beneath her eyes, eyes that gave Lizzie the creeps.

She could not reach her, could not touch her at all. She took to laying spiritual reading material on her nightstand, on the back of the commode. Mary tried to flush it down one night in a stupor, resulting in clogged drain pipes, overflowing commode, dripping through dry-walled ceiling into the living room.

And still Lizzie did not give up on her. Friends told her she was crazy, just send her back home. "You can't go on, you're too old, she's not your responsibility."

And Lizzie drew herself up to her full height and said God had placed her on her doorstep, and she was expected to step up to the plate and help that girl. She wasn't shirking her Christian duty. It was only a matter of time till she came to the end of herself. There was a mystery here, somewhere. Something had happened to send her over the edge, of this she was positive.

THERE WAS A voicemail on Sunday morning.

A professional from the medical field.

"We have Mary here. Your niece, I believe? She's on life support. We ask you to come as soon as possible to Lancaster General."

Lizzie replaced the receiver, had never felt Leroy's absence as keenly. A deep calm comforted her, a sense of capability, and she knew Leroy's spirit was on her side.

She dressed, called her neighbor, Cora, the Mennonite who drove a blue mini-van and was always available, any time of day or night. As they sped along a near empty freeway, Lizzie prayed with Cora, out loud, something she was not used to but found immensely comforting.

She walked through the glass doors alone, was shown to the fourth floor, ushered quickly to the ICU section, found Mary attached to countless tubes and wires, beeping monitors and squiggly lines lit by green lights, beeps and whistles sounding death knells.

She fought back panic, wiped tears with a crushed Kleenex when she wasn't aware she was weeping.

Two doctors. A handful of nurses.

"Ma'am?"

"Yes."

"You're the mother?"

"An aunt."

Quick explanations. She had been brought in unconscious. They would administer a substance, and if it worked, she'd awake within two minutes. If not, she'd be taken to Harrisburg to the toxicology unit. She had inhaled or swallowed a toxic substance, perhaps allergic to a form of a drug, most likely. Lizzie nodded, wiped her nose, bit down on her lower lip.

I must be brave, she told herself.

Suddenly, Mary struggled, sat up, laid back down. She tried to cough against the plastic tube. Vomit flowed through it. Trained nurses quickly began to remove it, wiped phlegm and spittle, residue of vomit. Mary's face was swollen, her eyes heavy with fluid, her hair matted. She opened her eyes, terror in their depth. She recognized Lizzie and began to cry, tears seeping from swollen eyes.

Quickly, Lizzie reached out, touched her arm.

The doctors stood by as the nurses performed the necessary maneuvers, carefully monitoring her vital signs. She was given ice chips, then the questions began.

She had no clear recollections after being in Kevin's care.

She was taken to a room on the second floor, Lizzie following, her black purse clutched in her hand, her solid black Skechers coming down softly on the polished tiles.

Ach, Mary, she thought. *Surely God is putting you through the fire, polishing you to some shining vessel. I mean it.*

CHAPTER 19

Winter sunlight flowed through large panes of glass, illuminating the drab walls, the white sheets and plastic bed rails. There was a dry erase board on the wall, with names of the two nurses and a doctor, a bedside table on wheels containing a pitcher and plastic cup.

Mary kept her eyes closed against the harsh light.

Lizzie found a brown chair, folded herself into it, set her purse on the floor beside it, and folded her hands. The only giveaway to being agitated was the whitening of her knuckles. She heard voices, rubber soles on polished tile, nurses going about their day work.

And she waited.

Finally, Mary opened her eyes and looked around before focusing on Lizzie. Her mouth formed the words, "I'm sorry."

Quickly, she went to her bedside, bent to kiss her forehead.

"It's okay. Mary, it's okay. You're alive."

Mary closed her eyes, and slowly, the tears seeped from between swollen lids.

"I don't know, I don't know," she kept whispering, so Lizzie stood beside her bed and held her hand to her shoulder.

"I'm so tired," she said finally, turned her head, and went to sleep.

Lizzie would not leave her vigil except to go to the bathroom. She would not accept a dinner tray, or a drink, but told herself she would be fasting and praying, which she commenced to do.

She gathered her supply of faith and she prayed for Mary's soul, for Kevin's, and for all the misguided youth of the world, who thought the wiles of evil were the way of acceptance, the way to conquer their insecurities. And she prayed for Amos and his well-intentioned superiority to the rest of the human race, caught in the spider's web of his self-righteousness.

And when Mary awoke, she smiled a small, wobbly smile, and said she was hungry.

They talked, then, really spoke about what was on their minds. Both of them. Mary cried softly, listening to what Lizzie had to say, then nodded her head in agreement, before the whole story tumbled out in broken bits and pieces, like a shattered vase tumbling off a stairstep.

She explained how she'd made the grade with her father, only to fail miserably when John King was not the person he wanted for her. The breaking point when he mocked him the next morning.

"Why didn't you tell me?" Lizzie cried, sick at heart.

"I don't know. Maybe rage consumed me, gave the devil a handhold," she said in a voice so broken it brought Lizzie to her bedside, soft arms around her.

They kept her for the night to watch her, but she was fully awake, talkative, unburdened. They were hungry. A kind intern brought them small bags of snacks, cans of ginger ale, and cups of ice, which they shared, talking quietly in the semi-darkened room.

A group of doctors came in the following morning, giving them the questionable verdict. As near as they could tell, she had smoked what she believed to be marijuana but it had been laced with fentanyl, a street drug.

Lizzie was terribly embarrassed, being Amish. Wasn't it awful? Here she was, dressed to be a conservative light to the world, extinguished completely by her niece being in this painful incident.

What did these English people think?

Well, nothing to do but hold her head up high, realize she was no better than anyone else.

Cora brought Mary's clothes, and they walked out of that hospital together, a cloud of thanksgiving following in their footsteps.

Mary did not go back to work that week, but sunk into a state of despair so deep, Lizzie was terribly alarmed. She wanted to get her into counseling, but Mary refused, saying she was going to be fine. She simply had a few issues to deal with.

She didn't realize how dependent she'd become on the alcohol and drugs to keep her mind quiet. At night, sleep was impossible, thinking of her soul's precarious perch on the pedestal she had made for herself. *Ungehorsam* (disobedient). She would not enter into Heaven with the remainder of her family, but languish in a state of unrest. God had to be thoroughly disgusted with her. She sought forgiveness feverishly, cried out in silent supplication, railed at the throne of grace, but found no rest.

She told Lizzie she wanted a new cape and apron, a white one, so she could return to church. Lizzie blinked back tears of joy and said they'd make a day of it, go to dry goods stores, shoe stores, wherever they chose. Eat at Bird-in-Hand. Lizzie loved the breakfast buffet there, so Mary agreed, but said she'd have to be moderate. She didn't want to gain back all that weight.

"How much did you lose?" she asked.

"I don't know exactly. A lot. I'm probably around one hundred seventy. Something like that. It makes me shudder to think of how I lost it."

A sad look crossed her features.

"I hope so much God can forgive me."

Lizzie gave her a penetrating look. She took a deep breath.

"You were forgiven over two thousand years ago. Way back when Jesus was nailed to the cross. That's why He was there, for human beings who do stupid things. Me and you."

"It's not that easy."

"What makes it hard? You're the one standing in the way."

Mary shook her head, unsure.

Lizzie let it go. The fact she wanted to return to church was enough for now.

She was afraid for Mary, so steeped in *ordnung* and being *gehorsam*, she thought they were her salvation.

There were letters from Mima, asking her to return, but not a single word from her father. It was unsettling, the size of him in her conscience.

SUNDAY MORNING LIZZIE and Mary walked side by side, the cold air unable to penetrate the thick, black shawls or the sturdy bonnets. Mary walked with a spring in her step, glad to be alive, even more aware of the goodness of it as the days went by. She was going to church again, and this time, she was going with an open mind, a searching heart.

She'd been down an awful road, and now it was time to sort out truth from deception.

They bent their heads to the stiff breeze, glad to turn in the drive to the place church services would be held. Mary thought of New York, the long buggy rides on gravel roads, the scent of pine and wet leaves, and felt a pang of homesickness.

But the wall between her and her father needed to be there. She couldn't return.

She met old friends, many of them married and moved to other districts. She was welcomed with a certain warmth, though, and felt a part of the congregation. She realized how much better she fit in, able to dress neatly, with a certain maturity, and now, an air of calm, of having been through storms, of upheavals, and times of redemption, muddled with rebellion and choosing the wrong turn in the road.

There was a young minister today, one with a strident voice, clear and unfaltering in his portrayal of the life of Jesus. She took great comfort in his stories, imagined himself to be the woman who touched Jesus's white robe when He felt the healing power leave His body.

Wouldn't it be great to be healed by merely reaching out? But Amish people didn't really qualify for that if they weren't obedient, did they? And so a portion of his message was absorbed, but the veil of her tumultuous upbringing hid most of it from her view.

She was happy, however, happy to be at a religious service, to wait on tables in the time-honored tradition of eating lunch after church. She bent to speak to small children, laughed at the antics of little girls sharing a roll of Lifesavers.

She was invited to a supper for the youth by a shy, blond girl from the Blue Jays, a new group that had separated from the Orioles. Mary had no knowledge of any of them, but did not want to spend the rest of the day alone in her room without a book to read, so she said okay, if someone would be able to pick her up.

"We will. My brother Ivan and I," she chirped.

What a little sparrow, with all that chirping going on, she thought. But she was flattered by anyone's attention, the way she'd ruined her reputation so thoroughly.

Later, while combing her hair, a sense of failure taunted her. Who did she think she was? Her life was a mess, a whole book of craziness, an up and down and roundabout road of dead ends and false starts.

Here she was at a ripe old age with still no idea of who she was. She took a deep breath, pinned her black apron over her blue dress, and grabbed her coat. She could hardly believe the black Mustang coming up the drive. She thought there would be a horse and buggy.

Aunt Lizzie was not happy. She warned her gently but firmly, and Mary assured her this was a new group, one she considered quite conservative, which seemed to reassure her.

She was greeted warmly by Ruthie and Ivan, a thin youth with a mop of blond hair, a quick smile, and easy conversation. As he steered the Mustang through traffic, Mary couldn't help but imagine what her father would say about this. A hat was a small thing.

Well, he wasn't here, so she put it out of her mind.

The cold winter weather kept them mostly in the large shop where games of ping pong, cornhole, and cards were underway, allowing her time to grasp the amount of youth belonging to this group, the way they were dressed, the level of behavior, and found she felt right at home. She enjoyed her Sunday afternoon immensely but was glad to return home early, much to Lizzie's delight, who had no intention of going to sleep until she returned safe and sound.

"I know, I know," she said, when Mary reassured her. "But that thing you were traveling in put up my warning flag."

Mary laughed. "Yes, my father would have a fit."

"Does his opinion still affect you?"

"It always will."

"It probably will. I agree."

"Does that really matter? I mean, can I live like this without stumbling over him continuously?"

"That is a good way of saying it, Mary. I don't always know what to tell you. I guess we'll take it a day at a time and see how you feel."

Mary went to bed and fell asleep immediately, a smile on her face.

WORKING IN THE bakery, her hands flying as she used the cookie scoop to separate the right amount from a mound of chocolate chip cookie dough, her thoughts were like clothes in an electric dryer, tumbling over and over.

Her life was a chaotic maze, one making no clear progress. She had no goal, and no change in the foreseeable future. She was back in Lancaster, had made another wrong choice driven by anger and rebellion, and now a sense of insecurity, of false starts, invaded her thoughts. Everywhere she went, anything she tried, all the events in her life, and still nothing was resolved.

BACK IN NEW York, Mima was in a quandary of her own. Amos had found the first letter from John King. He said he had a right to read his wife's mail, and then was outraged to discover what it actually was. Mima set her lips but made no argument and went about her duties with her mind churning.

It was high time the man met his match, but she wasn't sure she was up to the task. She was, after all, his wife, and had promised to obey him in her wedding vows, and this she could not take lightly. Brought up in a conservative family herself, there was a certain amount of guilt attached to any form of marital discord.

From her point of view, Amos held a deep seated grudge against Mary for disrupting the flow of "perfection," the appearance of righteousness through which his fellowmen could measure his impeccable discipline and control, an example of how children should be taught.

Mary had bruised his pride.

Another letter arrived, which Mima successfully pounced on and hid in her dresser drawer, planning to send it the next day. But he found it, destroyed it, and told her she was no match for him.

Mima bowed her head, felt her true place as a stepmother and took it to God, railing at the throne of Grace no more. She wrote to Mary, said her father destroyed the two letters and she had no address for her to reach him, but if it was the will of God, they would meet somewhere in Lancaster.

MARY TALKED TO Lizzie, the whole story tumbling out in fitful starts, long silences, and tangled emotion. She wanted a husband, of course she did. But every time she felt an attraction, or a nice young man noticed her, she was left high and dry, floundering for solid answers.

Why? Did God simply forget about her? Or was she meant to be alone?

Lizzie contemplated all this, all the events of her life, the casting about between two places, the unseen force that shaped her existence.

She decided to tell Mary.

"The root of your problem started the day you came into the world, which I know, sounds awful. But that is true. You were born different. You always questioned, always wanted more, even as a child. I remember Leroy commenting on it, when we were at a reunion. You were dressed as plain, but there was a spark, a difference in the way you viewed the world. And I believe this is no fault of your own, merely the way you were born, the DNA you carry. If your father was normal, which he isn't, your life would be different than it is now. You would be happily married to Ben Stoltzfus, living here in Lancaster, allowing your own conscience to decide how you will live."

Mary nodded.

Lizzie laughed. "But *ach*, Mary, now your life is, well, messy. Your reputation has taken a direct hit. In other words, you really ruined your good name. People will talk, things will be blown out of proportion, and well, I don't want to hurt you, but with your age and what you've done this last time, I'm afraid there will be consequences. I want to see you happy, Mary, I do. But I'm afraid you will need to have some help to get you to a better emotional and spiritual well-being."

Mary's green eyes flashed as she met the concerned eyes of her aunt. "I don't know what you're suggesting."

"Mary, listen to me. It is by the grace of God that you're here. You could have died quite easily, smoking that poisoned marijuana, and you know it."

"But I didn't."

"No, you didn't. Which means God isn't finished with you."

"Well, I'm done trying to find someone. Obviously, there is no one for me. And I need to build a life for myself."

"Mary, that's not what I was saying at all. I think you need a good counselor is all. There's no shame in getting a professional to help. I want you to stay here. I will be very lonely without you."

She was met by a cold, level stare.

THE FOLLOWING WEEK, she hired a driver and went to look at vacated market stands, houses for rent, places of business in need of a co-renter, but nothing was close to her meager budget. Visions of opening her own bakery, fresh doughnuts and cinnamon rolls, a charming area with tables, came alive in her mind once more. It gave her goosebumps, this dream.

All she needed was more money, and there was only one way to acquire it. Hard work.

So, she'd ruined her reputation, Lizzie said. If this was true, well, she'd quit running around. *Rumschpringa* was senseless at her age. It was time she faced facts, shored up her courage, and made something of herself. If John King was meant to be, well then, he'd come find her. She felt clear headed, clear-eyed, felt as if she'd finally obtained a purpose.

She did work hard, and she squirreled away every spare penny. Her savings account grew. She received a generous raise from Aunt Lizzie, more than she thought was possible.

She went home for Christmas with her family, glad to be among her own siblings, squeezing hands warmly, smiling as curious eyes raked up and down, taking in the much smaller head covering, the brilliant red hue of her long, tight dress.

Ach my, this open disregard for her father's wishes, they said to one another. So awful. They had no idea all that she'd done in Lancaster, Lizzie having agreed there was no need for them to know. But her clothing was enough to set their heads shaking again.

Her father's dire warnings rang in her ears again, but she did her best to tune him out. Mima squeezed her hand and whispered an Amish blessing in her ear. Tears filled Mary's eyes. She did not quite believe she deserved a blessing, but the kind words were a balm to her soul.

The old farm was stark and crumbling, paint peeling like old skin. Mima had spruced up the yard, the unkempt bushes and fences, but with her father's refusal to spend money or allow her to use her own money, things had not changed.

Covered in snow, the house looked bereft, yellowed, swaying on its foundation, the barn crippled with old, rusting metal on the roof and broken, loose siding.

Mary sighed, closed her eyes, and turned away. This was her childhood home, all her memories kept among these snow-covered buildings. She had been happy here, as a child, had known love and stability among her siblings, her mother moving from *kesslehaus* to kitchen, wash water steaming from the gas engine–powered wringer washer, the smell of homemade lye soap, white vinegar in the rinse water.

All these memories stirred a quiet longing to fit in. To be one of them, truly. To live among this beautiful scenery, to breathe in the purity of Pinedale Valley, to live in harmony among people who were absolutely content.

She felt the strong pull of her childhood roots, the old ways and traditions of her Amish faith. She had a moment of remembering standing in Eli and Sarah Allgyer's kitchen after their son Elam was home from the hospital. She could visualize where she stood, the linoleum, the kitchen cupboards, the glass canister set, the wooden cutting board. Light flooded through the windows. And there was something more that she couldn't put her finger on.

What hidden meaning was there in that powerful moment?

She got on the bus, her father's ominous warning ringing in her ears, his tall, bent figure dressed entirely in black, his broad brimmed black hat on his forehead, his sad, watery eyes pleading with her. Mima stood in her black shawl and bonnet, lifting an arm to wave as the bus pulled away, a colorful array of parked vehicles behind them.

She took a deep breath, relaxed, drew her warm woolen pea coat around herself, a chill going up her spine. Her eyes felt heavy, her shoulders weary, so she adjusted her seat and turned her head in the direction of the window.

This was her life. Back and forth. She would stay in Lancaster, would prosper, likely, but would always return to her roots, the room in her heart, the happiness of her childhood, when she was simple and innocent, had no knowledge of another time and place. So clear in her mind, the old farm, the place she'd come to be ashamed of in later years.

She took out her wallet, flipped through the pages of her checkbook, and studied the last deposit slip.

Soon enough, she would have enough to start her own bakery. She felt a stirring of excitement. Yes, this was almost attainable.

As the bus wound through the Adirondacks, the snow-covered mountains seemed to hold her, to reach out and cover her with their magnificence. From far away, the sun's rays hit a metallic object, glowed like a white sun's radiance, and she blinked back tears she could not understand.

CHAPTER 20

SHE WAS MEETING WITH THE REALTOR TODAY. AT LONG LAST, SHE had the amount needed for a down payment on the old brick building she'd found on the outskirts of Lancaster City. It was only a third of the building itself, the remaining sections housing a hair care business and a shop containing herbs and other natural health products. The busy side streets lined with old maple trees was quaint, perfect, the site of her dream.

Aunt Lizzie had not the faintest clue, and Mary felt no need to let her in on her secret, knew the outcome would not be good.

Armed with only her courage and sense of optimism, she saw the white car parked along the street, the man dressed in casual clothes. She greeted him with reserve, the way she had been taught, but was rewarded with genuine friendliness.

"Darrell Scott," he said, extending his hand. "I believe you worked with Hillary, right?"

"Yes, I did."

"She's unavailable, had another showing, so I'm filling in."

Mary nodded, "Great. Let's get started."

They went up a few cement steps. The door was in good shape, just needed paint. Two large windows out front. An empty, narrow room. Cavernous. Creaking wooden floors. A smell of mold, dead rodents, filth, peeling paint. The ceiling was covered in inexpensive suspended tile, much too low. An old brick fireplace had dust an inch thick.

The realtor began his sales pitch, the spiel she'd planned on. She walked around, questioned the commercial permits, sewer, water, rules of the borough. He cast her appreciative glances, stepped up his vocabulary. She gave him an offer, calculating the amount she would need for equipment, renovation.

Outside the window she saw the dappled shade of the maples, heard the hum of traffic from a distance, noticed a girl in running gear with a dog on a leash, and Mary took a breath.

She was a woman of means. She could stand right here, in this city, with intelligent plans of her own. She could gain respect and admiration from someone like this realtor. The feeling was heady, empowering.

HER OFFER WAS accepted, which she really had not counted on. Ecstatic, she could no longer hide it from Lizzie, and took the first opportunity to tell her, her nerves taut, her eyes downcast.

Lizzie pursed her lips, bright perceptive eyes on her face, then burst out laughing, a sharp, quick snort.

"Well, Mary. You should not have kept this from me."

"Why?"

"I would have been so relieved. Here I was, ready to give up my bakery, but afraid the responsibility for you to take on the business was overwhelming. So, this is what we'll do."

Out and running ahead, that was Aunt Lizzie.

Yes, yes, she'd sell the business to Mary. She knew Mary wanted her own location, which was fine. She'd work for Mary, run the register and wash dishes. A pure relief. Why hadn't she asked her for the down payment?

Lizzie was burned out, tired, and ready to retire, so Mary bought everything—mixers, ovens, stainless steel work tables, everything at below a reasonable price. She felt blessed, knew God's Hand was in this venture, and thanked Him every evening.

Mary was shrewd, frugal, sniffed out the best deals, and hired the Amish contractor most highly recommended, the one with the best hourly rate. She knew she had to open her business as soon as possible, to hire a worker with a vehicle for cheap, sensible transportation to and from work. She had all Lizzie's experience with pastries, but needed to learn the coffee and tea trade, so they visited many coffee shows, talked to owners, took in decor, the colors of paint, chairs, and tables.

Lizzie ran ahead with ideas, but Mary stood her ground. Finally, she was in charge. She was the one who could pick the colors, pay for chairs and tables, meet with the contractor, and tell him what she wanted. She slept little, except on the weekends, after taking a few Tylenol PMs, which Lizzie told her were addictive, not good for you.

No longer with any group of youth, she had few friends, content to rest on Sunday afternoon after church services. Since Amish services are held every other Sunday, she had long, lazy ones, when she told herself it was alright to be bored. Monday she'd be off and running.

They scraped paint, layers of it, off heavily grooved woodwork, washed and scoured the old windows and fireplace, waited on the day the Amish contractor would finally show up. Mary paced and fretted.

She needed to be careful or her funds would be depleted, having nothing left over for the signs or the actual décor. She knew the atmosphere was an important part of opening a bakery.

Lizzie stopped scraping paint, said she was hungry enough to eat herbs at that natural place. Why hadn't they brought food?

"I didn't think it would take this long."

"It's almost lunch time. Come on, Mary."

But Mary was watching out the window.

"They are actually here. I can't believe it. Sunnyside Builders."

She hurried to the door to meet an aging Amish man who introduced himself as Gideon Lapp. His hair was white, his beard neatly trimmed, his shirt a navy polo with the Ralph Lauren logo. He wore striped suspenders and well-fitting trousers.

"We don't have time for this, you know," he said, bluntly, his blue eyes taking in the suspended tile, the peeling walls.

"But you said you'd give me a price," Mary countered.

"I didn't say it."

"Well, you're here, so you may as well keep your word."

Unexpectedly, he punched a ceiling tile, pushed it off the inexpensive metal grid, then peered above the opening, saying nothing. He removed another, then turned to them both.

"Wouldn't take much to remove this ceiling and expose the old decorative metal tiles."

"What?"

Mary peered through the opening. "So, if you take this white tile away, the ceiling is what? Ten foot? Nine? What about heating and cooling?"

"It's a bakery. You'll need the space."

What about the cost?"

"Not much. If you paint."

Lizzie had maintained a respectful silence, but she spoke up now.

"I hope you know, I'm not painting ten-foot ceilings, Mary."

Mary laughed. "I didn't expect you to."

Gideon wrote on a legal pad, jotting down measurements, using a tape for square footage. They talked about flooring, Mary in favor of painting the existing pine. Gideon bounced up and down, shook his head at the amount of give, the squeaks.

"Should be replaced. New plywood, everything. Sub floor."

Mary grimaced, "How much?"

"Nine, ten thousand."

Mary shook her head. "I can't afford that."

He tried to persuade her, but she was adamant. No. Aunt Lizzie stepped up, offered to pay, but Mary refused. She thought the squeaking pine floor would be part of the attraction, give the place a quaint feel. Her head spun, changing the visual atmosphere. She'd create something entirely different, would scour antique markets.

Gideon muttered about jobs done half right, but Mary pretended not to hear. Lizzie agreed with him, said it would spite her in the end, the paint chipping off these old boards, and they both turned to stare at her with accusing eyes, eyes clearly telling her she was young and inexperienced, and why couldn't she see it?

When she told them of her plan, there was a collective eye rolling, but Mary went to work, painting the old, imperfect plaster a pure shade of grayish white, the old woodwork a shade darker, the floor a muted pewter gray. The Sunnyside men tore out the old ceiling, exposed beautiful metal tile work, which was painted white.

Counters were built, doors replaced. Plumbers, electricians, a new commercial sink, hand washing sinks, a bathroom installed. Mary paid bills, saw paint rollers and brushes in her sleep. Lizzie was impatient, tired, said her back hurt, she was getting charley horses in her calf.

So they took a few days off, went antiquing, ate lunch at a nice little cafe, drank coffee, and talked. Mary found a rustic sign, in chipped blue paint with white lettering: "Doughnuts 5¢." But she would not pay the exorbitant price. She bought old bakeware, cutting boards, anything at a bargain price to hang on the freshly painted walls.

She found a collection of inexpensive market baskets, rolling pins, and potato mashers.

They worked long hours, mopped and cleaned, tried out new equipment before setting the date for the grand opening.

ON THE SECOND week in November, on a rainy, blustery Tuesday, they were open for business. The rich smell of frying doughnuts was coupled with fresh brewed coffee. The refrigerator was stocked with supplies, milk, cream, flavorings, iced tea in gallon pitchers. Showcases were filled with pies, cupcakes, cookies, and turnovers. Balloons dangled from pink and white awnings, the rain melting down both sides.

Girls in white aprons moved around, experienced workers from Lizzie's bakery. Mary was more than nervous, but also excited.

They opened at seven to a quiet, tree-lined street dripping with rainwater, a few pedestrians with colorful umbrellas scurrying past without as much as a glance. Mary was sick with nausea, wild-eyed, could smell defeat. Lizzie gave her a weak smile at seven-thirty, polishing the oak tables and chairs, arranging and rearranging the wire trays containing small vases of oak leaves, crocks of sugar and dry creamer, and napkins in wooden holders.

No one said anything. It was too painful.

At seven forty-five, they heard car doors. Hope soared. When a gaggle of well-dressed ladies appeared, read the dripping sign swaying in the stiff wind, they nodded, peered through the door, then turned the knob and walked in.

Mary greeted them, saying, "Welcome to Mary's."

The largest of them boomed, "And you're Mary?"

"I am."

She looked around, found the exposed beam on the wall, the hooks for wet coats. "Smells heavenly."

They ordered coffees and chose pastries before sitting at one of the round tables. Engrossed in making sure they were comfortable, Mary was surprised to hear the tinkling of the antique bell above the door. A group of older men and ladies came through, then another.

Lizzie ran the cash register while Mary moved among the guests, smiling, chatting, asking them to spread the word to their friends.

They closed at three, locked the door, and sagged into chairs. Lizzie was almost crying with exhaustion, Mary so pumped she couldn't slow down, everyone making fresh cups of coffee, bottles of water poured over ice, ideas exchanged, and laughter ringing to the freshly painted ceiling.

"We need sandwiches, soups."

"And who, may I ask, will do all that?"

The day had been a huge success, exceeding their best expectations. They could only hope for the coming months, knowing you couldn't tell by the grand opening.

Mary realized she was busier at the coffee shop than she had ever thought possible. She hired another worker, couldn't keep up with Christmas orders, forgot about going home for Christmas that year. It was simply not possible.

They made platters of cookies, dozens of doughnuts, pies, and Christmas cakes. The cash register dinged, twenty-dollar bills piled up and were placed in bank bags and deposited. Mortgage payments were met, payroll was not a problem. Supply prices escalated. So did her prices for the finished product. No one blinked—customers assured her that her baked goods were worth the price.

She bought a new sign and hung it from a white beam. It was pink and white, their signature colors, with "Mary's" in decorative lettering. She stood in the wintry sunshine, awash in colors of success, realizing her dream. Taking a deep breath, she expanded her lungs, felt the widening of horizons, the endless possibilities in this city of opportunity.

Mary's. She clasped her hands over her heart.

IF THERE WERE empty spaces within, she had no time to think about them, no time to think of herself. From three in the morning till five in the evening, every single day of the week except Sunday, she was at her place of business. She controlled the quality of the baked goods, reprimanded anything below her strict standards, and it paid off in the end. The girls knew how to keep the frying oil at a certain temperature, or the heavy, greasy doughnuts could not be sold, something her mother had taught her. The small doughnut bakery earlier in life had served its purpose, certainly, and she smiled at this.

Glazed, filled, powdered, glazed and filled, lemon, apple, cherry, blueberry, coconut—so many fillings and flavors, all made by hand and perfectly done. They learned the art of making croissants, which turned into another success, added breakfast sandwiches and opened an hour earlier.

Between Christmas and Valentine's Day, Mary took a break and went to visit her family. Lizzie asked if that was a good idea. Why not take a vacation somewhere else? But Mary felt the draw of home like a magnet. It wasn't perfect, no, it wasn't, but it was home, and perhaps her father would show a bit of pride in her wildly successful bakery. Just a hint of happiness, anything to show his interest in her accomplishment.

She'd written a letter, and Mima had invited everyone for a Sunday dinner, so they could spend Saturday together, baking and cooking. They'd butcher a turkey, some of the old hens for *roascht* (chicken casserole).

Her father met her at the bus station, appearing like a thin black shadow as he stepped out from the crowd. There was no smile, no light of gladness, but the handclap and the "Mary" was as much as she could expect. The driver in his old Suburban shifted his bulk behind the steering wheel, coughed, and greeted her with far more enthusiasm than her father, but she'd expected that, too, so she kept up a lively chatter about her new business venture, elaborating on that first half hour when the rain pounded down, and no one came through the door.

Mima was glad to see her, the warmth genuine.

Oh, she was glad it was a success. "My oh, Mary." She smiled and shook her head and asked questions, put Mary right to work making cakes while she cooked tapioca pudding.

Mary looked around. "You painted."

"Yes, I did. New flooring, too."

"Oh my, it looks nice. I'm assuming you paid for it."

"I did. Glad I did. Johnny helped lay it."

"He did? I'm surprised."

"He was quite good actually."

Her father came in for an evening meal of scrapple and bean soup, one of his favorites. Navy beans soaked in salted water overnight, then parboiled before milk, salt, and browned butter was added, after which torn bits of stale bread were stirred into it. *Bona sup*. An old Amish staple, often eaten with dried apple pie.

He smiled at Jemima's offering, said nothing hits the spot on a cold day like *bona sup* and scrapple. Mima smiled, and his smile widened. Mary watched warily. During the course of the conversation, he asked more about her bakery.

"Where exactly is it?"

"It's in a building just outside Lancaster."

"I see. Not in the city?"

"No."

"Good. Evil abounds where wordly people are crowded together."

Silence met this statement head on.

He looked up sharply. "Don't you agree?"

"Yes."

"Well, then."

But that was the worst of his tirades, proving to be relatively mild-mannered all weekend. Mary was among her brothers and sisters most of the day Sunday, forgetting their differences and finding herself at ease, enjoying the camaraderie of times past. She went sled riding with the grandchildren, snow packed in her boots, her skirts wet, and her cheeks red from the cold and the exertion. She hadn't laughed like this in years.

She left the old homestead with warm circles around her heart, went back to Lancaster with the feeling of being welcomed back into the fold, no matter that her lifestyle was much more liberal. But in a few weeks time, there was a letter folded neatly in a business-sized envelope, a letter containing every warning and every depressing threat written in a crowded cursive script.

She read it all, to be fair, then threw it in the trash without a word to her Aunt Lizzie. She felt as if she'd opened a present and found a poisonous spider lurking in a corner of the cardboard box. Fear crowded out rational thinking till she calmed herself, went to her room, and spent the evening with her own Bible, trying to understand the words her father found so meaningful. Trying to understand him. Afraid of everything.

Fear of hell and its endless suffering propelled him in a safety net of ultraconservative living. Afraid of sin, afraid of being counted unworthy.

Was she any different, as long as she tried endlessly to win his approval, living in fear of his rejection? She was a victim of the parental chains, completely invisible, but the strongest bonds imaginable. His chains were cold, hurtful, far too tight, gouging scars into her flesh, something she could never change.

She devised a letter in her mind, countering the Bible verses he'd written down with some she'd read, but found it to be slander, wrong in an unexplainable way. Surely Jesus hadn't meant the Holy Scripture to be a weapon.

Perhaps in time, she could overcome her father's dire threats, finally be comfortable in her way of life. Was that a work in progress, or could a person merely flip a switch?

She only knew her night was fraught with howling voices, taunting her, silent screams of accusation that made her squeeze her eyes shut, put both hands over her ears. And still she heard them.

Past midnight, there was no rest. She felt caught in a steel trap, saw herself in the empty room, crying out in misery.

Ghosts of her sins, her lifestyle, the money she was earning, all piled around her until she had a panic attack, stumbling down the stairs to Lizzie, who handed her a box of Kleenex silently, listened and soothed, and assured her of her father's cruelty.

"Listen, Mary, you have to stop going home. Why do you go?"

"I want to go home. I miss my family," she hiccuped, blew her nose, and looked at Lizzie with swollen eyes.

"I don't think that's true."

"But it is. It's the only reason."

"Mary, I'm going to set you up with a Christian counselor. You need a trained person to help you sort this out. I'm not going to let you go this time. You are not well, emotionally or spiritually, stuck between what you are living and what your father expects of you."

"But if I sold the bakery, went back, and obeyed perfectly this time, I wouldn't need to pay for counseling. That would finally bring me peace. He liked me when the dogs attacked me that time. He did like me, Lizzie."

"Till you wanted to date this John King."

"That was my fault. His, too."

Lizzie sighed. There was no hope.

"Well, it's almost two, and we get up in an hour, so I'll make a pot of coffee."

She yawned and stretched, adjusted the small white dichly she wore to bed, buttoned her housecoat, and turned up the thermostat.

COFFEE AND ENERGY drinks got her through the day, her face pale, her eyes red with fatigue. She welcomed customers, smiled, and spoke kindly, but her thoughts were in turmoil.

Shame washed over her in waves, uncomfortable, causing her to writhe with embarrassment. She was a despicable person, lower than bacteria. Everything in her life was a lie, including the foolish pink and white sign with "Mary's" on it. No decent man would ever look at her again, ever.

She was quiet, moving about her dining room, cleaning tables, washing windows, battling the same inner conflict she'd fought for years.

By all appearances, she was a sturdy, almost pretty, striking figure with a ready smile, a gracious manner, but no one knew the times she cried silently for help when the battle raged. Lizzie knew, but only saw a fraction of the weight of self-blame and confusion.

Eventually, as always, she righted her small craft, rowed bravely through the worst of the raging waters, and found the one thing that helped her, confiding in the One who cared, her Father in Heaven. She had things to sort out, this she knew, but if He would have patience with her, surely she'd find what mattered most.

When she did come back to her usual self, she invested her profit into another commercial hood and a gas fired grill, added sandwiches and soups to her menu, enjoyed another wave of success.

Her happiness increased, for a time, carried on the wave of constant supervising, teaching, overseeing recipes, the quality of every sandwich. Aunt Lizzie made all the soup, expertly concocting her own recipes, her homemade soups selling out each day.

The girls who refused to take orders, the ones who stubbornly burnt toast, smashed bread with overloads of butter or mayonnaise, who refused to slice tomatoes the way she required, were let go with a small bonus and a firm explanation of why they could no longer work.

As her business expanded, so did her heart. She discovered the fact that she loved serving people, looked forward to her weekly customers, the regulars.

And yet there was a note missing in the music of life.

CHAPTER 21

SHE WAS DRESSED IN A BLUE DRESS, A WHITE CAPE AND APRON, drinking her coffee at Aunt Lizzie's table as she waited to walk to church. She had not slept well the previous night, tacked it up to too many leftovers consumed, and told herself for the thousandth time she had to go on a diet. As she told herself this, she helped herself to another portion of the breakfast casserole she'd put in the oven, poured homemade ketchup over it, savored every bite.

Breakfast didn't hurt, though. Your biggest meal should be the first one of the day. She wouldn't eat much in church, although she loved bread with cup cheese, snitz pie, and ham. Sometimes there were red beet eggs, which went well with sweet pickles.

"Are you ready, finally?" she asked, watching Lizzie tie her covering in the mirror.

Lizzie said there was no hurry, they'd be there in less than ten minutes.

"Where is church?" she asked, cutting off another small slice of the casserole.

"Benny Stoltzfuses."

Mary nodded.

"Lizzie, we're just like some old married couple. Did you ever think about it?"

Lizzie said soberly, "Well, Mary. I can tell you right now you are the biggest blessing to me. Since Leroy passed away. I honestly don't know how I could go through life without you. You'll never know how much you mean to me."

There were tears in her eyes, and Mary was overwhelmed with love for her aunt.

"Oh, Lizzie, you know I feel the same about you."

They walked together on the wide shoulder of the highway, Mary's spirits high, ready to face the day, to take it head on and see what God had for her. She felt in need of an inspiring sermon, something to bolster her courage to fight the good fight. To be the best person she could be.

She found stares of disapproval disconcerting, the curious peckish glances from good people appalled at her past behavior. But for the most part, her past was forgiven, she could tell. Most folks knew her bakery now better than they knew about her wayward months.

She stood in the living room, her arms crossed tightly at her waist, making small talk with Naomi Beiler, an acquaintance from church services in the past. She shook hands with countless people, smiled, nodded her head, but was glad when the lady of the house came to seat them on their allotted bench in the pleasant, open shop with windows allowing the space to be filled with light.

The ministers sat on folding chairs, facing one another, the ministers' wives behind them, also seated on folding chairs, with the aged grandmothers seated according to their age, followed by the middle aged, then mothers with children and babies. A bunch was reserved for the single girls, behind the older women. Everything was done decently and in order, following the traditions kept for centuries.

The men faced the women and girls on the opposite side, their hats on their heads, waiting till the single boys would make an appearance, the signal to remove their hats. As the young men filed in, they walked between the row of ministers and shook hands with them, a respectful way of greeting. They, too, filed in according to age, down to the nine-year-olds, the age considered to be the proper time to be taken away from the father's supervision, seated with the boys. Turning nine years old was a milestone, shyly or eagerly awaiting that first church service when you went in with the boys.

On with the girls, all in the same manner.

After the boys were seated, the opening song number was announced. A rustle of pages, a few whispers from those who hadn't understood, the *Ausbund* (hymnal) lifted to reveal the correct number, and then the space was filled with the undulating swell of plainsong, the slow, easy rhythm sung for hundreds of years.

Her thoughts wandered as she sang.

Here she was again, smack in the middle of her former life in Lancaster, ferrying from the other New York life like a vessel of indecision. Back and forth, back and forth, fruitlessly keeping up the endless cycle of melding both worlds. When home, she felt less Amish, a woman of the world, really. Catering to the public, a woman of substance, a lucrative establishment in the city of Lancaster. It was an honorable occupation, allowed by the church, so she should be at peace.

And she did feel at peace, except for the bullhorn of her father's voice at the edge of her conscience. Why did she always seek his approval even if she knew it simply was not available? Even now, listening to the words of the young minister, she wondered what he would say.

He used quite a few English words, mixed it in with Dutch and the old original dialect, high German. *Hoch Deutsch.*

Her father would frown, say the old original foundation was crumbling, the wolves were slipping through.

She banished him from her thoughts, tried to keep the true spirit of receiving the message as food for her soul, which she so sorely needed.

After services, there was a special meeting for those who were members of the church. A young couple wished to announce their desire to leave the confines of the Old Order and be excommunicated, allowing them to join the church of their own choice.

It was a solemn occasion, rife with heartbreak and tears, the parents' hopes and dreams smashed to a million pieces, the family circle broken. There was no outright condemnation, only sadness, a sense of loss, requested prayer as the couple left, their heads bowed.

In the coming months, they would sell their horses and buggy, select a vehicle of their choice, their driver's permit already underway. Electricity would be brought into their house and new clothing acquired.

They were no longer part of their former life, except for the teaching they had lived with, now ingrained in their being.

Mary had never experienced this, the formal manner of expelling someone from the church. Her curious mind was instantly pushed into overdrive. Her father's voice came first, the deep pit of this couple's doom. The casting into outer darkness, the wailing and gnashing of teeth. She heard him clear his throat, waiting for the onslaught of accusation and blame.

Were they lost, this couple who did not want to uphold rules?

As so BEGAN a whole new level of unrest. On weekdays, her energy was taken up by her business, the hubbub of keeping the bakery, grill, and coffee running smoothly. On weekends, however, when she was alone in a quiet house, her thoughts reached out into a thousand directions.

Who was she, really?

The runt of the litter, a round object unable to fit square orifices, a misfit. Everything in her life amounted to nothing as far as she could tell.

Then, unexpectedly, a thought popped into her head. Perhaps she wasn't meant to be Amish. Perhaps there was a whole new world out there, one that held her true love, someone she had no idea existed.

She began to search her Bible, to weigh one verse to another, tipping the scales in her favor, but always her father's voice dashed it all to the ground. No hope for the *ungehorsam*. "Take up thy cross, deny self. The way was hard. Broad is the way that leadeth to hell."

The premonitions, the dire threats were flashed before her eyes, creating painful scratches on old scars healed over. Would she be free of these things if she completely removed herself from the valley in New York? How did one go about acquiring perfect peace?

Aunt Lizzie banged the door, removed her gloves and shawl, divested herself of her bonnet before removing her steamed eyeglasses.

"Poo. So cold. That wind cut right through my shawl. That's one thing about these new shawls. They're not wool. Nothing warmer than genuine wool."

Mary folded the top of a page of the *Martyr's Mirror*, and smiled at her aunt.

"Where were you?"

"Didn't I tell you? Henry sie Eva had a get together for a bunch of us widows. Such a dinner. My oh."

"You walked to Henry King's?"

"I did. A good three miles, I'd say. I wore good shoes."

She lifted a foot to show her black Skechers.

"Pretty classy."

Mary smiled.

Her aunt nodded at the *Martyr's Mirror*.

"Looks like you're preparing for the ministry."

Lizzie laughed out loud.

Mary said nothing, but threw the warm blanket aside and went to make a cup of hot chocolate.

"You shouldn't spend your Sundays alone. I don't know why you quit running around. You aren't old enough to be considered a single girl for the remainder of your life. How will you ever meet anyone?"

Aunt Lizzie sat down, untied her covering, and threw the strings over her shoulders. Mary set down a cup of hot chocolate, her own secret recipe, and smiled. Stirring the steaming liquid, she told her aunt nothing ever worked out. It was time to give it up.

Lizzie shook her head. "It's not right. Now you tell me, what were you doing with the *Martyr's Mirror*? That's a bit depressing, holed up in here all by yourself on a dreary Sunday, no?"

Mary shrugged.

"Just curious about our beginning. The beginning of the whole Anabaptist movement. You know, Lizzie, what would happen now if someone would come up with a list of things and tack it onto the church bench wagon? Start a whole new way of thinking? Doesn't history repeat itself, over and over?"

Aunt Lizzie waved a hand, as if chasing a bothersome fly.

"*Ach*, Mary. Now you're going clear over my head. I don't even know what you're talking about. I'm not big on church history."

"What about that couple who just left the church, Bena and Amos? Where are they going, and what will become of their lives?"

Lizzie looked up sharply.

"Mary, young women shouldn't worry themselves about such things. You must remain contented with the spiritual food of our forefathers. It's not good to read too much about spiritual things. You'll only confuse yourself and start to doubt."

"Doubt what?"

"The Amish."

Mary was restless the remainder of that day, repeatedly going to the window to gaze across the windswept landscape. Horses ran fast, their heads held high, drivers drawing back on reins to control them better. Corn fodder blew across fence rows, onto the road, and skittered into ditches and frightened wary horses. A man pedaled his scooter furiously, his black hat jammed on his head. She watched as a car passed another buggy, causing oncoming traffic to swerve to the opposite shoulder.

She thought of all the couples throughout Lancaster County who would spend the evening together. Breathless young girls on their first date, young men agonizing over the big question, whether to ask an attractive young woman. There had been a time when she was one of them, had believed her story would unfold like all the rest, and been bitterly disappointed.

How did one go about deciphering God's will for one's life? Waves of hot rebellion toward her father accosted her, smacked her inner peace with the force of gathered anguish.

All the spiritual lessons fled in the face of her anger.

It was a very long time before she fell into a troubled sleep that Sunday evening, but by the sun's appearing on Monday, she was up and dressed, her troubles behind her, ready and willing to take on the world.

MONDAY WAS A slower day, a day to catch up on cleaning, ordering food, the girls stocking up on necessities as they prepared shelves for the upcoming week.

Mary buttered a roll, placed it face down on the grill, added a squirt of oil and a dipperful of blended egg. The perfect sausage patty from the steam table, a slice of white American cheese on the bottom and one on top, and her breakfast was complete. Plus a cup of coffee filled to the brim with a walnut cinnamon roll. She considered the overload of carbs, but figured she'd work it off by the time the fryer oil was changed, the kitchen cleaned. She never made the girls do this task without her help, truly enjoying her time scrubbing and scouring, the pots and pans cleaned and sparkling with an application of Bar Keepers Friend, her go-to for serious cleanup.

That was the wonderful thing about physical labor, the outlet for an accumulation of battering thoughts, doubt, and misgivings.

When your mind was filled with duties, your body using muscles and drawing on supplies of energy, the world and its complexities fell away.

Here she was in her element, here she knew she was someone worth knowing. She was Mary's. Mary's Coffee Shop.

No good can come of it, Mary.

She heard her father's voice, heard the rumbling in his throat as he prepared his lecture. Her stomach rumbled as her agitation increased.

The door opened, creating the welcome tinkling of the antique bell above it. A group of Amish this time. Mary took notice of their sober demeanor, the pale, stricken face of the oldest, heaviest woman.

Sunlight flooded the white walls, the clean hardwood floors and gleaming tabletops. There were tastefully arranged antiques on the walls, vases of red roses for Valentine's day. Mary felt the approval of the group and welcomed them warmly.

"You're Mary?"

"Yes."

"We'd like coffee, please. First of all."

She served it quietly and waited for introduction, questions about whose family she was from, but none were forthcoming. Bewildered, she asked if they were ready to order, but was brushed off with a brisk, "Not yet."

Soon, they were deep in conversation, the pale faced woman crying softly into her handkerchief, noticeably ironed to a perfect square as she unfolded it. Mary went away, leaving them to their troubled conversation.

Upon returning, she gathered the fact of someone being taken to Lancaster General Hospital. In a bad way.

She tried again.

"Ready to order?"

This time they did order, the woman's eyes brimming with tears. She felt for her, but didn't think it was her business to ask for details.

When they motioned her over for another waffle with strawberries, she nodded, jotted it down quickly, and left.

The next day, two of the women were accompanied by their husbands. Black hats were removed, hung on hat racks, before being seated. The faces were somber.

As Mary approached, she heard the one lady speak to her husband.

"But he said, there's a chance. Only a chance."

"Anna, listen. What good will an arm be if there is no muscle, no strength?"

Spoken kindly, but with conviction, one of the men pleaded.

"I think we need a second opinion."

"We already have three or four. How many do we need?"

Mary walked over, anxious now, asking quietly if they were ready to place an order.

When the man with a short gray beard ordered, he leaned in slightly and asked Mary if she'd heard.

Confused, she looked up, shaking her head.

"Our son drove his car into a guard rail, flipped over, and is seriously injured. The other couple's son was with him, has broken ribs, but they think Paul will lose his arm."

"I'm sorry."

"Don't be. God moves in mysterious ways, His wonders to perform."

Smiling, he left her there, watching him.

What was it about him? With so much conviction, with such ease, he'd told her the bedrock of his belief. From his eyes shone a warm radiance, a deep happiness.

When the bell above the door tinkled as they let themselves out, Mary yearned after them. After him. What was it about him?

All she knew was that he possessed a missing ingredient in her own life.

MARY CONTINUED HER search for truth, stuffing herself with hurried chapters of the Bible, reverting to Christian self-help books yet again. She continued to think about leaving the Amish church entirely, separating herself from the voice of her father, from tradition and *ordnung*, suspended between one world and another.

To finally make that clean break, to rid herself of the ties that bind, would that serve to be her answer? Or, would it prove to be the opposite? The voice of her father intensified.

She decided to attend the Mennonite church in Ephrata, hired a driver, and told Aunt Lizzie she was visiting her old friend Anna. A lie, perhaps, but a white one, knowing the Mennonites were derived from the Anabaptists as well as the Amish.

She found herself sitting on a wooden pew, in a clean, well-ordered church, the sermons much like the Amish, only spoken in English.

None of the single girls spoke to her, although a few of the older women shook her hand and thanked her for coming. She felt alone, a crow among songbirds, but reasoned to herself about this being the first time.

She'd try other churches. She wasn't about to give up.

SHE'D COMPLETELY FORGOTTEN the group of Amish with sons in the hospital, until she heard the bell above the door and looked up to see the kind man and his wife with the son in tow. Pale, sweating, dark eyes wild with fear. They seated themselves, waited expectantly.

"Hello."

"Hi. We finally got him out of the hospital," the man said warmly.

"Yes. I see."

"Paul, this is Mary. She owns the place. Quite an accomplishment."

To her surprise, Paul rose to his feet, came around the table, and offered his right hand. Mary took it. She glanced quickly at the dangling left sleeve of his jacket, then into his face.

"Good to meet you, Mary."

"And you. Sorry about your accident."

He grimaced, shrugged. "I have my right hand."

"Yes."

He sat down, took up the menu. Mary noticed he was breathing hard, his eyes too wide, his nostrils distended as if he'd been running and was out of breath.

"I'll just have coffee and a glazed doughnut. Thanks."

"It's so good to be here, Mary," the man said. "We really appreciated this place. Paul lost his arm, about halfway between shoulder and elbow. He's doing great."

"I think it's time we told her who we are," his wife said.

"How about that? We never did."

Mary smiled when he told her to go first, then told him her background, but he shook his head, not being acquainted with Pinedale, although he'd heard of it.

"I'm Jake Beiler. Sam's Ezra's, from the Gap. My wife Barbie."

Mary shook her head, told them she'd been in that area, but was not familiar with it, or the names he'd given her.

She left them to their food, but watched as the young man struggled to remove his jacket. His mother rose to help. He glanced up, thanked her. Mary saw the empty shirt sleeve, a striped blue and white. Saw the difficulty opening the small plastic container of coffee creamer.

Her mother extended an arm, waggled her fingers, but Paul shook his head.

"Sorry, Mom. I have to learn."

He wasn't a teenager. His hair was cut short to his scalp, an English haircut. He was of average height, dark haired, with good features, but like his father, neither handsome nor repulsive, merely another guy who wouldn't stand out in a crowd. There was something weary in the lines of his face, as if he'd run and run and found it unsatisfying.

So many times, Mary had thought perhaps this young man, or that young man had been sent by God, for her. She was so done with all of that. There was no feeling, no longing, no thought of being introduced to a possible husband.

So when the father looked up and asked if she liked to play Scrabble, she could honestly say she loved it, and he told her to come around the following Sunday afternoon. Paul would appreciate the company.

Mary agreed with a calm, but friendly, manner, and said she'd need an address, and did they have a Scrabble dictionary.

Of course they did, they played a lot of Scrabble.

When they left, Mary hummed as she wiped tables, looked forward to Sunday afternoon, but without any roller coaster ride of emotion of longing for romance. She had much more on her plate, the search to find out who she really was, and whether she belonged to the Amish church or if she didn't.

And the voice of her father would have to be dealt with sometime, although she had no idea how or when she would ever attempt it. She seemed to wear it like a second skin, viewed every choice through his lenses.

As she rode home, the sun was low in the sky, the highway choked with vehicles, houses built against neighboring lots, no mountains or wide open spaces, and she experienced genuine homesickness. A longing for pure, unfettered beauty, with the air so clean it made you want to breathe deeply, fling your arms wide, and embrace all of Creation. The future was ahead of her, the patchwork of her tattered past behind her, and she still had a long, winding road to travel.

Seize the day, she thought. Seize it.

THE END

ABOUT THE AUTHOR

LINDA BYLER WAS raised in an Amish family and is an active member of the Amish church today. Growing up, Linda loved to read and write. In fact, she still does. Linda is well known within the Amish community as a columnist for a weekly Amish newspaper. She writes all her novels by hand in notebooks.

Linda is the author of several series of novels, all set among the Amish communities of North America: Lizzie Searches for Love, Sadie's Montana, Lancaster Burning, Hester's Hunt for Home, the Dakota Series, The Long Road Home, New Directions, and the Buggy Spoke Series for younger readers. Linda has also written several Christmas romances set among the Amish: *Mary's Christmas Goodbye, The Christmas Visitor, The Little Amish Matchmaker, Becky Meets Her Match, A Dog for Christmas, A Horse for Elsie, The More the Merrier, A Christmas Engagement*, and *Love Conquers All*. Linda has coauthored *Lizzie's Amish Cookbook: Favorite Recipes from Three Generations of Amish Cooks!, Amish Christmas Cookbook*, and *Amish Soups & Casseroles*.

OTHER BOOKS BY
LINDA BYLER

LIZZIE SEARCHES FOR LOVE SERIES

BOOK ONE   BOOK TWO   BOOK THREE

TRILOGY   COOKBOOK

Sadie's Montana Series

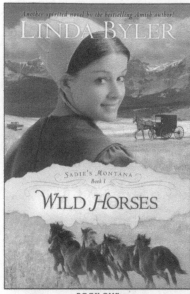

BOOK ONE

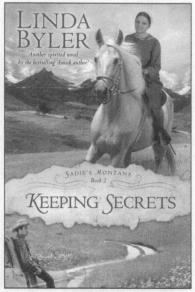

BOOK TWO

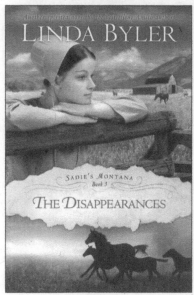

BOOK THREE

TRILOGY

LANCASTER BURNING SERIES

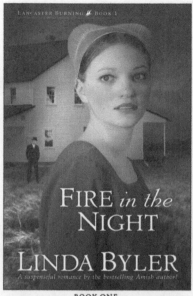

BOOK ONE

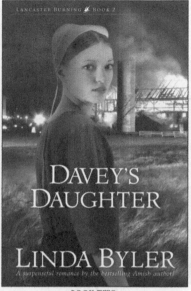

BOOK TWO

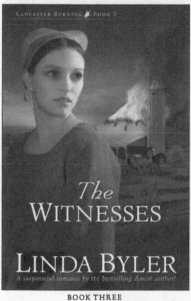

BOOK THREE

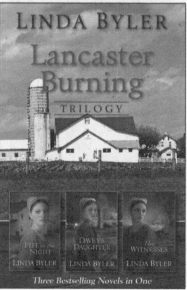

TRILOGY

HESTER'S HUNT FOR HOME SERIES

BOOK ONE

BOOK TWO

BOOK THREE

TRILOGY

The Dakota Series

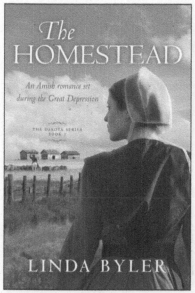

BOOK ONE

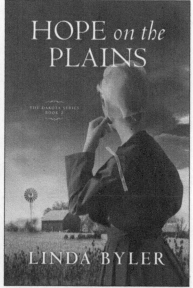

BOOK TWO

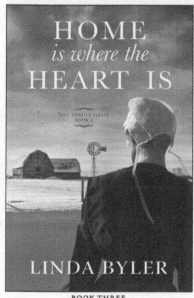

BOOK THREE

TRILOGY

Long Road Home Series

BOOK ONE

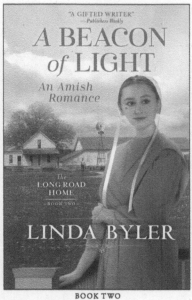

BOOK TWO

BOOK THREE

NEW DIRECTIONS SERIES

BOOK ONE

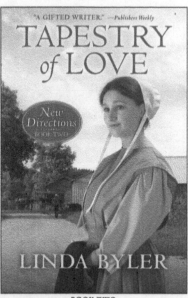

BOOK TWO

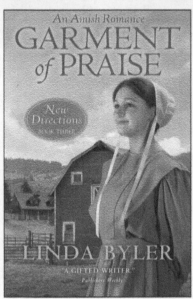

BOOK THREE

BUGGY SPOKE SERIES FOR YOUNG READERS

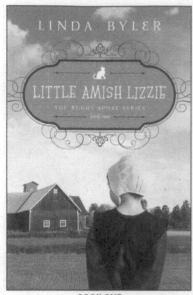

BOOK ONE

BOOK THREE

BOOK TWO

CHRISTMAS NOVELLAS

THE CHRISTMAS VISITOR

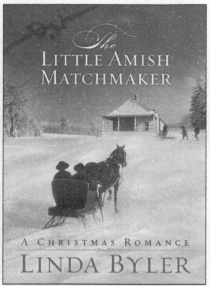

THE LITTLE AMISH MATCHMAKER

MARY'S CHRISTMAS GOODBYE

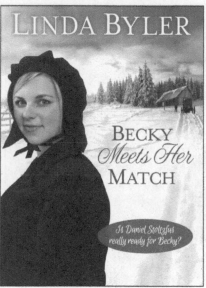

BECKY MEETS HER MATCH

A DOG FOR CHRISTMAS

A HORSE FOR ELSIE

THE MORE THE MERRIER

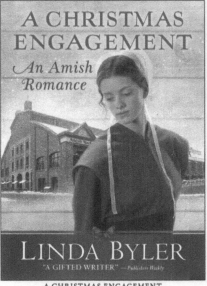

A CHRISTMAS ENGAGEMENT

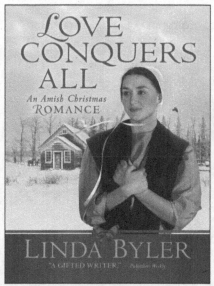

LOVE CONQUERS ALL

CHRISTMAS COLLECTIONS

AMISH CHRISTMAS ROMANCE COLLECTION

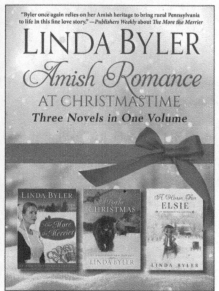

AMISH ROMANCE AT CHRISTMASTIME

STANDALONE NOVELS

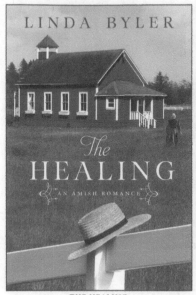

THE HEALING

A SECOND CHANCE

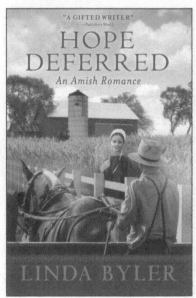

HOPE DEFERRED

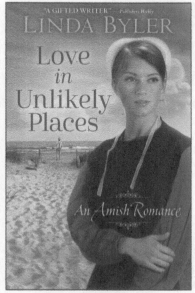

LOVE IN UNLIKELY PLACES